A Woman Scorned

China's eyes blazed. "You conceited, insufferable wretch! You flatter yourself!"

Gabriel chuckled. "I don't think so."

"If I cared enough to be jealous of you and my cousin," she snarled, mortified into recklessness by his words, "then why did I escape from you at Fox Meadow?"

"Because you were foolish," he replied. "And I think you know it now."

"Oh!" China ground her teeth. That smirk, that cocksure confidence! She longed to rake that smile from his face with her nails. "Get out of here!" she ordered. "I detest the very sight of you!"

"I don't believe that either," He told her frankly. "And I don't believe you really want me to go. Not just yet, at least."

He leaned toward her and, before China could react, brushed his lips against her throat. Her gasp, the involuntary shudder that shook her, confirmed his suspicions. His hand rose to her breast. . . .

Sandra DuBay
Winner of the *Romantic Times*
Swashbuckler Romance Award

"**Sandra DuBay** writes wonderful escapist fiction. It fulfills all her readers' fantasies!"

—*Romantic Times*

Other Leisure Books by Sandra DuBay

MISTRESS OF THE SUN KING
FLAME OF FIDELITY
FIDELITY'S FLIGHT
BY LOVE BEGUILED
WHERE PASSION DWELLS
IN PASSION'S SHADOW
BURN ON, SWEET FIRE
SCARLET SURRENDER
WILDER SHORES OF LOVE
TEMPEST
WHISPERS OF PASSION

SANDRA DUBAY

LEISURE BOOKS NEW YORK CITY

A LEISURE BOOK ®

August 1990

Published by

Dorchester Publishing Co., Inc.
276 Fifth Avenue
New York, NY 10001

Printed in the United States of America.

QUICKSILVER

One

New Providence, 1717

China Clairmont sat on the tattered lilac velvet cushions of the windowseat in the captain's cabin of the *Black Pearl*, pride and joy of her captor—the pirate they called Le Corbeau.

China sighed as she twined a lock of her thick, ash blonde hair around her long delicate fingers. She'd been aboard the ship for more than a week, ever since Le Corbeau had attacked the passenger ship, the *Amity*, on which she'd been traveling to Virginia.

She hadn't been particularly surprised when the lookout high in the *Amity's* rigging had spied the pirate ship following in their wake. It was only the latest in a series of disasters that had befallen her in the past year.

Only to think, she mused as she looked out at the lights of the settlement in whose harbor Le Corbeau's ship rode at anchor, a mere twelvemonth before, she had been the pampered only child of the elegant and fashionable Baron Louis Clairmont and his wife, Emilia. Their home in London had been a gathering place for the cream of London society. Princes and dukes, diplomats and visiting royalty, had passed through its doors. And their country seat—Clairmont Court—nestled in the verdant beauty of Derbyshire had been universally admired as the epitome of elegance and grace.

And then . . . China's beautiful oval face clouded at the memory of that night, that dreadful night when her life had shattered around her. The fire that had destroyed the London house had not only robbed China of her parents, it had stolen away any hopes for a brilliant marriage in the aristocratic circles in which the Clairmonts moved.

For the Baron Clairmont's estate had been entailed away from his female descendants. Upon his death, having no son to succeed him, everything he possessed had gone to his younger brother, Arthur. Lord Clairmont's untimely demise had left his daughter destitute. China had no home, no dowry, no prospects. She was entirely dependent upon the charity of the new Baron Clairmont, her uncle.

For six breathless weeks she had waited to hear if her uncle was disposed to be kind to his brother's orphaned daughter. For six sleepless, endless weeks her future hung in the balance.

The reply, when it came, contained both good news and bad. China's uncle was indeed prepared to provide his niece with a home and, when the time came for her to marry, a dowry. That had been the good news. The bad news was that the new Lord Clairmont, an ardent colonial, had no interest in returning to England nor in owning and maintaining an enormous country seat he had no intentions of ever visiting. China, if she wished to avail herself of his offer of a home, would have to go to Virginia, to Montcalm, the plantation her uncle was building near Yorktown on the York River.

And so China had set out aboard the *Amity*, a small, lightly armed ship owned by her uncle that carried supplies and indentured servants for his plantation. Their voyage had been uneventful, with calm seas and a brisk wind to fill the sails. They were two and a half weeks out of Portsmouth when Le Corbeau had attacked them.

They had been easy prey for the pirates. A mariner like the *Amity* carried a crew of less than two dozen men and fewer than a half-dozen guns. A brigantine like the *Black Pearl*, on the other hand, though not so very much larger, often carried a hundred men and more than a dozen guns.

China had huddled with the others, herded onto the deck by the filthy, riotous pirates for their captain's inspection. She had shuddered with revulsion at their leering glances and recoiled from the sly, groping hands that bedeviled her and the other women passengers.

Le Corbeau, a small, swarthy native of Martinique, had glared at them, malice and contempt glittering in his dark eyes. It was a meager prize he'd won in reward for a full day's dogged pursuit. He'd expected a bounty, gold, goods, perhaps jewels adorning wealthy passengers. And what had he found? Tools, plows, seeds, a cowardly crew most of whom were locked in a storeroom below, and a cringing band of would-be servants who eyed him as if he were the Devil himself made flesh.

"Whose ship is this?" he demanded of the trembling captain who'd been dragged before him.

"She belongs to Mr. . . . that is to say, Lord Clairmont, master of Montcalm of Virginia," the captain replied, his eyes fastened to the saber in the pirate captain's hand. "We are bringing supplies and servants for his plantation. From England." He looked toward China and would have said more but her pleading gaze silenced him.

A hiss of disgust puffed Le Corbeau's lean cheeks. "Supplies and servants! What am I to do with a pile of seeds or a plow? What need have I of debtors and thieves who escape a prison sentence by selling themselves into servitude?"

His withering glare swept over the little group clustered meekly at the rail. His eyes narrowed as they lingered on China, who stood nearly hidden between two brawny men.

"What is this?" the pirate murmured. "Who have we here?"

With a nod to one of his crewmen, the pirate ordered China pulled away from the rest. She was nearly dragged across the deck and deposited at his feet. Trying hard to conceal her fear, China pushed herself up to stand before him.

He circled her, his appraising stare moving quickly over her. The examination seemed to go on forever, but at last he came round to face her once more.

"Who are you?" he asked sharply.

China thought quickly. If she admitted to being Lord Clairmont's niece, the pirate might try to hold her for ransom—a ransom China was not at all certain her uncle would be willing to pay. Her only salvation, as she saw it, seemed to lie in convincing the pirate she was merely a servant like the others with no means of providing him with any ill-gotten gains.

"My name is . . . Meghan," she lied, praying the others would understand and not give her away. "Meghan Gordon. I am to be lady's maid to my Lady Clairmont."

Le Corbeau smirked. Though she wore a simple gown and a muslin mob-cap that hid her hair, her beauty shone like a beacon setting her apart from the plain, homely people behind her.

"You are to be Lady Clairmont's maid, are you?" he sneered. "That may be why you are hired, but I would wager my life you will end as Lord Clairmont's doxy."

"Doxy!" China's blue topaz eyes blazed. "I'll be no man's doxy!"

"Oho!" The pirate glanced at his crew, smiling at their mocking laughter and low whistles. "She has spirit! Perhaps this day's work has not been for nothing!"

China felt the blood draining from her cheeks, leaving her starkly pale. "I have no money," she told him honestly. "Nor jewels. I have nothing that could be of value to you."

"You have something very rare and precious," Le Corbeau contradicted. "You have a beauty such as I have seldom seen. And if I am not mistaken—" Before China could recoil, his hand shot out and snatched the concealing mob-cap from her head. "Aye," he murmured as the shimmering cascade of silvery curls tumbled over her shoulders, "I thought as much. Hair the color of moonlight. Eyes like the summer sky . . ."

"There are many who could boast the same," China assured him.

"In England, perhaps," the pirate agreed. "But there are places in this wide world where such women are rare and therefore highly prized. And there are men in those places who pay dearly for them."

A sick feeling quivered in the pit of China's stomach. Was it too late, she wondered, to tell this vile man who she really was? And if she did, would her uncle in Virginia pay any ransom that might be demanded for her return? She might be left by her uncle at this man's mercy and be more vulnerable for his knowledge of her true identity and rank.

"What men?" she demanded, a noticeable tremor in her voice. "I am no animal to be bought and sold."

"You are an indentured servant," Le Corbeau reminded her. "What does that mean if not to be sold like an animal?"

China would have protested further, but the pirate waved an impatient hand. "Enough of this! We will take what little there is of value and this girl." He fingered a shimmering strand of China's hair, laughing when she snatched it away with a jerk of her head. "She will help pay for our trouble today."

And so China had come to share the captain's cabin aboard the *Black Pearl*. A week and more had passed since that day. Le Corbeau had not harmed her. When, soon after her abduction, he had discovered that she was untouched, a virgin, he had left her alone. He knew that her innocence would only increase her value in the seraglios of the East for which she was destined.

From the first, China had vowed to find a way to escape. Hope had flared inside her when she'd heard they were to make port in order that the ship might be readied for a voyage across the Atlantic.

She scowled now as she looked out at the ramshackle village that crowded the ship-choked harbor of the pirate stronghold of New Providence in the Bahamas. From her place at the window, she could see nothing but other pirate ships riding at anchor. On shore, makeshift huts housed the island's few permanent inhabitants. The only buildings of any substance were the taverns that offered every imaginable kind of ale and wine and liquor, all captured from this brigantine or that mariner or some sloop. Dirty, slovenly trollops plied their trade on shore brazenly competing for the ships' crews with a fierce enthusiasm that spread the diseases running rampant through the pirates' ranks.

Escape? A small smile filled with bitter self-mockery curved China's lips. Not bloodly likely! At least aboard Le Corbeau's ship she was a valued and protected commodity. Ashore, vulnerable and alone, she would fall prey to the first brigand she passed. And, no doubt, the second, and third, and . . .

Shuddering, she leaned back against the wall. Escape to New Providence would be tantamount to suicide. Doubtless there were men there who would make Le Corbeau look like the country vicar who came occasionally to dine at Clairmont Court.

In the gathering darkness outside the window, China saw a tender boat being rowed out toward the *Black Pearl*. In it sat the small, swarthy figure of Le Corbeau. Opposite him, his back to the ship and to China, sat another man, far larger, dressed in dark clothing.

Curling back into the corner of the windowseat, China drew the heavy velvet draperies halfway across the window. Le Corbeau, it seemed, had brought back company from New Providence. China hoped he would not bring the man below to the great cabin, but in case he did, she made herself as hidden as possible. One pirate's acquaintance was all she wished to make.

From her place of concealment, she heard

the rattle of the key in the lock of the cabin door. Booted footsteps, muted in the thick pile of the fine carpet covering the cabin floor, entered the room.

"Come in, damn your eyes," Le Corbeau's voice said in the soft, exotic drawl of the isle of his birth. "Take what you will for what I owe you."

China listened as the slow steps of Le Corbeau's companion circled the room. The cabin was littered with the choicest pieces of the pirate's plunder. Jeweled goblets, gold and silver plate, caskets of gold and jewels, ropes of pearls yards long lay in shining abundance, mute testimony to the success of the brigand and the misfortune of his victims.

"Where did you get this?" a low, deep, masculine voice rumbled.

"I took that off Madagascar," Le Corbeau replied. "An East Indiaman homeward bound from Bombay." The concern in the pirate's voice was evident. "But I do not owe you so much."

Behind the draperies China smiled, realizing what it was Le Corbeau's guest held. The Great Mogul, Le Corbeau called it, an Indian ruby of some two hundred carats. Many times he had shown it to her and, without reserve, she had admitted it was the most magnificent jewel she'd ever seen. It was Le Corbeau's pride and joy, worth more than everything else combined. He would sooner part with his life, he told her, than with the Great Mogul.

"What is this?" the other man was asking. "A watch?"

"Very fine," Le Corbeau told him, relieved to see his ruby laid safely back in its ornate brass and mother-of-pearl casket. "French. Enameled. Those are rubies and diamonds, my friend."

The stranger chuckled skeptically. "Garnets and paste, more like. But it's pretty and I know a lady who might like it."

"Oh!" China moaned, realizing which piece he must be holding. It was a delicate, beautiful watch on a matching chain that she'd adored from the moment she'd seen it among Le Corbeau's hoard of booty.

"Who is that?" the stranger demanded, his voice lazily amused. "You did not say you had a companion."

China clasped her hands over her mouth, wishing she had contained her dismay. Please, she prayed silently, please make him think he was mistaken! Tell him it was no one. Nothing. Please—

But at that moment the velvet drapery was pulled aside and China found herself gazing up into a pair of black-lashed green eyes set in a sharp-planed face that was brutally handsome.

A long dimple appeared in one tanned

cheek as the stranger smiled. "I see you keep the loveliest of your treasures well hidden, Le Corbeau."

China's apprehensive gaze went to her captor's swarthy face. He seemed unconcerned.

"Her name is Meghan," he told the stranger. "I took her off a ship bound for the Americas. I am taking her East when my ship is seaworthy."

"Why?" the stranger asked, holding out a calloused hand to China who had no choice but to take it and come out of her hiding place.

"Why?" her abductor repeated. "Why do you think? In the slave markets such women can make a man's fortune."

"You mean her for the harem of some fat Turk?" The tall man's voice dripped disdain.

Le Corbeau shrugged, turning away. Behind him China stood, trying not to tremble, feeling small and helpless, a pawn in a game over which she had not the slightest control. On the one hand, there was Le Corbeau to whom she represented only the gain her beauty would fetch when auctioned to the highest bidder. Her fate after the sale was something in which he had no interest. On the other hand, there was the stranger who stood beside her, his tanned, work-hardened hand still imprisoning hers which lay dwarfed in his palm. He was tall, so tall her head barely reached his shoulder. His sable brown hair was caught at the nape of his neck with a carelessly tied ribbon the same color as the forest green coat and breeches he wore. There was about him an air of confident strength that frightened China even as it attracted her. In his disconcerting green eyes there was a glow of frank admiration. He grinned as she ventured a glance up at him, and she felt an icy shiver snake up her spine.

"I'll take her," the stranger decreed. "And we'll call it even."

Le Corbeau whirled. "Her? Damnit, Fortune, that's a high price to pay for an unlucky turn of the cards. She's worth—"

"You should not have played if you were not prepared to lose," the stranger interrupted, unconcerned by the other man's chagrin. "She's what I want."

Le Corbeau's appraising stare raked China from head to foot. "It would save me sailing to the East," he reasoned.

"Indeed it would," the stranger agreed. "And there's always the risk she might die on the way. Then where would you be?"

The pirate nodded. "All right, Fortune. You win. Take her and be damned."

His opponent laughed. "I will take her," he chuckled. "And no doubt be damned as well."

"Go with him, *chérie*," Le Corbeau told

China. "He won our game fairly. There is honor even among thieves."

"But . . . no . . ." China protested, appalled. "You cannot . . ."

"Go on," Le Corbeau ordered. "His name is Gabriel Fortune. He is master of the *Golden Fortune,* and you are his now."

Helpless, stunned, China looked up into that handsome, smiling face. Gabriel Fortune grinned down at her, his emerald eyes sparkling.

"That's right, m'dear," he said softly, the crease in his cheeks deepening as his brilliant smile broadened. "You're mine now."

Two

China tried hard to ignore the catcalls and remarks Gabriel Fortune's men shouted as she was ushered aboard the *Golden Fortune*. But the hot flush that flooded her cheeks was evident to Gabriel who walked beside her.

"Don't pay them any mind," the pirate captain comforted as he led her across the gleaming deck of his two-masted schooner. "They don't mean any harm. They're good men."

"They're pirates!" China reminded him haughtily.

Gabriel sighed. "Aren't we all?" His brilliantly white grin split his tanned face at the indignant glare she turned on him. "Your pardon, milady," he mocked, standing back and gesturing, with a bow, toward the door he wished her to enter. "I hadn't realized you bore such a keen dislike for men of my profession."

"If it had not been for men of your 'profession.'" China snarled as she preceded Gabriel along a narrow companionway, "by now I would have been with my—"

"With your?" Gabriel prompted when she let the sentence dwindle into nothingness.

"With my new master and mistress," she finished, deciding the wisest course lay in going on with her masquerade as Meghan Gordon, indentured servant.

"Ah, my dear," he said as he stopped before a door and produced an ornate brass key from his pocket, "you are far too lovely to spend your days polishing furniture or cleaning grates." Opening the door, he gestured for her to enter. "A young woman of your beauty should not be wasted on such menial pursuits. I should not like to see you with soot all over that lovely nose."

"What I have on my nose is none of your affair, Master Fortune," she told him coldly.

Gabriel's green eyes bore into her for a long, awkward moment. "You claim to be a servant, Mistress Gordon, even while you have the airs of a duchess." He noted the way China's defiant glare wilted and slid away from his face. "There is a mystery about you," he mused aloud. "I will look forward to solving it. But for the meanwhile, make yourself comfortable. I am going above to see us out of this pesthole and on our way home."

China watched as he left the cabin, carefully locking the door behind him lest she get any foolish notions about escaping. When he was gone, China rubbed at the gooseflesh that had risen on her arms.

"Take care," she cautioned herself softly. "You've been with him little more than an hour and already he suspects you are not what you say you are."

Sobered, concerned that this pirate would not be so easily duped as the other had been, China wandered around the cabin in which Gabriel Fortune had imprisoned her.

It was smaller than Le Corbeau's, and there were no prize pieces of pirate's booty lying about to be gloated over as her previous captor had done with his rubies and gold. Whatever treasure Gabriel Fortune had taken from his enemies was either stored elsewhere on the ship or kept from sight in one of the cabinets built into the walls of the darkly paneled cabin.

Against one wall a walnut writing desk stood open. Papers lay strewn across its marquetry surface, and China, casting a wary eye toward the locked door, went to it.

Most of the papers were lists, notations

such as one might make in a ledger or log. Headings, landmarks, ships sighted both merchant and military, the value and description of prizes taken, the names of the men killed, the names and injuries of the wounded. A pirate's ledgers, China reflected, all itemized and ordered like any other business.

A half-unfolded sheet of thick, creamy paper caught China's eyes. As she picked it up, a lock of pale gold hair fell out onto the desk. The pink satin ribbon that bound it trailed over the pirate's papers. Curious, China tilted the page toward the lamp that had been lit to dispel the gathering darkness.

"My dearest heart," she read,

"So many weeks have passed since I last saw you. So many lonely nights when I have lain awake remembering that night in the garden when you asked me to be your wife. . . ."

Wife! China's eyes rounded. A thousand questions filled her mind. He was engaged! That sable-haired, green-eyed buccaneer! Did his fiancée know what he was? Did she approve? Was she content to live her life surrounded by the spoils of a life lived as a predator? Wearing clothes bought with stolen gold? Living in a home bought and furnished with the misery of her husband's victims? What sort of woman could she be? China remembered the trollops who lived on New Providence island, blowsy, hard women, toughened by the rough, often dangerous existence they eked out on the pirate isle.

China could not picture one of them writing the letter she held in her hand. Except for the merchants and their clerks and the sons or daughters of the nobility, there were few who could read and write. China doubted that one in a hundred of the women she'd glimpsed on the pirate stronghold could do more than make a distinctive mark that passed for their signature.

China picked up the lock of hair that had fallen to the desktop. It was long and softly curling, of a pale blonde not quite so silvery as her own but very similar in texture. As she fingered the lock, the delicate scent of jasmine wafted upward. This was no lover's token from some New Providence harlot. This was a memento from a lady of breeding if not of the aristocracy. Who was she, then, that she would deign to marry a pirate?

Another thought entered China's mind. She remembered hearing the stories they told of the great pirate Captain Kidd, who had been hanged at Wapping in 1701. They said that when not at sea plying his villainous trade, he had lived as a gentleman in a fine house on the corner of Pearl and Hanover streets on Manhattan island. They said he had a wife whom he adored and two children to whom he was a devoted father. Did Gabriel Fortune, like William Kidd, have another life waiting upon his return to his home port? Did he, when not aboard his ship, live as a gentleman, courting well-bred young ladies, whispering sweet nothings to them in flower-scented, night-shrouded gardens?

China found herself unexpectedly beguiled by such a thought. He was handsome, she admitted grudgingly, very handsome, with his thick dark hair, his eyes the color of the first leaves of spring, and his smile—that pearly flash against the sun-kissed flesh of his face.

What would he look like, she wondered, dressed in a gentleman's clothes rather than the rakish—and, she had to admit, becoming—pirate's garb of tall boots, dark breeches, and loose shirt that gave him enough freedom of movement to use his weapons with ease in a fight. Would the fall of a linen stock over a delicately embroidered silken waistcoat detract from that threatening masculinity? Somehow she thought not.

The iron rattle of the key turning in the lock of the cabin door sent China scrambling. She dropped the letter she held loosely in her hand and laid the beribboned lock of hair across it. Retreating to the other side of the cabin, she pretended to gaze out at the black expanse of the sea where the shores of New Providence had long since faded from view.

"Are you hungry?" Gabriel Fortune asked as he entered.

China turned toward him. He was carrying a tray on which rested a steaming bowl of stew, a spoon, fork, glass, and a bottle of wine.

"I am, actually," she admitted, crossing to the table where he'd placed the tray. "Aren't you going to eat?"

He shook his head. "I'll join you in a drink, though," he promised.

Taking up her spoon, China warily tasted the stew. Unlike the abominable fare served aboard Le Corbeau's ship, this was delicious. Great chunks of beef swam in a thick aromatic broth with potatoes and carrots.

"It's good," she told him honestly, pausing for a sip of the sweet red wine he poured into her glass.

"One of the things I demand on my ship is a decent cook," he said. "We take on provisions as often as we can. I don't think men fight well when they're hungry or sick. I don't want to see my crew with their ribs poking out." He paused long enough for

China to nod. "Or all yellow with jaundice." She nodded again. "With their teeth falling out from scurvy . . ."

"I see your point," she told him sharply, anxious for his litany to end.

Gabriel's eyes sparkled. "Or eyeing the rats in the holds as if they were Sunday hams."

"Enough!" China hissed. "I am trying to eat!" She shuddered, muttering under her breath: "Rats!"

Picking up her fork, she speared a piece of meat and Gabriel mocked: "Squeak! Squeak!"

"Will you stop!" China snarled.

Laughing, Gabriel leaned back in his chair and took a long draught from the bottle of wine. He watched China as she ate, noted her manners, the air of practiced gentility that surrounded her. When she had finished, he asked her:

"Who are you?"

The question should not have taken China by surprise. She had suspected before that he had not accepted her at face value.

"Meghan," she told him after too long a hesitation. "Meghan Gordon."

"Indentured servant," he finished for her.

"Aye," she confirmed. "I was to be a lady's maid to a gentleman's wife."

Gabriel stared at her. He did not believe she was some lowly servant nor even some gently-born girl reduced by poverty to sell herself into servitude. But who or what she was, he knew, was a secret she would guard carefully. He would let her keep it, he decided, for the moment. But one day he would know the truth.

"Have some more wine," he invited casually, refiling her glass.

"Why, Mr. Fortune," she teased, already feeling the effects of the strong red wine more than she realized or would have admitted, "I do believe you are trying to make me drunk."

"And if I am?" he countered, an unmistakable gleam in his leaf green eyes.

"It's very wicked of you," she told him primly. "Very, very wicked, indeed!"

"I'm a wicked man," he retorted with a shrug of his wide shoulders. "I'm a pirate, a brigand. Or hadn't you heard?"

China giggled, hiccoughing softly. "Someone told me that, but I did not know if I should believe him."

Gabriel leaned forward, his eyes sparkling with a fire she hadn't seen in them before. All the playful, bantering air of a moment ago was gone. "Believe him," he counseled seriously. "And don't ever—ever—cross swords with me, for I am a deadly adversary."

China gazed at him, his words not quite penetrating the warm, wine-soaked haze that seemed to have gathered around her. "Are you trying to frighten me?" she asked, unwilling to admit that if he was, he was succeeding admirably.

"No," Gabriel disagreed. "Merely warning you."

They fell silent then, Gabriel rising and leaving the table, leaving China to watch him over the rim of her refilled glass. He went to the desk as though sensing for the first time that the papers there might reveal more about him than he cared to have known. Gathering the papers—with no particular regard for the letter or its pale blonde, beribboned token, China noticed—he closed the desk and turned the tiny key in its chased silver lock.

China burned to ask him about the letter and his fiancée but could not. She would not admit to him she'd been snooping in his papers and did not think he would be willing to tell her anything of his personal life. Instead, she asked casually:

"Where are we going?"

"Home," he replied shortly, a troubled look crossing his brow. He wondered how much she might have learned about him from those carelessly left documents. She did not have to admit having looked at the ledgers and letters on the desk; he would have been surprised if she hadn't.

"And where is home?" she persisted.

He turned toward her, his expression now

one of lazy amusement. "Do you always ask so many questions?"

China felt a flush of embarrassment rising into her cheeks. Eyes studiously downcast, she drained her glass only to have him come to the table and fill it once more.

"No more," she decided, shaking her head. "I'm getting dizzy."

"Perhaps you should go to bed," he told her. "It's late and it's been a long day for us all. Get some sleep. I've got to go check our heading and see the night watch is on duty."

China watched him leave, her eyes drawn to the fluidity of his movements, the powerful animal strength that seemed so much a part of him. Her eyes went to the locked desk as the door closed behind her captor. The tiny keyhole was empty. He had taken the key with him, thus ending China's chances of learning more of who—and what—Gabriel Fortune might really be.

Rising from the table, China clutched at the back of her chair for support. She hadn't been lying when she'd told Gabriel she felt dizzy. The shadowy, half-lit cabin swam before her eyes. The bed, nestled into one corner of the low-ceilinged cabin, seemed so far away, and the pitch and roll of the ship seemed to have increased tenfold since she sat down at the table to eat.

Moving slowly, carefully, she reached the bed. Her wine-soaked brain did not stop to ponder where the bed's owner intended to sleep. All she knew was that she wanted to lie down in the warm softness of the bed and wait for her head to clear. She fumbled with the laces of her gown and petticoats. Undressed to her chemise, she slid beneath the covers.

The darkness in the cabin was complete when China emerged from the depths of her intoxicated slumber. She was warm, so warm, and the bed felt smaller now, with a wall close on either side of her. Her senses swam, with the wine she thought at first, but then she realized it was something more.

The wall at her back was no wall at all. It was a body, hard, unyielding, far larger than her own. The warmth that felt so luxuriant was the heat of strong, muscled flesh curved around her. The languid, delicious sensation that set her senses swimming came from the arms that held her, from the hands, large, work-roughened, long-fingered, that had eased up the skirt of her chemise and now explored her soft, alabaster skin with practiced skill.

China shuddered as the hand that rested for a moment at the inward curve of her narrow waist slipped up to cradle her breast. It held her, weighing the quivering flesh in its palm while the thumb traced lazy circles around the taut, pale pink crest.

Through the tipsy, bemused haze that clouded it, China's mind shouted a warning. But her will, her senses, fell all too easily under the spell of the new, hitherto unimagined sensations those hands were evoking. Sheltered, protected, destined for marriage with a nobleman who would insist upon being the one to awaken his bride's passions, China had been told nothing of men and women, of love and lovemaking. As she lay in those arms, she knew only that she'd never felt as she did at that moment, only that she thought she would die if he stopped touching her, holding her.

His hand slid down to her hip, down over the gentle rise of her belly, over the long, lean curve of her thigh and back up again. China gasped, shuddering, as he found her, touched her, his fingers moving rhythmically against her flesh. A feeling was growing inside her, blossoming, burgeoning, she felt frightened and enthralled at the same time. Surely, surely, she told herself, arching back into the curve of his body, nearly weeping with the sheer pleasure of his caresses, she could not bear much more.

And then Gabriel was turning her, moving her. He lay above her, his face in the shadowy half-light of the cabin was flushed, sweat beaded his brow and the full chiseled curve of his top lip. China gazed up at him uncertain, curious. His glittering green eyes saw the innocent bewilderment in her eyes and realized too late what it meant.

For China the sudden, sharp, tearing pain that shot through her cleared her senses. She screamed. Her hands pushed at him, she writhed, trying to escape him, her nails gouged at his shoulders. She felt as though her body were being torn apart as he took her, as he tore asunder that veil of virginity her parents had intended for some marquis or earl.

Still, his breathing broken, harsh in the quiet cabin, Gabriel lay above China. He realized what he had done. He knew he had hurt her, frightened her. But he could not stop then, his body ached with a fire that only time could quench—time spent in making love to the trembling, beautiful, tearful girl in his arms.

Murmuring soft, meaningless words to China, he began to move against her. He heard her weeping, felt the hot wetness of her tears against his throat, his shoulder. He could not fathom her thoughts—truth to tell, he had never lain with a virgin. He supposed her behavior was nothing unusual. And he hoped that with time, with patience and gentleness, he could atone for whatever fear, whatever pain he had caused her.

But those thoughts, those intentions, were forgotten as his body shuddered in the throes of his rapture. He knew only the moment, only the pleasure so intense it was almost pain.

It was only afterward that he had some clue as to China's emotions. Only when he sat on the edge of the bed at a loss to know what to say to her and he found her blazing, sky-blue glare upon him. Only when her sobbing quieted and her voice rang out clear and filled with loathing in the silent cabin:

"I hate you, Gabriel Fortune!" she hissed. "I'll hate you till the day I die! And if it's the last thing I do, I'll pay you back for what you've done to me!"

Three

If any of the crewmen aboard Gabriel's *Golden Fortune* noticed the change in their captain's mood, the frown that seemed to perpetually furrow his brow, the air of tension that hung over him, the way he seemed to find no end of things to do above decks, they made no mention of it. At least not aloud. But below decks in the communal sleeping quarters where they lay in their hammocks and on their pallets when not on duty, speculation ran rife as to the cause of their captain's ill temper.

It was a woman, they agreed, it had to be, for their fortunes at sea had been good on this voyage as they had on the last. It was a woman, and what was more, it was the woman who even then was residing in the captain's cabin.

"I said we shouldn't take her aboard," a young sailor reminded his shipmates. "I said it when I seen him bringin' her from that Frenchie's ship."

"A woman aboard ship's bad luck," decreed an older pirate with a grimy patch where his left eye should have been. "The cap'n would be a sight better off if he just threw her to the sharks."

There was a murmur of agreement, but a single voice rose in China's defense:

"I seen her when she came aboard," Tom, the youngest member of Gabriel's crew remembered. "She was the prettiest woman I ever seen."

He ducked, covering his head with his arms as shoes, bits of half-whittled wood, and anything else laying loose at hand came flying from every direction. Shrinking back into his bunk, he said no more. But in his mind he pictured the silver-haired girl he'd seen come aboard with the captain he respected—and feared—and he remembered thinking to himself that that was what success must be; a fine ship, a loyal crew, and a woman who took your breath away.

"It has to be the woman," a grizzled seaman decided, "but why? I've been with the cap'n more'n just about anybody. I ain't never seen him in this kind of lather before. He's always been like the rest of us. When he needs a woman he finds one. When he's had his fill of her, he sails away."

"That's the only way to be," a red-headed gunner asserted. "Don't let them get their hooks into you. First thing you know, you're a landlubber scratchin' out a livin' on an acre of rocks with a wife and a half-dozen brats tuggin' at her skirts. An' the sea only a memory."

They fell silent then, unable to fathom such a fate, for they were all sailors first and foremost and the thought of leaving the sea for the life of a farmer was too horrible to comprehend.

"You think that's what it is?" a tall, gangly rigger wanted to know. "You think that woman's got her hooks into the cap'n?"

"Can't have!" a gunner's mate snarled. "The cap'n's too smart to let any woman snare 'im!"

But Gabriel's change of mood had begun the morning after they'd left New Providence—the morning after they'd taken the girl aboard—and though none of them cared to consider the possibility, all of them wondered what there was between their captain and the girl whom none of them had seen since Gabriel had taken her below three days before.

The truth would have been more difficult

for them to believe than any of their theories. The truth was that nothing had happened between Gabriel and China since that first night. No touch had passed between them, scarcely a look, and certainly no words. Gabriel had not known how to approach her, and China had not deigned to address so much as a syllable to him. The few times that he found her eyes upon him, her look was filled with such reproach, such repugnance, that any intentions he had of trying to bridge the chasm between them withered and died unspoken.

He stood at the railing with only the ship's lanterns for light on a night when the moon and the stars hid behind coal-black clouds. The sea beyond the rail was inky, impenetrable, black as the dark, dense feeling in his heart. He thought of China below in his cabin—the cabin he could scarcely bear to visit now. A part of him chafed with angry impatience at her stubborn ill humor. After all, she had seemed willing enough in those languid, sensual moments when he'd held her, caressed the petal-soft flesh whose memory still moved him to desire whenever he thought of it. He had not known she was a virgin. She was so beautiful and no mere child. It seemed ridiculous to think no man had possessed her.

The scowl his crew had come to know twisted his handsome face. She should not be humored. If she was going to sulk like a child, perhaps he should treat her like a child. A good spanking might teach her to act like a woman and not like a spoiled schoolgirl.

But then, even as those thoughts were swirling in his mind, another, less welcome notion crept its stealthy way into his consciousness. Spoiled. That was how she acted. Like some pampered puss used to having her own way, unused to being crossed. There was nothing humble about her, nothing of the servant, meek and biddable. He had seen enough of women to know that servants, even indentured ones, even gentle-born girls forced into servitude, did not sulk for days, refusing to speak, throwing their silent tantrums and waiting for whomever had offended them to come crawling to them with apologies.

What then, did that tell him about the girl who was even then locked in his cabin? He'd suspected from the first she was not really the person she claimed to be. But then, if she were some cosseted daughter of rich and influential parents, what was she doing traveling on a ship that had fallen so easily into a pirate's hands?

Running his hands through his sable hair, heedless of the long, waving locks he pulled free from their confining grosgrain ribbon at the nape of his neck, Gabriel found himself with a new worry. It was getting dangerous for pirates in colonial waters. The British were taking harsher measures against them, and the Royal Governor of Virginia, Alexander Spotswood, had declared that nothing would keep him from pursuing them, driving them out of American waters. Even North Carolina, whose governor, Charles Eden, had a comfortable, and profitable, arrangement with the pirates, could not guarantee their safety. Not with Spotswood's ships ignoring boundaries and territories in their vendetta against the brigands haunting the coastal waters.

And now—this. If the girl he'd taken a few nights ago turned out to be the daughter or sister or betrothed of some—God forbid—Virginia planter, Spotswood would single him out to be made an example. Everything he'd dreamed of, worked for, all his hopes and ambitions would end on a scaffold before a crowd of jeering spectators.

He could almost picture a teary-eyed beauty testifying how he had won her on the turn of a card, taken her to his ship, forced himself upon her (leaving out the fact, of course, that up until the time he'd actually entered her she'd been enjoying their loveplay as much as he himself).

He could hear himself being portrayed as the vilest of men, a fiend, a ravisher of helpless young women, a defiler of innocence. He had no doubt that of all the testimony the law might muster against him, that of "Meghan Gordon" would be the one to put the noose around his neck.

Absently, he rubbed his throat as though he could already feel the rough caress of the hemp against his skin. Lost in thought, he did not hear the approach of his first mate, Edward O'Meara.

"Evenin', cap'n," he said, coming to stand at the rail beside Gabriel.

Gabriel started at the sound of his voice. Then with a self-mocking smile he returned his mate's greeting.

"We should be makin' port by this time tomorrow," O'Meara observed. "I expect you'll be glad to be back home."

"I will," Gabriel agreed. "But—"

The first mate glanced sideways at his captain. He, like the rest of the crew, had noticed the change in Gabriel's temperament over the past few days. And, also like the rest of the crew, he had thought it the wisest course to say nothing about it.

"But, cap'n?" he ventured now, his position as first mate and his long years of association with Gabriel giving him the right to at least try to discover the captain's dilemma.

Gabriel sighed. "It's the girl," he said quietly. "I don't know what to do with her."

"If ye let her go," O'Meara questioned,

"would she be like to call the law down on us?"

"As soon as she could," Gabriel admitted. "She hates me. She's vowed to pay me back for—"

O'Meara nodded, suspecting he had a fairly clear notion of what it was the girl in the captain's cabin wished to be revenged for.

"Then ye can't turn her loose," he observed. "Ye could always—"

Gabriel looked at his first mate and saw O'Meara draw one scarred finger slowly across his throat.

"No," he insisted. "I could not kill her." His first mate started to speak, but Gabriel went on: "Nor could I let someone else harm her."

O'Meara frowned, shaking his head. "God help ye, cap'n, she may be gettin' her hooks into ye."

"I think she may be," Gabriel agreed. "I do think she may be."

Pulling his cap from his head, O'Meara hung his grizzled head as if a dear friend had died. "'Tis a fine shame, cap'n. A fine shame."

Leaving his captain at the rail to ponder his dreadful fate, Edward O'Meara went below to break the terrible news to the crew of the *Golden Fortune*: their captain had been laid low by the one adversary neither canon nor saber could defeat, the siren's call of a woman.

Left behind, solitary, downcast, Gabriel knew the situation was far more serious than even his first mate knew. For Edward O'Meara, trusted comrade though he might be, knew nothing of the letter in his desk accepting his proposal of marriage—a proposal he'd regretted almost from the moment he'd made it. So now he was engaged to a woman he did not love and obsessed with a woman who vowed to destroy him. How could he explain either to the other, and how could he rid himself of one and break down the barriers of resentment and disgust that separated him from the other?

"Damnation!" he muttered to the vast emptiness around him. "I'd rather face a dozen British men o' war than one vengeful woman!"

Leaving the deck, he went to the storeroom where he'd slept the past two nights, not caring to brave China's self-righteous loathing by going to his own bed. Curling up on a Turkey carpet taken from a Portuguese merchantman, he tried to sleep and longed for tomorrow when he would be home.

China jerked her arm out of his grasp as he helped her down the gangway and onto the dock built along the bank of a river. She stumbled—after the long weeks at sea she felt oddly disoriented on dry land—but her icy glare kept Gabriel from lending assistance.

"Where are we?" she demanded as they left the dock where Gabriel's ship was being unloaded.

"Home," he replied simply, gesturing toward a deeply rutted road where a simple one-horse shay waited.

"Your home, not mine," she hissed. "But where, I will ask again, are we? Are we in America, at least?"

"At least," he admitted, but would say no more.

He bundled her into the carriage, then climbed in after her. Driving away from the dock, they crossed a wide, cleared expanse of lawn. In the distance, illuminated by the moonlight that appeared suddenly from behind the gathering thunderheads of an approaching storm, China saw the skeleton of a sprawling house. It was not far along. It would be some months before it was habitable. But China could see from the shape, the size, that it would be as large as many of the grand country houses she'd visited with her parents in England.

"Yours?" she asked, seeing that his eyes lingered on the house sitting on a rise of ground.

"Mine," he admitted.

"For your fiancée?" China pressed a hand to her mouth but it was too late, the words she had not meant to utter had been said.

Gabriel only smiled. "I suspected you'd seen that letter." He thought quickly, trying to remember if his betrothed had signed it with her entire name—he wanted nothing to give China a clue to the secrets he hid behind his pirate's persona. Then he remembered that the letter had been signed with an initial only and he relaxed. "And yes, the house was meant to be finished by the time of my marriage."

"Was meant to be?" she repeated. "You mean it won't be?"

"Materials and labor are not so easily come by in America as in England."

"Hmmm," China sighed sympathetically. "I suppose very few of the ships you plunder are carrying nails or lumber or shingles."

Gabriel threw her a sideward glance and found her eyeing him with an expression of high amusement. Slapping the reins, he drove them past the half-finished house and into the surrounding forest.

When they emerged into the next clearing, China saw their destination. It was a cottage, built of brick, with an enormous chimney on each end. Three dormer windows pierced the steeply pitched roof, and two diamond-paned windows pierced the front and the back of the cottage.

"This is where you live?" she asked as he lifted her out of the carriage and set her on her feet near the three steps leading to the door.

"When I am not at sea," he confirmed.

"And this is where you mean me to live?"

Gabriel said nothing as he unlocked the door and led her inside. In the near darkness, he went to a table near the door and, striking a flint, lit a candle which he used to light others around the central hall. Motioning for China to follow, he went into the parlor and lit candles there. Logs had been stacked in the fireplace and he lit them, kindling a fire that would soon take the damp chill out of the room.

China came to the fireplace, drawn by the flickering light and the warmth of the fire. The room around her was white-walled with a heavy, beamed ceiling. The furnishings were, for the most part, old, well-worn. Here and there a piece stood out—a fine marquetry table, an exquisite chased gold box, a pair of fabulous silver candlesticks—and China could not help wondering if they had come from one of Gabriel Fortune's victims.

Looking over her shoulder, she noticed he had left the room. She crossed the central hall and found him in the other of the two downstairs chambers. Having lit the candles, he was kindling a fire in a gaping fireplace obviously used for cooking.

"You mean me to stay here with you?" she asked as he rose and dusted his hands.

"I don't see any alternative, do you?" he countered.

There was a knock on the front door, and Gabriel opened it to allow two of his men to enter, each bearing a leather-bound trunk. Nodding to the captain, they fixed China with such angry, resentful glares that she involuntarily stepped back and behind Gabriel.

"Why do they look at me that way?" she questioned as they returned to the parlor.

"I've no idea," Gabriel lied. Having received solemn condolences from several of his crew on his misfortune at having been "netted" by a woman, he knew they regarded her as a threat both to their continued success on the sea and, if she made good her vow to destroy Gabriel, to their very lives.

China did not believe him for a moment, but there seemed little point in disputing the point. She watched as he sat beside the fire and stretched his booted legs out toward it. Though she'd vowed never to speak to him again, the change in their surroundings meant that certain questions had to be asked and, hopefully, answered.

"What do you mean to do with me?" she wanted to know, standing only near enough to feel the warmth of the fire.

"Keep you here," he replied. "I could

hardly let you go, could I?"

"You could," she disagreed. "It would be the decent thing to do."

"But then I am not a decent man, am I?" he countered. "Isn't that why you vowed you would avenge your lost honor?"

The last two words were said with a cold harshness that stung China. Swearing he would not see how they hurt her, she turned her back to him.

"And if I promised I would say nothing about you to anyone?" she ventured.

"I could not risk believing you," he replied quietly, his leaf green eyes following the tumble of shining silver curls to that slender waist he'd caressed on the night he'd made her hate him. Unbidden, the memory of that night, the softness of her skin, the silken tickle of those curles against his skin, the sound of her pleasure in those blissful moments before he'd known that her passion was that of awakening innocence filled his mind.

Those memories moved him, roused him, with a sudden violence that startled him. Rising, he left the fireside and went to a table where a bottle of wine waited.

"Do you want some?" he asked her, holding up the bottle.

"I think I'd better not," she replied stiffly. "Considering . . ."

Gabriel's face flushed. "I had no intention

of . . . I did not mean . . ." A harsh sound of exasperation escaped him. "I did not bring you here tonight intending to make you my mistress."

China rubbed at her arms. Despite the now-roaring fire, she felt cold. "What am I to be, then, your prisoner?"

His eyes glimmered slyly. "You could be a servant here. Little difference—here or in someone else's house."

"There would be a great deal of difference," she disagreed. "The master to whom I was indentured is not the man who raped me."

Gabriel held his tongue, biting back a sarcastic reply, resisting the urge to remind her that she'd derived more than a little pleasure from those initial caresses and that by the time she changed her mind it was simply beyond his strength to stop. Instead, he asked:

"What makes you think any master who had a servant as beautiful as you beneath his roof would not sooner or later give her a choice of either gracing his bed or leaving his employ?"

China chafed impatiently. The argument was pointless since she was not a servant at all. But since she could hardly use that to end the exchange, she retorted:

"Not all men are as wicked as you, Mr. Gabriel Fortune."

With a haughty lift of her chin she turned away, satisfied that she had had the last jab in their battle of jibes. But even as she did, she remembered his words—"a servant as beautiful as you"—and to her annoyance she found her heart beating faster, felt a little thrill that he found her beautiful, obviously desired her.

Sharply, crossly, she banished such thoughts from her mind. He had ruined her without a thought, without a care for her future. He, a man with a fiancée, a man who knew he belonged to another woman. And now, to offer to make her a servant in his house!

Gabriel watched the play of emotion across her face. He had deliberately offered to make her a servant hoping her pride would force her to tell him she was no lowly scullery maid. That had not happened, but from the expression he'd seen in her eyes, her face, he believed he was right in assuming she was merely masquerading as an indentured servant. In time, he was confident, he would learn the truth.

The pounding at the front door caught them both by surprise. Gabriel went to answer it, and China crept as close as she dared to the chamber door in order to hear what was happening.

"The storm's comin' up, cap'n," O'Meara told Gabriel. "She looks to be a bad 'un. Most of the cargo's unloaded. "I told the men to lash 'er down and go home till it passes."

"That's fine," Gabriel approved. "But tell me, Edward, is there anyone about you can send to the inn for some food? There's none in the house and I'm deucedly hungry."

"There's young Thomas," O'Meara replied. "He's no family to go to, so I told him he can come home with me. But he's a mite fuddlebrained, y'know."

"Surely he could find the inn," Gabriel decided. "It's practically at the end of the lane. Send him. Tell him to bring back whatever they have ready. For two. Give him this and tell him there's another for him if he gets the food back before the storm breaks."

"Aye, cap'n," O'Meara agreed.

Pulling open the door, both men gasped at the sudden chill of the inrushing wind. O'Meara left, and Gabriel stood in the doorway staring up at the thick black clouds filling the night sky. It was going to be a bad one. He knew he should go down to the dock and make certain the ship was lashed tightly. If it was driven against the dock it could do extensive damage both to the dock and to the hull of the ship.

But could he leave his guest alone there? It was true she had no notion of where she was, but that might not stop her trying to escape. Perhaps if he told her he was posting guards around the cottage . . . She knew his men did not like her. It may be that she would rather stay in the cottage and have only her captor to deal with than take her chances if she were captured by one of his crewmen.

Deciding that was the best course, he went back into the parlor to tell her he was going to the dock but leaving some of his crewmen around the cottage. When he entered the room he saw that all his planning was for nothing. The back window stood open. The crewelwork draperies fluttered as the wind swirled about the room extinguishing the candles and sending sparks from the fireplace dancing dangerously over the carpet.

Gabriel ran to the window. Outside the night was black as pitch and the surrounding forest concealed the beautiful refugee who had fled into it.

"Damn!" he muttered. "Damn! Damn! Damn!" He punctuated his words with sharp blows of his fist against the window jamb.

He cursed himself for having left her alone, but how was he to know that she would be so stupid—or so bold—as to brave the wild, storm-swept forest by night?

Four

The storm broke overhead as China stumbled blindly through the black tangle of the forest. Frightened by the blinding flashes of lightning, deafened by the crashing bursts of thunder, she went on and on. Her skirts grew sodden and heavy, her hair trailed in lank, dripping skeins over her head and shoulders, her face and arms were lashed by branches, her feet in their thin, soaked slippers were bruised by rocks and fallen limbs littering the floor of the forest. But still she did not stop, and in spite of the cold and the wet and the pain she was grateful for the storm. As hard as it made her flight, it also made it harder for Gabriel and his men to find her.

Tripping over a fallen tree, China sprawled. The breath rushed from her burning lungs as her hands scraped the rocky ground. A pain shot up her thigh as her knee struck a stone half-buried in the sodden earth. Gasping, compressing her lips to stifle a cry that she feared might bring Gabriel or his men swarming down upon her, China knelt there as the rain sheeted down on her.

Cold, frightened, lost, she wished for nothing more than a warm, dry shelter where she might seek refuge from the storm roaring about her. But she could not regret having taken her one chance of escape. She knew, for all Gabriel Fortune's smug offers of servitude in the grand manor he was building, that all he was truly offering her was a place in his bed. He might think that "Meghan Gordon" would leap at the chance to escape a life of drudgery. Perhaps, had she been "Meghan Gordon" she might have agreed. But she was a baron's daughter—she would never be mistress to a pirating scoundrel who obviously thought himself heaven's gift to any woman.

She had to go on. Pushing herself to her feet, she wiped her hands on the wet, dragging skirt of her gown and forced herself to resume her flight through the forest. There was no moon to show her the way. She had long since lost any sense of direction. She could only pray she was going in the right direction and that her arduous, painful flight would not lead her back to the cottage and to the sensual servitude Gabriel had in mind for her.

The storm seemed to be abating when China, bone weary, chilled, her arms and throat and cheeks crosshatched with scratches from the tangled underbrush of the forest, sank down in the relatively dry shelter of a young oak tree. She longed to stay there. Fatigue had taken hold of her, fatigue born of the tension and fear and shocks of the past few weeks. She desperately longed to curl in a ball on the soft bed of damp leaves and go to sleep, but she knew it would be folly of the most dangerous kind. With the storm letting up, Gabriel was almost certain to be looking for her and with his pirate's cunning would no doubt realize she had heard him speak of the inn near the end of the lane. Her only hope lay in reaching the inn and pleading for sanctuary from Gabriel and his men.

Her determination bolstered by that thought, she ran her fingers through her dripping hair, pushing it out of her face, and moved on. With each step she took, each minute that passed, the storm was easing. The black clouds were moving on, and China knew she had to reach the shelter of the inn before the glow of the moon helped Gabriel Fortune find her.

"Please, oh please," she whispered, "let me escape from him! I can't go back there, I can't!"

As if in answer to her plea, she saw a flickering light filtering through the rain-heavy, dripping branches of the trees around her. China's heart thudded heavily in her chest. If that should be Gabriel . . . If she should find she had merely wandered in a circle, lost in the storm, confused by the pelting rain . . .

But it was not Gabriel. As China crept closer to the light, she heard voices unlike any she'd heard while in the company of Gabriel and his crew.

Poised like a skittish doe, ready to take flight, she moved nearer and found herself on the edge of a rutted road cut through the forest. The flickering lights she had seen were torches, their flames hisses and faltering as the last drops of the passing storm threatened to extinguish them.

"Put your shoulder to it, man!" a man was commanding.

China studied him in the wavering light. He was not so tall as Gabriel Fortune nor so powerfully built, but just then, in her eyes, that was in his favor. He wore light jackboots that reached to his black breeches. His coat was of fawn cloth and the frills of his linen shirt showed beneath the wide, turned-back cuffs. A black beaver tricorne rested on wavy, dark auburn hair worn loose about his shoulders. When he turned and his face came into view, China could see he was not unhandsome though he had none of the brutal masculine beauty that had both frightened and enticed her in Gabriel Fortune.

Trembling with the cold and her own uncertainty, China hovered there in the shelter of the concealing undergrowth. She knew that once the coach wheels were freed from the boggy mud into which they'd slid, the man and his companions—coachman and outriders, by the look of them—would be gone, and along with them a perfect opportunity for escape from Gabriel.

But did she dare place herself in this man's clutches? Who was to say he was not as great a scoundrel as the man from whom she was fleeing? What if he, too, was a pirate? What if he knew Gabriel Fortune—was his friend—and would return her to him? Perhaps she'd be better served to try and find the inn. And yet, might not the innkeeper be a friend of Gabriel's? Might he not wish to win Gabriel's good will by returning her to him?

Wracked by indecision, China watched as the man in the fawn coat urged the horses forward while his three companions pushed at the large, dark-painted traveling coach from behind. The horses strained, their hooves sinking into the mud, sliding, and the coach inched forward, little by little rising from the mud that had trapped it.

Once they tried. Twice. On the third attempt they succeeded and the coach rolled out into the relative safety of the road's center.

"Damnation!" the coachman swore, wiping at his sweaty brow with his sleeve. "I never thought she'd come free!"

"Nor did I," the auburn-haired man agreed. "But she has. At last. Now, let us be on our way."

From the side of the road, the two outriders retrieved their tethered horses and swung up into their saddles. The coachman climbed up onto the box and took up the reins. And the gentleman with the black tricorne lifted a foot onto the coach step.

China knew she must reveal herself at that moment or lose the opportunity. Stumbling out from her hiding place, she cried:

"Wait! Please, I beg of you, sir!"

Startled, the man turned toward her while his two outriders stared, too surprised to draw their weapons.

Seeing the look on their faces, China flushed. What a sight she must be after her soaking in the storm and mishaps in the forest! Self-consciously, she pushed the wet hair back from her face and tugged at the drenched and dirty skirts of her gown.

"God's teeth!" the man muttered. "What's happened to you, my child?"

Trembling, China stepped closer. "Please, sir!" she breathed, brought close to tears by the kindness in his dark eyes and the concern in his voice. "Don't let him find me! Take me away with you, I beg of you! If he finds me . . . If he should recapture me . . ."

A sob caught in her throat and she wrapped her arms about herself. The man, moved by her distress, came to stand nearer.

"Who?" he asked, looking over her head toward the dark forest from which she'd emerged. "Who is after you? What do you mean, 'recapture' you?"

"Gabriel Fortune!" she hissed, shivering.

"Gabriel—the pirate?"

China nodded. "He kidnapped me from the ship I was aboard. I escaped. He'll come looking for me! He must not find me! Please, don't let him. Say you will help me!"

Reaching out, she seized a handful of the soft woolen cloth of his sleeve. Her great blue eyes, awash with unshed tears, pleaded with him.

"Hush now," he soothed. "I will help you, of course I will. Come, get into the coach. We'll be away before this villain can find you."

Climbing into the coach, China found herself wrapped in the warm folds of a heavy greatcoat. She settled onto the velvet seat of the coach scarcely daring to believe she was even then being borne away from Gabriel

Fortune and the life he had planned for her.

Shivering despite the warmth of the garment that enveloped her, China slipped her feet out of her ruined slippers and tucked them into the folds of the coat. She managed a wan smile for the man who sat opposite her.

"I am obliged to you, sir," she said. "I had heard there was an inn hereabouts and thought to ask for shelter there."

The man nodded. "Likely the first place he would have gone to look," he said, confirming China's earlier fears. "Allow me to present myself. I am Ian Leyton—Dr. Leyton."

"I am—" China hesitated. It might be wise, she thought, to keep her name a secret until she knew more of what kind of man he was. "Meghan Gordon," she finished. "Your servant, sir."

"Your servant, Miss Gordon," he returned. Frowning, he pulled off his tricorne. His dark auburn hair shone in the wavering light of the coach lamps. "You say this varlet abducted you from your ship?"

"That is not precisely true," China admitted. "Another pirate took me from my ship. Gabriel Fortune took me from him."

"They prey on one another now, do they?" he asked.

"I believe they were gambling. On New Providence island. Gabriel Fortune won me."

"Barbarous." Ian Leyton shook his head, his face the picture of disgust. "These wretches are far too bold. It shouldn't be tolerated. But I daresay as long as Charles Eden is governor of North Carolina . . ."

"North Carolina?" China interrupted. "Is that where we are?"

"Aye," he confirmed. "Is that where you were bound?"

"No. I was bound for Virginia."

"Ah. That is to the north. I, myself, am bound for Virginia. Williamsburg. I . . ." He paused, his dark eyes softening at the sight of her shivering despite the warmth of the coat he'd wrapped around her.

From the depths of his coat pocket, he brought out a small flask and handed it to her. "Drink some of this," he told her. "It will warm you."

China did as she was told. The brandy startled her, burning her throat, blazing a path down to her empty stomach, then seeming to go straight to her head. She coughed and gave him back the flask.

Ian tucked it back into his pocket. There were questions he longed to ask her—questions about Gabriel Fortune and the other pirate, the one who had kidnapped her in the first place. But when he would have spoken he noticed she had fallen asleep, lulled by the rocking of the coach, the warmth of the coat about her, and the brandy lying on her empty stomach.

Smiling, Ian took a fur-lined lap robe from the seat beside him and tucked it about her. His questions could wait. In the meanwhile it was pleasant to ride through the night wondering at the adventure she'd had and admiring her beauty, which, despite the half-dried, tangled locks of her silvery hair hanging about her pale face, was quite remarkable.

The inn was called the Blue Dovecote and the room in which Dr. Ian Leyton sat was the best it had to offer. Its furnishings were dark and in the ornate, heavily carved style of the later years of the previous century. But they were clean, the room well aired, and the sheets on the bed were fresh and smelled of lavender.

In the muted light of the late afternoon, Ian Leyton gazed at the supine figure in the bed. He was excited, intrigued, apprehensive.

She was beautiful, his fugitive from Gabriel Fortune. He'd known that two days before when she'd stumbled, sodden and bedraggled, from the forest. But he hadn't dared to imagine what she'd be like once the mud was washed from her alabaster skin and the twigs and tangles combed from her cascading, silver-pale hair.

She had not awakened from the slumber

into which she'd fallen as they rode through the forest in the darkness. The rain had chilled her to the bone and she'd taken cold. For the next day and all the following night she'd lain, shivering uncontrollably, while he cared for her, applying poultices to her beautiful, velvet-soft skin, burning aromatic herbs in a pot hung over a fire that made the room unbearably hot. He'd watched her scrupulously, pulling the blankets over her when she, in her fevered thrashings, kicked them off. He'd soothed her as best he could when she moaned and cried out fending off the attentions of Gabriel Fortune, who haunted her unconscious mind with unremitting regularity.

His diligent care had been rewarded late in the night when her fever had broken. With the wife of the innkeeper, he'd undressed China and bathed her, changed the sweat-soaked sheets, and kept watch, relieved, as she fell into a sound, quiet sleep uninterrupted by the nightmares that had bedeviled her during her illness.

Ian sighed as he thought of that incredible, creamy skin—soft, so soft—of her breasts, pink-tipped, nestling in his hand for an all too brief moment when he bathed her. If only—

But no. Sternly, he turned his thoughts from the memory of her beauty. His hand shook as he went to his traveling case and took out a carefully packed bottle more than half full of absinthe.

He poured a glassful of the green liqueur and lifted it to his lips. In the back of his mind, he heard again the warnings. Absinthe, so they said, affected the mind when taken in too large a quantity over a period of time. Well, that might or might not be true, he told himself. But he was a doctor, after all, and he knew how much was too much.

A stirring in the bed behind him made him replace the precious liqueur in its padded case. Turning, he found China struggling to push herself up in the bed.

"Rest quietly, my dear," he told her, going to the bedside. "You have been very ill."

China groaned. She felt leaden, dizzy, her very bones seemed to ache. "Where are we?" she asked.

"At an inn. The Blue Dovecote. You fell ill. I thought it best to stay here until the crisis had passed."

China gazed up at him. He was not as handsome as Gabriel, but then how many men were? And she was grateful to him for his consideration and care. He had rescued her from Gabriel and now he had broken his own journey for—she was startled to realize she had no idea what day it might be. In any case, he had delayed his own trip to care for her, a total stranger.

"You are very kind, sir," she murmured, flushing when she noticed she wore only her diaphanous shift and its wide, beribboned neck was hanging far off one bare shoulder.

"Not at all, Miss Gordon," he said, pretending not to notice as she pulled the garment into place. "I am, after all, a doctor and a gentleman. I could hardly leave you, ill and alone, with strangers."

China smiled, her cheeks pinkening prettily. "You and I are strangers, sir," she reminded him.

"I feel as though we are not," he told her. Sweeping forward the long tails of his embroidered white silk waistcoat, he sat down on the chair beside the bed. "I do not know where you were bound when you were abducted, Miss Gordon, but I should like to help you reach your destination. I, too, am bound for Virginia, as I told you. Williamsburg. If I could see you safely to your home, I should feel satisfied you were in no further danger."

China said nothing. She felt embarrassed that she had told him her name was Meghan Gordon. Now she must admit to her lie, for his kindness did not deserve to be repaid with falsehoods. She hoped he would understand her reasons for telling him less than the truth.

Ian took her hesitation for reluctance.

"You know, Miss Gordon," he said, "that I mean you no harm. I simply wish to know you will fall prey to no other brigands such as—"

"I comprehend your motives, sir," China said quickly, suddenly unable to bear the sound of Gabriel's name. "It is not out of suspicion of you that I hesitate. I fear I misled you." She felt her cheeks flush. "As to my identity."

"I do not understand."

"Bear with me, please," she asked. She picked at the binding of the blanket covering her legs, unable to meet his eyes. "When I was taken from my ship, I told my abductor my name was Meghan Gordon and that I was an indentured servant bound for my master's plantation in Virginia."

Ian Leyton tried to hide his chagrin. An indentured servant! He knew there was a little more equality between classes in America than in his native England, but even so! He was not merely a doctor—he was Lord Ian, younger son of the Earl of Denniston. For all that this girl was the most beautiful creature he'd ever seen, the thought of courting her now seemed ludicrous.

"I see," he said at last, trying to hide his disappointment but not succeeding. "Even so, I will take you to your master if you will allow—"

"Dr. Leyton," she interrupted. "I said I told my abductor that. I was afraid he would try to hold me for ransom if he thought there was a chance someone would pay for my return. They is why I lied to him."

"You lied?" Ian repeated, hope reborn.

"Aye," she admitted. "I am not Meghan Gordon. Nor am I an indentured servant. My name is China Clairmont. I was traveling to Montcalm on the York River. My uncle and aunt, Lord and Lady Clairmont, live there."

Ian's relief was almost comical. "Clairmont," he said thoughtfully. "I was once presented to Lord Clairmont in London."

"That must have been my father, sir, the previous Baron Clairmont. He and my mother perished in a fire."

"My condolences," Ian said sincerely. "And you were left alone in the world?"

"I was. My uncle, having inherited my father's estates, graciously offered me a home with his family. It was from his ship, the *Amity*, that I was taken."

Smiling broadly, Ian rose to his feet. "Well, then, Miss Clairmont, if you will allow me, I should be honored to escort you to your uncle's plantation."

"I should be glad of your company," China replied. "And I should be grateful if you would summon someone to help me dress so that we may be on our way."

Bowing, his manner suddenly courtly, Ian left the room to search out the innkeeper's wife. Behind him, lying back against the pillows, China frowned thoughtfully. She had the uncomfortable feeling she had just gained not only an escort but a suitor.

Five

China and Ian Leyton reached Yorktown just before noon the following day. The town bustled with life. As the principal port between Philadelphia and Charles Town, it attracted both the prosperous merchants who inhabited graceful, elegant homes on the bluffs overlooking the York River and the seamen who inhabited the rougher, less genteel settlement near the wharves "below the hill."

Since the Royal Governor had decreed that all goods entering and leaving Chesapeake Bay had to pass through Yorktown's customhouse, the wealth of the burgeoning colonies was there to be seen on Yorktown's wharves. There seemed no limit to the heights the town could achieve, for as the colonies prospered, as the number of ships sailing to and from America and Europe increased, so too did the wealth of the merchants, seamen, and craftsmen of Yorktown.

Arriving in the city, China and Ian Leyton went to the Swan Tavern on Main and Ballard Streets. There China waited in the ladies' parlor while Ian went to bespeak a room for her. He would also, he told her, dispatch a messenger to Montcalm to let China's uncle know she was safe.

"I'll stay with you until someone comes for you," Ian told her when they'd been conducted to the room upstairs.

"It's very kind of you," China told him. "I know my uncle will be grateful to you for postponing your business in Williamsburg to bring me here."

"It was a pleasure," the young doctor told her.

China turned away, made uncomfortable by the unconcealed admiration she saw in his dark eyes. Catching sight of herself in a gilt-framed looking glass, she lifted her hands to her hair.

"I look a sight," she fretted, pushing back one waving, silver lock of hair. She plucked at the skirts of her gown. Though the wife of the innkeeper at the Blue Dovecote had done her best to clean and mend China's gown, it was stained and bedraggled. "What will my uncle and aunt think of me, arriving like this?"

"You've been held captive by two pirates," Ian reminded her. "You escaped in a thunderstorm, fled through a pitch-black forest. You've been ill. They won't expect you to look as if you've just stepped from a bandbox."

"Even so . . ." She let the thought end on a sigh.

"You rest," he urged her. "I've asked for a maid to be sent to help you refresh yourself after our journey. I'm going to step out for a bit. But I'll be back long before anyone comes from Montcalm for you."

Smiling, China watched as Ian left the room. But her smile faded as the door closed behind him. Ungrateful though it might be, she wished he would simply accept her thanks and go on his way to Williamsburg. He had obviously appointed himself her protector, and, from the tone of his voice and the expression in his eyes, China feared he hoped to be even more than that.

A maidservant arrived with a jug of warm water and clean towels. A small cake of soap sat on the washstand. When China asked the girl if she could find her a comb, the girl bobbed a curtsy and left the room.

Stripped to her shift, China washed away the dust of the journey. When the maidservant returned, carrying a small ivory comb, China carefully worked the tangles from her long, curling hair and tied it back with a length of ribbon the innkeeper's wife at the Blue Dovecote had given her. Much as she hated to, China had no choice but to allow herself to be relaced into the mended, stained gown in which she'd escaped from Gabriel Fortune.

Gabriel. She hadn't allowed herself to think of him since the stormy night she'd run away from his little cottage. But now thoughts of him, disturbing, unwelcome thoughts, flooded her mind, filling her senses until she scarcely noticed the maid taking the dirty wash water and leaving the room.

In her mind's eye China saw his face, so handsome, his eyes, those amazing, leaf green eyes beneath the dark slashing brows that were as bold, as vivid, as the man himself. She saw him as he'd first appeared to her, dwarfing Le Corbeau in the cabin of the *Black Pearl.* She saw him in the little cottage kindling the fire to warm them both. But most disturbingly, she saw him in the master cabin of his own ship, the *Golden Fortune,* saw his green eyes glowing as he gazed at her, saw his face as it loomed above her in that breathless, aching moment just before he—

"China?" Ian's face appeared around the partially opened door. "I knocked but you did not answer. I was concerned . . ."

China's cheeks glowed red; she felt mortified, ashamed, as though the young physician could somehow fathom her thoughts of a moment ago.

"My mind was elsewhere," she offered by way of explanation.

"I brought you something," he told her, entering the room. In his arms he carried a large painted box. The maidservant who had brought China her wash water and comb followed him into the room.

"You've done quite enough for me already," China assured him, wishing he would not make her feel quite so beholden to him. All the same, her curiosity was piqued and she came to the chest at the foot of the bed where he'd laid down the box.

"I got it from a dressmaker a few streets away," he told her, lifting the lid to reveal a delectable pile of sky-blue damask and creamy linen.

China watched, astonished, as the maid emptied the box of the blue damask gown with its neck frill of cream-colored linen and double ruffle trimming elbow-length sleeves. It was worn over a hooped underpetticoat and a whisper-thin, lace-trimmed chemise. Fine embroidered stockings lay at the bottom of the box.

"But how . . . I cannot imagine . . ." she stumbled.

"The gown had been ordered," Ian explained, "then the order was canceled. The dressmaker was pleased to find someone who could use it." He saw no reason to tell China that the gown had been ordered by one of Yorktown's prosperous merchants, intended for his mistress. The order had been canceled after the sizable bill had been sent by mistake to the merchant's home—and his wife.

"It's lovely," China admitted. Much as she hated being obliged to her rescuer, she had to admit she much preferred meeting her relations in a new and fashionable gown to greeting them looking like some waif washed up on a seashore.

Pleased with her admiration of his gift, Ian left the room so China, with the help of the maidservant, could discard her stained and patched gown for the new one.

With the maid's help, China was soon dressed in the blue damask gown. The laces had to be pulled tight—apparently the nameless merchant's mistress was slightly more buxom than China. Once gowned, China sat before the looking glass while the maidservant gathered the hair about her face and pinned it into a cluster of curls. The rest she left hanging in long silvery ringlets down China's back.

"What shall I do with this, miss?" the maid

asked, pointing to the patched, stained gown China had discarded.

"Get rid of it," China told her. "I don't want it—any of it."

Gathering the old gown as well as China's shift, torn stockings, and mended petticoat, the maid left the room just as Ian returned.

"There's a carriage below just arrived," he told her. "I do believe it's your uncle, for I heard someone mention the name 'Clairmont.'"

China pressed her hands to the fluttering in her stomach. Though she had no reason to expect her uncle would be anything other than kind, she felt unaccountably nervous at the thought of meeting him.

Flying to the looking glass, she examined the fall of the linen ruffles at her elbows, the drape of her blue damask skirts. Pulling one long silvery ringlet over her shoulder, she let it fall over the swell of her bosom above the low, square neckline.

A tap at the door brought her self-conscious perusal to an end.

Ian opened the door. The innkeeper himself announced:

"Lord Clairmont."

Turning away from the looking glass, China clasped her hands in the folds of her skirts to still their trembling. She watched, breathless, as her uncle appeared in the doorway.

Arthur Clairmont, now Baron Clairmont, bore very little resemblance to the tall, urbane father China still grieved. He was shorter than his brother, but altogether larger, with broad shoulders and a powerful build that made him seem as solid as the very earth on which he stood. His face was square, jowly, with thick, bushy eyebrows of the same dark chestnut brown as the shoulder-length hair that was, apparently, his own rather than a wig. He was dressed plainly, his tall, spurred boots were well worn, his clothes—dark breeches, a russet coat, and brown waistcoat—were well cut and of quality materials but unadorned by the elaborate embroidery so popular in cities like Yorktown. Only his eyes, the same startling blue topaz as China's, marked him as a Clairmont.

Those eyes twinkled as they came to rest upon his niece. Tossing his three-cornered hat on a table, he came to her and enfolded her in his arms.

"Here you are at last!" he boomed, a surprising amount of emotion in his deep bass voice. "When the *Amity* docked and we heard what had happened . . ." He held China at arm's length. "I don't mind telling you, my dear, I thought we'd never see you again. I cannot tell you how I felt . . . my dear brother's only child . . ."

China was touched, moved by the emotion in his voice and his face. But she was bewildered. The letter in which she'd been offered a home at Montcalm had seemed cool, had made it plain the offer was tendered more out of duty that any genuine desire to see her rescued from destitution's door.

"I escaped my captor," she told him. "Dr. Leyton found me and has interrupted his own journey to Williamsburg to see me safely delivered to you."

"We owe you a great debt of gratitude," Lord Clairmont said, offering his hand to Ian. "Will you come to Montcalm, sir, and help us celebrate my niece's safe arrival?"

"Alas, milord," Ian replied, to China's secret relief, "my business in Williamsburg can be delayed no longer. I must leave at once."

China was content to leave it at that. But to her chagrin, her uncle went on:

"You must take care on the road, sir. Though Williamsburg lies less than four leagues distant, the road passes Black Swamp. The weather of late has been wet, the road is like to be a mire. Tell your coachman to take especial care."

"Thank you, sir," Ian replied. "I will do as you suggest."

"Good. And when your business is finished? Will you consent to be our guest? Allow us to repay your kindness with our hospitality, I pray you."

Ian's dark eyes lingered on China's face

too long and too warmly. "An opportunity to see Miss Clairmont once more will be payment enough," he said softly.

China's uncle glanced from the young doctor to his niece and back again as though in sudden realization of the doctor's feelings. His low chuckle was far too pleased for China's comfort.

"Good!" he boomed. "We'll be looking forward to it, doctor. And now I think I should take China home."

With murmured farewells and assurances that Ian would conclude his business in Williamsburg with all possible haste, China and her uncle left the Swan Tavern and climbed into a coach drawn by four matched grays.

"I believe that young man has tender feelings for you, my dear," Arthur Clairmont said as they left the city and rode toward Montcalm.

"It may be possible, sir," China replied, turning her reddened cheeks toward the passing scenery.

"Sir?" Arthur scowled, though the twinkle in his blue eyes belied the expression. "Come now, enough of that, I am your Uncle Arthur and that's what I'll be called." His teasing tone faded and his eyes were filled with compassion. "My child," he said softly, taking her hand which was dwarfed by his. "I do not plan to ask you what you suffered at the hands of those wretches. It cannot be a subject on which you care to dwell. But I hope if you feel the need to speak of it, you will not hesitate to come to me or to—" He paused as though reconsidering what he'd been about to say. "To me," he finished.

"Thank you, Uncle," China murmured, but she could not imagine herself describing to him anything about Gabriel Fortune. She could scarcely bear to think about him. Images of his face, his form, their night aboard the *Golden Fortune*, tormented her and she banished them from her mind the moment they began to creep their stealthy way into her consciousness.

They rode in silence then, each lost in their own thoughts. China was enchanted by the lush greenery of the countryside; there was something primeval about it, almost as if the land had looked exactly this way at the dawn of time. And yet she occasionally caught glimpses of the steep-pitched, dormered, tall-chimneyed roofs of stately houses poised on the bluffs and promontories overlooking the estuary that was the York River.

"Here we are," Lord Clairmont suddenly announced when the coach turned between a pair of brick gateposts surmounted by realistically sculpted pineapples, the traditional symbol of welcome. "Montcalm."

The drive curved through a forest that concealed most of the more businesslike aspects of the thriving tobacco plantation. It rolled in a long, lazy curve toward the fine Georgian manor whose gardens stretched down toward the York shimmering in the distance.

Perfectly and beautifully symmetrical, the house rose two stories to a steep roof. Two tall chimneys stood at either end, and the stately brick house with its pedimented-and-pilastered doorway boasted keystone arched windows spaced evenly all around its long rectangular perimeter.

As the carriage neared the house, China saw a small black boy run up the front steps and into the house. A slave, she reminded herself. Such children had often been kept by the nobility in England, dressed in gaudy silks, to trail in the wake of great ladies cradling small, snapping lapdogs in their arms. In America, she knew, they were imported, brought from their native lands far away, to work in the fields doing the back-breaking labor of cultivating and curing the tobacco that was the font of Virginia's blossoming wealth.

The door opened a second time as the coach rounded the final curve of the drive. Two women appeared—China's aunt,

Frances, Lady Clairmont, and her cousin, Rebecca. It took no more than a glance as she descended from the coach for China to realize that neither her aunt nor her cousin were as pleased with her rescue as her Uncle Arthur obviously was.

Six

The long green fronds of the spreading willow floated gracefully on the water at the river's edge. China, her back braced against the thick, gnarled trunk of the tree, watched them, her thoughts far away and strangely melancholy.

The first month of her stay at Montcalm had come and gone. She could not say she had not been made welcome. She'd been given a lovely room with windows overlooking the gardens and the river beyond. Her belongings, delivered upon the docking of the *Amity* along with the news of her abduction, were ready and waiting for her. Her uncle went out of his way to make her welcome, and if her aunt was not quite as warm, she was none the less cordial.

In fact, after initially disliking the thin, sharp-faced woman her uncle had married, China came to find her more than a little amusing. Frances adored being Lady Clairmont. Every second word addressed to her by her servants was "milady." She could not get enough of hearing herself addressed by her title, and China imagined she must have been bitterly disappointed when her husband would not take her back to England where she could have entered society and moved in the fashionable circles of the English nobility.

But then, China reasoned, as a baron, Lord Clairmont was at the lower end of the English aristocracy. In America, where there were fewer bona fide noblemen, anyone with the right to be called "milord" or "milady" was treated with the deference accorded a duke in England. It was, perhaps, not so surprising then that Lady Clairmont was content to remain in America.

"China?" The voice came from the gardens near the back of the house where several slave children were delegated to keep the geese away from Lady Clairmont's flowers.

China sighed. It was Rebecca, her cousin. Come, no doubt, to boast a bit more, to tell her cousin of the wonder that was her fiancé.

She had heard little else since her arrival. On the very night Arthur Clairmont had brought his niece home, Rebecca had come to China's room and regaled her with the details of her courtship and betrothal. Still, China supposed, if she were to be married to a man she adored as much as Rebecca adored her suitor, she would want to talk about him too.

"Over here!" she called back, waving the willow frond she held in her hand.

"What are you doing down here?" Rebecca demanded, ducking beneath the green drapery of the willow.

China shrugged. "It's cool. And pretty. If you lean over you can see the docks down there."

She pointed in the direction of Montcalm's docks jutting out into the York. The *Amity* lay moored there, the sight of her unleashing a flood of memories in China. Like sepia-toned images, they flitted through her mind. The *Amity*, Le Corbeau, the *Black Pearl*, the fabulous Great Mogul, and Gabriel, his savagely handsome face in an ever-changing montage of expressions.

"What is it, China?" Rebecca Clairmont asked.

China looked at her cousin. Sitting there in the dappled shade of the willow, the two girls looked more like sisters than cousins. Rebecca was like a slightly less perfect version of China. Her skin was not quite so flawless, her cheeks lacked that rose-kissed blush, her eyes were not so deeply blue, her hair, though pale blonde and thickly curling, lacked the silvery highlights that made China's so startlingly beautiful. Lady Clairmont, Rebecca's mother, had noticed the difference. It bespoke what the aristocracy would have called superior breeding—as if China's bloodlines were that significant fraction more pure, her antecedents a bit more noble. Frances Clairmont, having always believed her daughter a creature of magical beauty, was forced to see now that there was another, lovelier version to be found. It was a grudge she nurtured against China in the private confines of her heart.

But Rebecca, blissfully content in her betrothal, securely basking in the affection of her adored fiancé, felt none of the jealous resentment that so gnawed at her mother. To her, China was the potential source of a most satisfying envy. She was certain that once China laid eyes on her cousin's husband-to-be she would be stricken with such intense jealousy that Rebecca could afford to be generously condescending.

"China?" Rebecca repeated when her cousin did not reply. She reached out and touched the yellow linen sleeve of China's gown. "What is it? You turned so pale all of a sudden."

China smiled apologetically. "It is nothing. The sight of the *Amity* at the docks reminded me . . ."

Rebecca said nothing. She knew, of course, that China had been taken from the *Amity* by force. She knew of her captivity first with *Le Corbeau* and then Gabriel Fortune. But she knew only those bare facts. There was so much more she longed to know. Details, descriptions. She was dying to know what life had been like aboard the pirate vessels. She wanted to know how the pirates looked, how they lived. And she wanted to know what had befallen China at their hands.

In her daydreams Rebecca tried to imagine it. She had heard stories of pirates who took women from ships, who made them—willingly or unwillingly—their doxies. She remembered the feelings of helplessness, of being weak and small she'd experienced when enfolded in her fiancé's arms. She remembered how his lips crushed hers in a kiss that seemed so savage, so demanding it took her breath away. When she thought of some pirate, some brigand used to taking what he wanted be it gold or goods or flesh, taking her in his arms, forcing her to his will, she felt almost faint, felt a delicious, forbidden thrill.

But of course she did not dare ask China for the particulars. Manners, good taste, and her father forbade her to pry into so shameful and painful an episode. She could only hope that time and closeness would make it possible for her cousin to tell her what she wished to know of her own free will.

"I almost forgot," Rebecca said, changing the subject as she reached into a pocket in her voluminous skirts. "This came for you. Mama said to bring it out."

China took the letter and broke the wax seal. Opening it, she scanned the contents. Her face fell.

"He is coming back," she sighed, raising exasperated eyes to her cousin's face. "Ian Leyton."

"Is he so terrible?" Rebecca wanted to know. "Papa said he seemed quite the gentleman."

"I suppose he is," China was forced to agree. "He is not unhandsome. And his kindness to me was extraordinary. But he is not . . . not . . ."

"Whom?" Rebecca prompted. "Did you have some beau in London? Oh, China, were you torn from him when you had to come to Virginia?"

China had to smile. "Nothing like that. Your engagement has made you see romance around every corner."

But her smile faded. In her mind's eye she saw Gabriel Fortune's face, looked again into his leaf green eyes, felt again his—

"It was nothing like that," she repeated, stubbornly forcing those tormenting images from her mind. Gabriel Fortune was a pirate, a villain, a ravisher of helpless women. The fact that he was handsome, that the sound of his voice seemed to set some chord inside her aquiver, was contrary to all good sense. She was a fool to romanticize him even in her weakest moments.

"You could write to Dr. Leyton and tell him you would rather he did not come to Montcalm," Rebecca suggested.

"No, I could not," China disagreed. "Your father has already invited him. And I owe it to him to see him."

"But you will be pleased when his visit is over," Rebecca surmised.

China nodded. "Very pleased," she agreed. "And you? What of your fiancé? When am I to meet this paragon of every manly virtue?"

Rebecca giggled, her cheeks pinkening becomingly. "Soon," she answered. "He has written to say he is coming to Montcalm at the end of the week. Mama has decided to invite several of their friends to a *soirée* in honor of our engagement."

"Short notice, isn't it, to plan such an affair?" China asked, remembering the weeks of complicated arrangements that went into her mother's entertainments in London.

"I suppose," Rebecca admitted. "But Gabriel has so much to keep him at Fox Meadow. He seldom has time to come calling. It is possible he will not be able to come again before our wedding." She shivered, biting her lower lip. "Oh China! I cannot wait to be Mrs. Gabriel St. Jon."

China smiled wanly, pleased for her cousin, but inwardly she was thinking: Gabriel St. Jon! Is every other man in this benighted land named Gabriel?

Ian Leyton arrived late in the afternoon three days later. He apologized for taking so long in Williamsburg, apparently unaware that he was the only one disappointed by the prolongation of his business in that city.

His dark eyes shone with admiration when China was summoned to greet him. He took her hand in his and bowed over it with courtly grace.

"I had remembered you as lovely," he told her, unabashed by her relatives standing nearby. "I had not remembered how very breathtaking you truly are."

"You flatter me, sir," China managed, her cheeks hot with embarrassment. Pointedly she drew her hand from his grasp.

"I am no idle flatterer," Ian assured her.

Frances Clairmont, delighted to have a potential suitor for her niece's affections so conveniently at hand, spoke up.

"Dr. Leyton, you will not be hurrying away again, I hope? We are giving a dinner in a few day's time in honor of my daughter's betrothal. Perhaps you would deign to join us? You could escort China."

China's heart sank at the delighted glow that suffused Ian's oval face.

"My dear Lady Clairmont!" he replied, "you are too amiable! You must know it would be my honor and pleasure to be Miss Clairmont's partner at dinner." His eyes swept to Rebecca's face. "Allow me to offer my congratulations, ma'am, on your engagement."

China's eyes met her cousin's, and in Rebecca's clear blue eyes she thought she saw an expression that said all too clearly: Thank heaven I am marrying Gabriel St. Jon and not a simpering buffoon like this!

Sighing, feeling Ian's weighted gaze upon her, China swallowed the feelings of envy that welled inside her.

By the time the day of Rebecca's engagement dinner arrived, China thought if she saw Ian Leyton's face once more she would scream. From morning till night, from breakfast until the time when each of the household, lit candle in hand, mounted the stairs to their rooms, Ian was at her side. He complimented her, flattered her, courted her with a dogged persistence that left her no time for privacy or reflection.

How strange it seemed that, only a few days before, she would have welcomed some diversion to keep her mind off the tormenting memories of Gabriel Fortune. Now she wanted only a few moments to herself to think of anything—anything!—but Ian Leyton.

It was the afternoon of the engagement dinner when China and Ian returned from a drive along the tree-shaded lanes near Montcalm. China's maid, a pretty, shy girl called Kitty, was the first to notice the coach sitting in front of the elegant brick house.

"Miss Rebecca's gentleman must be here," the girl observed. "That is Mr. St. Jon's coach."

China leaned out. The coach was a handsome one, the horses beautiful, sleek creatures, their coats a deep, gleaming russet.

"Rebecca must be delighted," China said. "She's been so looking forward to Mr. St. Jon's arrival. She's so anxious for their wedding."

"When one finds the person they desire to be the companion of their lifetime, they are naturally eager for marriage," Ian decreed.

China's stern glance at Kitty stifled the giggle that so obviously bubbled beneath the surface. She herself felt exasperated, frustrated. Ian's courtship was bad enough, but her aunt was shamelessly pressing for a match between the attractive young doctor and the niece she was only too ready to see married and out of her house.

Their coach drew up behind Gabriel St. Jon's. Ian stepped down first, then helped China and her maid out. With Kitty trailing behind, China and Ian went in and relinquished their hats and cloaks to the servant waiting in the hall.

"Milady and Miss Rebecca are in the drawing room, miss," the servant told China. "With Mr. St. Jon."

"And my uncle?" China asked.

"Milord has not returned from the fields."

"Thank you, I . . ."

"China!" Rebecca's voice echoed in the entrance hall. "China! At last!"

China smiled as her cousin appeared in the doorway of the oak-paneled drawing room. Rebecca's cheeks were flushed, her blue eyes sparkled. In her excitement she was prettier than China had ever seen her. In that moment, in the happiness and pleasure of her fiancé's arrival, Rebecca's beauty approached China's own.

"Come in," she urged. "Come meet my Gabriel! I've been telling him about you since we first learned you were coming. I know he's longing to meet you!"

Stepping closer to China, she said in tones meant for her ears alone: "I've told him nothing of your misfortunes at the hands of those pirates. I thought that was something you would wish kept within the family."

China smiled her gratitude. She wished to meet people in the normal way and have them judge her for herself, not look upon her as some curiosity plying her with embarrassing questions or, what was worse, saying nothing but regarding her with searching, and prurient, stares.

She linked her arm through her cousin's. "Well then, cousin, take me to meet this paragon of yours."

Giggling happily, Rebecca led China across the entrance hall to the drawing room that overlooked the garden.

"Remember," she teased as they crossed the threshold, "I saw him first."

China laughed as she entered the room. Her aunt was seated near the fireplace. Opposite her, a man sat in a matching chair. He rose as the women, followed by Ian, entered the room.

China's first impression was that he was a large man, tall with broad shoulders. His shoes had gold buckles that caught the slanting sunlight falling through the two tall windows on the garden front of the room. His stockings, of oyster silk, encased long, muscular calves. His breeches were of dark cloth, snugly fitting over long thighs. His waistcoat was of deep brown silk embroidered with pale cream tracery and his coat, with its edging of chased gold buttons, was a startlingly dark background for the fall of ecru linen at his throat and wrists.

Raising her eyes to his face, China smiled. She was prepared to find him handsome—surely Rebecca's boasting of his masculine good looks could not be all a product of her lovestruck mind. But as her eyes reached his, as her gaze met and locked with that of Rebecca's fiancé, China felt as if her heart had stopped, as if a jagged fork of white-hot lightning had impaled her.

Nor was she alone in her reaction. Gabriel St. Jon's handsome face, tanned by the sun, framed in a fall of waving sable hair, paled when he beheld this English cousin his fiancée had spoken so much of. The shock of seeing her, of meeting her eyes with his own, was plain to see in the moment before he managed to collect himself.

"Miss Clairmont," he said, his voice low, soft, with a breathy hush he could not quite conceal. "Your cousin has told me much of you."

The cool politeness of his words, the piercing edge of warning in his eyes, silenced the shocked exclamations that sprang to China's tongue. After a moment, after a deep, tremulous breath and a nervous, furtive licking of lips suddenly gone dry, China found her voice.

"And you, sir," China managed, though

she would never know how. "She has told me so much about you, I feel as if I know you."

Humor, deviltry, and amusement twinkled in his eyes as he alone understood the irony of China's words. He took her hand in his and bent over it, his lips lingering on the soft, creamy flesh he remembered only too keenly.

Even as he kissed her hand, he lifted his eyes to hers. His eyes, grass green, were sparkling and alive. China realized with a start that he was enjoying the potential danger of the situation.

China jerked her hand away. His kiss seemed to have burned her flesh, branded her in some way she did not understand. Her body quivered with a trembling she could not suppress. It was clear to her in that moment that the persona of Gabriel St. Jon, gentleman planter, master of Fox Meadow, was only a façade, a thin veneer. To the casual onlooker he was Gabriel St. Jon, but behind that mask, in his heart, in his soul, he was Gabriel Fortune, a pirate, a rake, a ravisher of virgins.

China longed to expose him, to scream the truth at her aunt and cousin. But as she looked up into the face that had haunted her days and nights, as she felt herself sinking into the depths of those miraculous green eyes, she could not seem to find the words.

Seven

Gabriel St. Jon, master of Fox Meadow, alias Gabriel Fortune, master of the pirate ship *Golden Fortune*, stood at the window of his room at Montcalm. His windows, like those in China's room down the hall, overlooked the garden. But he had no eyes just then for the formal beds bordered by neatly clipped hedges. The artfully planted trees and terraced beds running down to the sparkling river had no charm for him. His mind was filled with images of a face out of his dreams, a form that had haunted him for weeks.

He'd thought he'd lost her, his "Meghan Gordon." He'd thought, on that night she'd run from his cottage in the forest at Fox

Meadow, that she'd disappeared from his life. He'd been tormented by fears that she'd fallen into the hands of some villain who would use her and abuse her and possibly kill her when she ceased to amuse him. He was not, after all, the only pirate carving out a home for himself in the lush, fertile land near the Pamlico Sound. And there were still Indians in the area, Indians who loathed the white men who claimed their lands and cut their forests, who dammed their streams and killed their game. The fate of a beautiful white woman at their hands was too horrible for Gabriel to contemplate.

He'd made inquiries in the area but had found nothing. The innkeeper at the inn near Fox Meadow had seen nothing of her. The masters of plantations near Gabriel's reported no strangers on their lands. It seemed she had vanished into thin air like a will-o'-the-wisp. Were he the superstitious type, had he believed in the folktales of those who believed in sprites and fairies, he would have thought her some mad illusion, some dream, some fantasy of beauty sent by a cruel fate to show him the mistake he was making in settling for less than love.

That thought brought him back to his present predicament. Meghan's—no, he told himself, her name was China. China's appearance in his life had shown him the folly of marrying for the wrong reasons. He had proposed to Rebecca Clairmont for what she represented—respectability, social connections, stability. She would make a proper mistress for Fox Meadow, he had assured himself. Her family was of noble lineage, her father was heir to a title and estates in England. And she was beautiful. He winced to remember that he had once thought her very beautiful. But that was before he had seen China. They were very similar, China and Rebecca, but Rebecca's beauty was a bland imitation, a muted reflection, of China's pearl and silver radiance.

Leaning an arm against the fluted window jamb, Gabriel heaved a sigh. He had given up the dream of ever finding his beautiful escaped captive. He had resigned himself to never seeing her again except in the tormenting images that filled his mind whenever his efforts to keep them at bay weakened. He came to dread going to sleep at night because he knew he would soon awaken, drenched in sweat, his body aching with desire for a girl who had vowed to destroy him, whose slim, petal-soft body he had held in his arms all too briefly.

When Rebecca's letter had reached him at Fox Meadow, a letter telling him of her cousin's arrival from England and pleading with him to come to her soon so they could formalize their betrothal, he had brutally beaten back his longing for the girl who had become a plague, a curse, a threat to his very peace of mind. He reread Rebecca's letter and tried to recapture the feelings he had had for her before he'd met "Meghan Gordon." They were very similar in looks, he mused. He wondered if Rebecca was enough like "Meghan" to soothe his longings, slake his gnawing desires. It was unfair to Rebecca, he supposed, to use her as some sort of substitute, but he would be giving her what she wanted. She would be his wife, the mistress of his plantation, the mother of the son he wanted to inherit the fortune he'd earned at sea and the estate he intended to build at Fox Meadow.

He'd forced down any misgivings, any thought of what was fair or unfair, and wrote to Rebecca telling her the date he expected to arrive at Montcalm and adding politely that he was looking forward to meeting this cousin of whom he'd heard so much.

A smile rife with self-mockery curved his full lips. How could he have guessed that Miss China Clairmont, orphaned daughter of the seventh Baron Clairmont, niece of the eighth, and Meghan Gordon, indentured servant, were one and the same? His smile softened as he remembered the shock in those topaz blue eyes when Rebecca had introduced her cousin to her fiancé in the drawing room below. China was as shocked as he, it was plain. Having escaped Gabriel

Fortune, the pirate, she now found herself faced with her nemesis once more, now in the guise of Gabriel St. Jon, master of Fox Meadow. How had she gotten there, he wondered. How had she made her way from Fox Meadow, in North Carolina, to Montcalm on the banks of the York?

There were so many questions to be answered, he reflected, leaning forward as he noticed China moving slowly along one of the flagstone paths in the garden. His face flushed with anger, his brows drew downward in two angry slashes as he noticed the man who moved swiftly along an intersecting path, obviously intending to join China. Gabriel had dozens of questions he longed to ask China, but first and foremost he wanted to know the identity of that man who seemed so comfortably ensconced at her side.

Below in the gardens, China's thoughts too were centered on that awkward, stunning meeting in the drawing room. It was all so astonishing. Beyond belief.

She thought back to the earliest moments of her captivity when Gabriel had locked her in the master cabin of the *Golden Fortune*. She remembered the letter she'd seen lying on his desk—the letter accepting his proposal—the letter with its beribboned lovelock—the letter from her cousin.

Rebecca! China remembered the tales her cousin had told her of her courtship. The perfumed nights she and Gabriel had spent strolling hand in hand through these gardens. The stolen kisses, the professions of love. . . . It had all seemed charming and romantic when the man in question had been but a faceless stranger who meant nothing to China. But now he had a face—the face she could not get out of her mind. The thought of Gabriel courting Rebecca was not charming, not romantic. The taunting images of Rebecca and Gabriel together made China feel ill.

China glanced back toward the house. The guests for the *soirée* had begun to arrive. Among them were several gentlemen from Williamsburg—gentlemen who had access to Governor Spotswood. A word in their ears would be enough to put a noose around Gabriel's neck.

China sighed. She had once vowed eternal hatred of the man who had seduced her. She had pledged vengeance. Now she had it within her grasp. Why, then, did she hesitate? Did he not deserve to hang? Should he not pay for his crimes? Could she allow her cousin, all unwitting, to marry such a vile, unprincipled, treacherous . . . handsome, virile, bold . . .

She scowled, furious with herself for those thoughts. Gabriel St. Jon! Master of Fox Meadow! That was merely a pose. He could play the fine gentleman if he wished, but it was a sham. She should expose him! She should reveal his secret to everyone! She should . . .

But she wouldn't. China wilted, her shoulders slumping wearily. Something inside her, some traitorous, foolish part of her, would not allow her to set his downfall in motion. And what was worse, she believed he knew she could not.

She remembered the look on his face, the devilish, conspiratorial twinkle in those magnificent eyes when he'd bent over her hand in the drawing room. There had been no concern there, no fear. He knew his secret was safe. He knew some unfathomable emotion would seal her lips.

China clenched her fists. It was infuriating! He was so smug, so sure of himself. Well, that was all well and good. Perhaps she would not be the instrument of his destruction. It may be that she did not have it in her to sign any man's death warrant. But she would exact a price for her silence.

She had come to like Rebecca in the weeks of her stay at Montcalm. She could not, knowing what Gabriel was, stand by and watch while Rebecca married a man who was not what he pretended to be. She would not!

Her lips pressed in a prim line, China

vowed to have a little talk with Master Gabriel St. Jon. She would tell him that in exchange for her silence, in exchange for his freedom and his life, he would have to break his betrothal to Rebecca. He would have to leave Montcalm and never return.

Feeling better, China smiled as she walked along the flagstone path. A new determination filled her. She felt more confident, more sure of herself. All the conflicting emotions—the doubt, the feeling that, on the one hand, she should have her revenge on Gabriel Fortune for what he had done to her and, on the other hand, the strange reluctance to be the catalyst of his destruction—now vanished. It was as if the sun had suddenly appeared in a sky that was brilliant, flawless, breathtaking . . .

"Miss Clairmont?" It was Ian. "I have found you."

. . . with only one cloud. China's mood deflated. She turned toward Ian, a wan smile painted across her lips.

"I was not hiding, sir," she told him.

He fell into step beside her. "Could you not call me Ian?" he asked. "Would you not allow me to call you by your Christian name?"

China felt suddenly that she had been uncharitable toward him. After all, she owed him a great deal. And it was not that she disliked him. He was a pleasant, obviously kind, not unattractive man. It was only that his presence at Montcalm . . . in her life . . . at that moment was, well, inconvenient.

"Of course you may," she told him. "And I will call you Ian."

Pleased, the doctor clasped his hands behind his back as they walked toward the river. "It is a pleasant thing, is it not, to see someone as happy as Miss Rebecca over her betrothal?"

"Indeed it is," China agreed. "But all too often such happiness does not last. I fear . . ." She glanced up and found Ian's dark eyes questioning her. She shook her head. "Sometimes people are not what they seem," she finished softly. "Not at all what they seem."

Gazing off toward the river, China did not see the look of alarm that flitted across Ian's face.

"What do you mean?" he asked, too quickly.

Suddenly aware that she was on the brink of saying far too much, China made a vague, dismissing gesture with one hand. "It's nothing," she told him. "I am rambling. Pay no attention." Smiling apologetically, she laid a hand on the forest green cloth of his sleeve. "I pray you excuse me, sir. I fear I have a headache. I must lie down if I am to be fit company at my aunt's *soirée* tonight."

"I have a draught—" Ian began.

"No, no. It's nothing, truly. A few hours rest will work wonders."

With a sweet smile, she left him and retraced her steps back to the garden front of the house.

Above, in his window, Gabriel saw her approaching. His eyes narrowed, glittering dangerously. He felt suffused with an emotion he'd never known. It was a possessive jealousy that seized him, making him want to charge out to the garden and attack the auburn-haired doctor who dared to speak so intimately with China, who dared to meet her in the gardens, speak to her with his head so close to hers.

But that was ridiculous, he told himself, leaving the window. He was in the home of his intended bride. He rolled his eyes at the thought. What could he do? He had vowed to forget "Meghan Gordon" and marry Rebecca Clairmont. But now . . . Egad! Was ever a man ensnared in such a tangle?

China climbed the stairs intending to go to her room. She had not been lying when she told Ian she had a headache. All her scheming and planning, combined with the shock of seeing Gabriel again, had wound her nerves tight as a spring.

But her determination had not weakened. Though there seemed little she could do to prevent the formalizing of Gabriel's betrothal to Rebecca, she resolved to see that the wedding never took place. The cousin she had come to regard as the sister she'd never had would not marry a pirate—and particularly not this pirate—if she had anything to do with it!

She pressed the latch of her door and was about to enter when the sound of another door opening in the hall captured her attention. She looked up the corridor in time to see Gabriel in his own doorway.

"China?" he said, and the mere sound of his voice sent a quiver of sensual remembrance snaking up her spine.

China gazed at him, returning the stare he could not seem to break. Silence reigned in the corridor. There were volumes each longed to speak to the other, but neither was able to put words to the jumble of thoughts and emotions swirling inside them.

"I—" Their voices blended as each began to speak.

China bit her lip. Opening her mouth, she was about to try again when the sharp clack of heels mounting the stairs shattered the tense silence in the hallway.

"Gabriel?" Rebecca, climbing the stairs, saw him standing in his doorway. "Here you are. Come walk with me. Come down to the river; I've been so longing to be alone with you."

Gabriel glanced toward the sound of her voice. By the time he looked back—by the time Rebecca reached the head of the stairs and would have seen China standing in her own doorway further down the hall—he was alone in the long, pale blue corridor.

Eight

"Is something wrong with your cousin?" Gabriel asked as he and Rebecca walked in the gardens.

"With China?" Rebecca murmured, frowning. "What do you mean?"

"That doctor is always with her. He follows her wherever she goes. I assumed she must be sickly. If she requires a doctor in constant attendance . . ."

Rebecca laughed and took his arm to resume their stroll toward the river. "Ian Leyton! But, darling, no! He is not here to care for China's health."

"Then why is he here?"

Rebecca glanced about to make sure they were alone and so missed the tight scowl on

Gabriel's face. Leaning close as she held tight to his arm, she dropped her voice to a whisper.

"I suppose, since we are to be married, since you are soon to be a part of the family, it would be all right if I told you," she said. "Come, let's sit over here."

Gabriel sat beside Rebecca on the bench, his long, maroon-stockinged legs stretched out before him.

"You see," Rebecca told him, her voice low and conspiratorial, "no one is supposed to know, but Ian Leyton rescued China. He saved her life."

"Rescued her?" Gabriel leaned toward her, his green eyes glittering. "What can you mean?"

"She was kidnapped. From Father's ship. By a pirate!" Rebecca's breath caught. "They took her to a cottage deep in the forest, but she escaped. They might have recaptured her but for Ian who was traveling in the area. He found China and brought her to Yorktown. Papa went to fetch her there. So you see, China has reason to be beholden to Ian Leyton."

"Indeed," Gabriel murmured. The doctor's face appeared in his mind's eye. So he had been the one! If it had not been for Ian Leyton, he might have found China that night at Fox Meadow. If it had not been for Ian

Leyton, China would be with him now. One day, he promised himself, he would repay Leyton's misplaced generosity.

He returned his attention to Rebecca. "But why has he stayed so long at Montcalm?"

Rebecca dimpled. "He left after delivering China to Papa. He had business in Williamsburg. But when his business was finished, he came back. Papa had invited him to visit, but he has stayed to court China. Between us, I do believe Mama is hoping it will end in a match."

Gabriel felt the blood pounding in his temples. A match! China hadn't been at Montcalm two months and already that ferret-faced, interfering aunt of hers was trying to marry her off to the first man who came courting! What was wrong with that meddlesome old crone! Wasn't inheriting everything China's family owned enough? Did she begrudge her niece a roof over her head and the food in her mouth? Was a little hospitality too high a price to pay for a title and a fortune? She was nothing but a—

"Gabriel?" Rebecca patted his arm. "Gabriel, what can be the matter? You look as though you're ready to strangle someone."

Looking away, Gabriel tried to force himself to remain calm. Resolutely he pushed the outrage out of his mind. After all, it was only natural for Lady Clairmont to try to find a husband for her niece.

But could it be possible that China welcomed Ian Leyton's attentions? She did not seem to be hiding from him. They were always together. Could it be that she . . . no, she couldn't . . . could she? Was it possible that she was in love with the man who had stolen—no, rescued—her from her captor?

Smiling, feigning an indifference he was far from feeling, Gabriel launched into an insipid conversation with Rebecca. But in the back of his mind, he determined to corner China at the first opportunity and demand to know what there was between her and Ian Leyton.

As the string quartet Lord Clairmont had hired from Williamsburg played, China danced in the too tight embrace of Ian Leyton.

"Are you enjoying yourself?" he asked, forcing her to look up at him.

"Of course," she replied automatically. But it was a lie. She had enjoyed none of the farce this evening had been. The dinner had tasted like sawdust, the wine, though praised by one and all, seemed stale and did nothing to lighten her sour mood. She could take pleasure in none of it, not the beauty of the long salon lit by the golden glow of a hundred candles in candelabra and chandeliers, not the sheen of the candlelight on silk and satin nor the glitter of the jewels sparkling on ladies and gentlemen alike. The room was aglitter as the Clairmont's guests strove to outdo one another in the beauty of their dress. China found herself repeatedly asked how a Virginia *soirée* compared to one of her parents' London entertainments. And what could she say but that they were quite as lovely. But it was hardly the truth. Oh, the room was beautiful and the costumes were obviously copies of London fashions. But there was none of the glamour that went with the princes and archdukes and diplomats who had frequented her mother's salons. And there was Gabriel . . .

All through that interminable dinner, China had felt Gabriel's eyes on her, boring into her. She had forced herself to concentrate on the food before her, the dinner she only pretended to eat, and on the dull conversation of Ian who sat on one side and the neighboring planter seated at her other hand.

With the rest, she had raised her glass in a toast as Rebecca and Gabriel's betrothal was announced. The look on her face was one of polite attention, but beneath the surface her emotions were in turmoil. She wanted to scream out the truth, to expose Gabriel before them all. But she couldn't. That in itself puzzled her, frustrated her. But the deeper feelings, the feeling of betrayal, as though she were watching a lover being unfaithful before her very eyes, the feeling of—no, she refused to call it jealousy—it was only concern for her cousin, anger to see her being led on by an unprincipled villain who was representing himself as something very far from the truth.

Her thoughts were muddled as she moved stiffly in Ian's arms. She did not notice the tall, broad-shouldered figure in lilac blue velvet approaching them across the gleaming parquet floor.

"May I?" Gabriel's deep voice, soft as the silver-embroidered velvet of his coat, asked.

Gallantly Ian relinquished China into Gabriel's arms. "Your future cousin, China," Ian said, smiling at her as he moved aside.

China looked up into those changeable green eyes and felt a quaking in the pit of her stomach. "How do you dare come among these decent, unsuspecting people?" she snarled.

Gabriel's eyes narrowed. He'd meant to reassure her, to tell her he was glad she was well and safe, to let her know he meant to find some way to extricate himself from a betrothal he knew was a foolish mistake, and to sound out the depths of her feelings toward Ian Leyton. But her question, her tone, froze all those good intentions. One sable brow arched sardonically.

"I dare anything I please," he informed her. "As you well know . . . cousin."

"You mean to marry Rebecca, to drag her into the sordid tragedy you call your life?" China hissed. "Have you no conscience? Are you so wicked that you would ruin yet another innocent life?"

Gabriel smiled, glancing over China's head toward his fiancée who stood speaking with the wife of an elderly merchant from Yorktown. The expression on his face did not change as his eyes fell to meet China's.

"And what innocent life did I already ruin?" he asked wryly. "Yours? You seem to have recovered. Here you are, nestled in the bosom of your family, with a devoted lapdog trailing your every step."

"Lap . . ." China flushed as she realized who he meant. "Ian is a friend. He found me that night when I . . ." She glanced around, wondering if they were being overheard. ". . . that night in the forest," she finished. "Had it not been for his kindness—"

"You would not be here tonight," Gabriel ended for her. "Nor would I, my sweet."

China frowned up at him puzzled by his words. But at that moment the music ended, and China saw Rebecca crossing the floor toward them.

"I'm so pleased the two of you like one another," she said, winding her arms possessively about one of Gabriel's. "China? What is it? You look flushed."

"It is intolerably hot in here," China told her, unfurling her fan. "I believe I will step into the garden for a moment. If you will excuse me, Mr. . . ." Her eyes glinted up at him. ". . . St. Jon."

Turning with a rustling of peach silk skirts, China made her way out of the room. Hurrying along the entrance hall that ran from the front of the house to the back, she went out into the torchlit gardens.

Breathless, her senses and thoughts a hopeless jumble, China sank onto the bench at the end of one of the yew-bordered walks. Neither the night air nor the cool, almost chilling breeze that seemed so refreshing after the heat of the crowded ballroom could restore any semblance of order to her befuddled mind.

Her heart told her that Gabriel's snide remark about Ian stemmed from something far removed from contempt, but her rational mind argued against such a notion. Gabriel cared nothing for her. It was not jealousy that had prompted his sneering words about the man who had rescued her from his clutches. It was merely that the pirate in him, that predatory, unprincipled part called "Gabriel Fortune" begrudged her her freedom, chafed at the thought of being beaten, robbed of any part of his ill-gotten gains. No doubt he would have liked to keep her at what she now knew had been his home—Fox Meadow. No doubt he held Ian responsible for her escape, for without his help she could easily have been recaptured, returned to his possession. That was all his antagonism against Ian amounted to, surely.

The velvety voice in the darkness took her by surprise. "China?"

She gasped, starting violently. Her head jerked up and she found him there—Gabriel—standing before her.

Shaking, she rose to her feet. "Go back!" she hissed, astonished at his audacity in following her into the dark seclusion of the gardens. "Are you mad?"

"We must talk," he told her.

China knew it was true. Now was the moment for her to serve him with her ultimatum—leave Rebecca's life, leave them all in peace, or she would expose him, lay him open to charges of piracy, which could end in his death on the public scaffold.

"All I have to say to you," she snarled, her eyes measuring the distance between him and the yew hedges bordering the path, planning her escape from this secluded, intimate place, "is that I will not see you hurt Rebecca. I know she cannot be aware of who, of what you really are. I won't stand by and watch as she, all unwitting, becomes the wife of a man like you."

She started to pass him, holding her body away to avoid touching his on the narrow path. She felt Gabriel's hand closing on her arm and jerked away. His fingers caught at the delicate fabric of her sleeve and she heard the stitches at her shoulder give way, but even that did not stop her. Snatching up her skirts, she fled into the darkness and hurried back to the house, entering through a little-used door and retreating to her room upstairs.

She said nothing as her maid helped her undress and brushed out her long, shimmering silver-pale hair. Climbing into the high tester bed, she blew out the candle and lay in the darkness listening to the muffled sounds of music and laughter from the salon below.

In her window she could see the flickering light of the torches in the garden. An image of Gabriel standing before her at the end of that dark, narrow garden path appeared in her mind. He was wicked, deceit personified. And yet, in that moment when she'd seen him there, when he'd spoken her name and she'd looked up to find him standing before her, a spasm of pure emotion had pierced her to the heart. It was as if a current, some unfathomable, undeniable electric charge, had passed between them.

China felt it again as she lay there, a quivering, fluttering sensation snaking down her spine and coiling in the pit of her belly.

With a smothered groan, she rolled onto her stomach and buried her face in the softness of her down pillows. How could he do this to her? How could she loathe him for his masquerade even while her body reacted to violently to the mere sight of him? It was so far beyond anything in her experience as to be inconceivable.

When she awoke, the darkness outside the window was complete. The torches had gone out, the house lay still around her. The guests who lived nearby had gone. Those whose journeys home were longer had retired to guest rooms for the night.

China lay in the darkness, the cool breeze riffling the drapes at the open window bathing her face. She was disoriented, having been startled from a deep sleep by . . . She frowned in the shadows. By what? What could have—

A sound so faint she could not have said with certainty she had heard it brought her upright in the bed. She was not alone in the room. Someone . . .

Her gasp of surprise and fear was muffled as a hand, hard and calloused, closed over her mouth. Her eyes, wide and staring, found the shape of a man in the concealing darkness beside her.

"It's only me," Gabriel said. "Don't be afraid." His lips touched her ear, his breath was warm on her cheek as he spoke. "I'm going to take my hand away. Will you be quiet and listen to me?"

China nodded, and the smothering hand was removed. She leaned as far away from him as she could in the bed.

"What are you doing here?" she demanded. "You must be insane!"

"I told you in the garden," he murmured. "We have to talk. You would not talk to me there; I had to try again."

"And I told you everything I had to say to you," she retorted. "I won't see you ruin Rebecca's—"

"Your concern for your cousin is touching," Gabriel sneered. "Or would be if I thought it was genuine."

China's eyes narrowed. "What are you saying?"

He shrugged one shoulder. The silken embroidery of his belted banyan tickled China's arm. "I am saying that I believe there is another reason for your objections."

"What reason?" she challenged.

A maddening smile quirked the corners of his mouth. "Jealousy?" he suggested.

"Jealousy!" China's eyes blazed. "You conceited, insufferable wretch! You flatter yourself!"

Gabriel chuckled. "I don't think so," he disagreed.

"If I cared enough for you to be jealous of

you and my cousin," she snarled, mortified into recklessness by his words, "then why did I escape from you at Fox Meadow?"

"Because you were foolish," he replied. "And I think you know it now."

"Oh!" China ground her teeth. That smirk, that cocksure confidence! She longed to rake that smile from his face with her nails. "Get out of here!" she ordered. "I detest the very sight of you!"

"I don't believe that either," he told her frankly. "And I don't believe you really want me to go. Not just yet, at least."

He leaned toward her and, before China could react, brushed his lips against her throat. Her gasp, the involuntary shudder that shook her, confirmed his suspicions. His hand rose to her breast.

As if touched by fire, China flung herself away. Nearly falling, she scrambled off the bed and stumbled toward the door. But Gabriel was after her. His reflexes honed to perfection by life aboard the *Golden Fortune*, he was beside China before she could reach the door.

His arm snaked about her waist. He pulled her hard against him, lifting her off her feet. One hand covered her mouth as he carried her back to the high, curtained bed.

He lay half across her, his weight pressing her deeply into the yielding feather bed. His hand left her mouth only to be replaced by his lips, hard, demanding, parting China's own. His hand caressed the satiny skin of her thigh, progressing higher as her struggles threw back the trailing skirt of her nightdress.

China felt her will yielding beneath the onslaught of his hands, his mouth. She drew a ragged breath as his mouth left hers and found the taut, pink-tipped breast laid bare by the wide neck of her disarranged nightgown.

"Let me go!" she hissed, struggling beneath him, trying, to no avail, to ignore his hands caressing her, his fingers parting the tender flesh that moistened to his touch.

She felt his lips on her belly, her hip, her thighs, and time stood still for a breathless moment. Surely, her bemused mind told her, he could not . . . would not . . .

Her body leapt as his mouth found her, his lips kissed her, his tongue teased her. She writhed, fingers clutching at the bedclothes, thinking she would shatter with the force of her pleasure if he did not stop—and die in agony if he did.

His mouth, his hands, drove her toward sweet madness and she lay, shuddering, helpless to fight the new and unimagined sensations he gave her.

But then, without warning, he stopped. China moved beneath him, body burning with unfulfilled desires, mind reeling, knowing he had felt the first breathless tremblings of her rapture and had deliberately denied it to her.

Frustrated, angry with him and her own weakness, she squirmed beneath him trying to escape. Her hands pushed at his shoulders, his arms, trying to force him to release her.

"Let me go!" she repeated, perilously close to tears. "Leave me alone! All I have to do is scream and the whole house will awaken!"

Gabriel's face loomed above hers. His grass green eyes glittered. With the flick of one hand, he tugged at the belt of his banyan. The robe fell open and he pressed his body to hers.

"Then scream," he challenged, pushing his body against hers.

China felt him against her, his body parting her thighs, his flesh invading that moist, traitorous part of her that ached despite her protests.

"Scream," he breathed again, his mouth against her cheek as he pressed himself slowly into her.

But China could not scream, could not summon help. A sob caught in her throat as she was filled with a pleasure so intense it was almost pain. Her tears slid unheeded down her cheeks to stain the lace-trimmed pillowslips. Unable to stop herself, she arched against him.

"No," she moaned, though whether in entreatment or in denial of her own emotions even she could not tell. "Please . . . please . . ."

The knocking at the door shocked them both. China smothered a cry as Gabriel withdrew from her. Together they lay on the bed staring mutely at the door.

"China?" Rebecca's voice was muffled by the thick panels. "China, are you awake?"

"Rebecca," China breathed. "Oh, my God!"

Scrambling away from Gabriel, China slid off the bed. In the darkness, she went to the door.

"What is it?" she asked, her lips close to the space between the door and doorjamb.

"I can't sleep," Rebecca answered. "Can't I come in and talk to you?"

"I . . ." China leaned her forehead against the cool wood of the door. Now was the moment. If she threw open the door, Rebecca would see at a glance what kind of man she proposed to marry. She would see him there, naked but for the banyan, in her cousin's room in the dead of night. There would be questions, no doubt a scandal, China might well find herself sent from Montcalm in disgrace. But at least Gabriel

St. Jon would no longer be able to dupe the innocent girl on the other side of the door.

Taking a deep breath, China pressed down the latch and threw open the door. Rebecca stood there, candle in hand.

"How pale you are," she said, entering the room. "You look quite guilty, China. One would think you had a lover in here."

China tensed, unmoving, waiting for the cry of disbelief, of dismay. But there was nothing. Turning, she saw Rebecca set her candle down on the table near the open window. China's eyes darted to the shadowy corners of the room. They were empty.

"You retired so early tonight," Rebecca was saying, unaware of her cousin's concern and confusion. "I was afraid you were ill. But Gabriel said he saw you just before you went up and you were only a little tired and overcome with the heat of the salon."

"I . . ." China crossed the room to the tall armoire. Surely Gabriel could not have hidden . . . She jerked open the doors, but there was nothing inside but the exquisite wardrobe her uncle had ordered for her shortly after her arrival.

"China?" Rebecca eyed her curiously. "Whatever is the matter with you?"

"Nothing," China sighed. "Nothing at all. It's only . . . That is to say, I thought . . ."

Moving to the window, China leaned out. She caught her breath, for there, in the shadows at the foot of the rose trellis that reached to just below her window, Gabriel stood.

Grinning, a wild red rose clenched in his teeth, he swept her a mocking bow. Taking the flower from his mouth, he kissed its petals, then tossed it up toward her. By the time it fell to the flagstone path, he had disappeared from view.

Stunned, China turned back toward the room. She sank wearily into the armchair next to the window.

Rebecca leaned forward. "What is the matter?" she demanded. "You look as if you've seen a ghost."

"Not a ghost," China corrected, shaken, pale. "The Devil, cousin. The Devil himself!"

Nine

Ian Leyton sat on the blanket chest at the foot of his bed and contemplated the gilt buckles on his brown leather shoes. His prolonged visit to Montcalm had not been what he'd hoped it might be. He had made no progress at all with China. He had thought that her gratitude to him for taking her away from the clutches of her pirate captor would form the foundation of an attachment that might, with a little encouragement, blossom into something far stronger and long-lasting.

That had not happened. As far as he could see, she tolerated his attentions, accepted his company with an air of resignation that seemed more politeness than any real desire to spend time with him. It was a blow to his pride and, more than that, it was puzzling. In the past, he had never had any difficulty attracting women once he had made up his mind to do so. Quite the opposite was true, in fact. On more than one occasion he had had to find ways to discourage women who pursued him long after he had finished with them. It was ironic, then, that the one woman upon whom he had finally set his sights seemed to find him eminently resistible.

Sighing, he went to the traveling case where he took out the carefully cushioned flask of green liqueur.

"Absinthe," he whispered, swirling the liquid as he held the flask up to the light. "Liquid emeralds." He knew he was addicted to it but he did not care.

Savoring the liqueur, he replaced the flask and closed and locked the traveling case. Absinthe was not as easily obtained in the wilds of America as in his native England where it was known as Green Ginger. He intended to guard his dwindling supply like gold until he returned home to London.

And now, fortified, his thoughts returned to China. Perhaps she was simply more trouble than she was worth. It might be just as well to pack his bags and go on his way. It would be better for his self-esteem, certainly, if he were to leave rather than face any more of her casual indifference.

But he knew he could not leave just yet. The girl, for all the frustration she gave him, was special. She affected him in a way few women did—in a way he had not been affected in a very long time. He had to get closer to her, touch her, kiss her, test the strength of her effect on him, the strength of his own feelings. If he found she could touch him, arouse him, then he would move heaven and earth to make her his own.

Buoyed by that possibility, Ian pulled on the maroon coat with its double row of chased gold buttons that matched those at the knees of his light brown breeches. Glancing into the looking glass, he brushed back a trailing auburn curl before leaving his room to find the object of his desire.

China, meanwhile, sat in a downstairs parlor, a crewelwork sampler lying ignored in her lap. Her wools, dyed in jewel tones, spilled over the skirts of her lavender silk gown and onto the polished wood floor. Her thoughts were not on the needlework she'd begun in order to occupy her mind but on the very subject she'd thought to banish by busying her fingers—Gabriel.

She was appalled by what had happened in her bedchamber the night before. If only she'd been able to scream, to summon help.

If only Rebecca had come to her door a minute earlier! Then they would never have . . .

Her cheeks flushed scarlet with shame at the thought of what had happened. She remembered the almost painful rush of pleasure that had shot through her when Gabriel took her. How could she have felt anything but horror? How could she have known any emotion but shame? Her own body had betrayed her. In that split second before they had become one, she had wanted him, craved him as she had never wanted anything before.

Oblivious to the cascade of cloth and wool, China covered her face with her hands. It was madness, but such sweet, pleasured madness. And he had known! Gabriel had known full well that she would not call out. He had known without her telling him that she would succumb to him; that he could take her with impunity, force her to want him as much—perhaps more—than he wanted her.

Damn him! Damn him! China's eyes were fierce as her hands fell to her lap. It would never happen again! She would die before she let Gabriel St. Jon touch her! And he would marry her cousin Rebecca—ruin another innocent life—over her dead body!

Ian appeared in the open doorway as China raised her head. The angry determination still burned in her eyes, and he, misunderstanding, was taken aback by the loathing look. He wondered what he could have done to so offend her.

But China, suddenly aware of Ian there, watching her, let her face relax. Ignoring her spilled needlework, she rose and came toward him, hands outstretched.

"Here you are," she lied, smiling. "I've been wondering where you were hiding."

"I've hardly been hiding," he replied, baffled by the swift change in her expression and mood. "You've been . . . well . . . it seems you've been avoiding me."

"Avoiding you? Nonsense. How can you say such a thing?"

China gave him a sideways glance full of coquettish charm. She realized that the answer to her dilemma had been there under Montcalm's roof all along. Ian was eager to spend time in her company. So be it. His presence would not only take the edge off Gabriel's maddening confidence that he held her senses—if not her heart—in the palm of his hand, it would also help keep her from being alone with Gabriel.

"Still," Ian was saying, ignorant of China's new resolve toward him, "you seem less than enamored with my company. I thought you might prefer to see me leave Montcalm—"

"Leave?" China wound her arms about one of his. "How can you think of leaving? I depend on your escorting me to the ball at Bramblewood. Oh, Ian, say you will."

Ian felt that maddening, elusive tingle, that all-too-rare, much-longed-for sensation China provoked in him. All thoughts of leaving Montcalm and China vanished when he gazed down into those thick-lashed, blue topaz eyes.

"I would be honored to escort you to Bramblewood," he said thickly, drowning happily in those eyes.

"You're so kind to me," she cooed demurely, veiling her gaze modestly. "May I ask another favor?"

"Of course," he replied, too quickly.

"Will you go riding with me? Rebecca tells me there are some trails along the river. She says the countryside is beautiful."

Ian agreed, and China left him to go to her room and change into her black riding habit with its billowing skirts, gold grosgrain waistcoat, and ivory stock. Her hair was drawn back and woven into a single thick, black-beribboned braid. A black tricorne trimmed with gold braid perched atop her head.

Together the two of them rode through the forest, one behind the other, on winding trails too narrow to let them ride abreast. As Rebecca had promised, the forests surrounding Montcalm were beautiful, wild and untouched, affording glimpses of darting animals scurrying out of their path, of snowy white birds startled into flight from the river's shallows, of wildflowers blossoming like scattered jewels in the dappled shade of the gnarled, interlacing trees.

Montcalm was far behind them, the forest surrounded them. It was as if they were the only two people in a lush, virgin paradise. China reined in her spirited chestnut mare and smiled at Ian as he rode up beside her, his grey gelding dancing skittishly, eager to feel the wind blowing in its long mane once more.

"You can just see the river through there," China remarked, nodding toward the water shimmering in the distance framed by an undulating pattern of greenery.

"It's beautiful," Ian agreed, though his dark eyes left China's face for scarcely a second. "Shall we stop for a bit?"

China nodded and waited while Ian dismounted and tethered his horse's reins to a sapling. Coming to China, he tied her mount's reins, then, spanning her waist with surprisingly strong hands, lifted her down from the ornate little sidesaddle she had borrowed from Rebecca.

Leaving her waist, Ian's hand slipped down her arm to her own gloved hand. He clasped it in his own as they walked toward the steep bluff overlooking the York.

China felt Ian's gaze upon her, weighted,

heated. Her hand trembled in his. She could not bring herself to look up from the russet cloth of his gold-buttoned coat and somber ivory waistcoat. She thought she knew what she would see in his eyes—desire—and she did not know how to answer that desire. She was aware—only too aware—that it was not Gabriel who held her hand, that Gabriel was not the man standing beside her, burning her with his eyes. And yet she needed to be there with Ian, she needed to know if it was Gabriel who truly held the key to her senses or if it was merely the sensual side of her nature that he had awakened. Would her senses, her body, respond to Ian as they had to Gabriel? If they did, she reasoned, then she could face her erstwhile captor with more confidence, secure in the knowledge that he did not have some unique hold on her heart, her mind, her body. She had to plumb the depths of her own emotions, her desires. She had to compare her reactions to Ian to the responses Gabriel elicited so effortlessly.

And so, as Ian released her hand, as his own hand slipped about her waist, nestled in the small of her back, drew her toward him, China made no protest.

China tipped back her head, lifting her face, her lips, to receive Ian's kiss. His mouth on hers was gentle, almost tentative. His lips were warm and dry. He kissed her tenderly, with none of the savagery, the fire, she had known with Gabriel. There was nothing demanding in his kisses, he did not exact a response, force her own body to betray her. Even when his hand, first cupping her cheeks and then sliding down to her throat, her shoulder, her breast, was like a butterfly's touch compared to the masterful, almost ravenous fury of Gabriel's lovemaking.

It was Ian who broke the embrace. He stepped away, turning from her. His hand trembled as he reached out toward a spreading live oak for support.

"Sweet heavens!" he muttered, trying to bring some semblance of order to his dazed mind. He breathed deeply of the warm air rich with the redolent perfume of the forest around them. He'd never imagined . . . he'd never dared to dream . . .

Realizing that China must be wondering at his reaction, he composed himself as best he could. When he turned back to her he found her watching him. Their eyes met, then hers fell, a delicate flush suffusing her cheeks.

"I hope I have not offended you," he managed, trying manfully to hide the unsteadiness of his tone. "If I have, let me please beg leave to apologize. It was unpardonably forward of me—"

"Please." China stopped him. She paused, trying to soften the impatience in her voice. Though she had known a moment's fear, wondering how far she could allow her experiment to go and still escape unscathed, she felt cheated, unaccountably insulted. Ian's restraint was, she supposed, the mark of a gentleman. But how could she compare her reaction to him to her reaction to Gabriel if he did not behave like Gabriel? "There is no need to apologize. Perhaps we should go back now."

They rode in silence to Montcalm. China was grateful when, upon their arrival, her Uncle Arthur engaged Ian in conversation, giving her an opportunity to slip upstairs and change out of her habit. From her bedroom window she saw Ian ride away beside Lord Clairmont. They were heading toward a newly cleared field, and China imagined that Arthur meant to question Ian about farming techniques in his native England.

China could not help smiling. What Ian, a doctor, the son of an earl, knew about preparing land for the cultivation of tobacco she could not imagine. Still, if it gave her a respite from his company and time to ponder what had happened—or, more precisely, had not happened—between them in the forest, she was grateful.

A housemaid entered to tidy China's room, and China, seeking privacy, went downstairs to the library that was her uncle's domain. Her aunt and cousin were more concerned with matters of fashion and society than with improvement of the mind.

The aroma of candlewax and old leather greeted China when she entered the room. The library was plain, almost severely furnished compared to the beauty of the rest of the house. The furniture was solid, built for comfort rather than looks. Glass-fronted cabinets held Arthur Clairmont's precious store of books, and draperies kept drawn at the windows prevented sunlight from fading their bindings. A screen, forming a kind of alcove near the fireplace, provided a warm, private retreat where Lord Clairmont spent many hours immersed in the wisdom of the ages.

Moving from cabinet to cabinet, China perused the titles. Though she had come for meditation, not entertainment, she could not help opening one or another of the glass-paned doors and examining several of the prizes of her uncle's collections.

When the library door opened, China looked up impatiently. If it was that bothersome housemaid . . . But it wasn't. And when she saw who it was, she wished it had been the maid after all.

Gabriel shut the door behind him. The glint in his green eyes warned her. The closed, taut expression on his face made her instinctively step back.

"So, you've returned," he said tightly,

moving toward her. His black coat rippled as he walked, its gold buttons glinting dully in the muted sunshine that glowed behind the drawn draperies.

China lifted her chin. "Did you think I wouldn't?" she countered. "There is no reason for me to escape from Montcalm—unlike some places I've been."

A muscle ticked in Gabriel's jaw. "You went riding with Ian Leyton." It was more than a statement, it was an accusation.

"I did," she confirmed, turning with a cool indifference that was mostly feigned, to replace the book in the case. "If it's any of your business."

She looked back at him and saw his eyes narrow dangerously. "Or have you forgotten that you are betrothed? My cousin should be your concern, not I."

"I told you," he snarled, "I plan to break with Rebecca."

"Oh?" China's tone was frankly skeptical. "And when will this happen? On your wedding night?"

"Dammit, China—" he began.

"No!" she hissed. "I don't believe you intend to end this betrothal at all. You're lying! You're lying to buy yourself time! You mean to marry your way into respectability. Well, you can't! You're a villain, Gabriel, a thief and worse! And I will believe you mean to break with Rebecca when I see it." She tilted her chin haughtily at him, feeling strong, confident, determined to have her say before the feeling deserted her.

"And as for me," she finished, "I will do as I please with whom I please, and be damned to you, Mr. St. Jon!"

Gabriel closed the distance between them in the breadth of a second. His hands closed painfully about her upper arms, his fingers creased the pale blue silk of her gown and pressed deeply into her tender flesh.

"Is he your lover?" he demanded of her, shaking her, his face mottled with jealous rage. "Is he? Have you taken that . . . that meddler into your bed?"

"Meddler?" China snapped. "Why? Because he freed your prisoner? Because he—"

"Have you!" Gabriel growled, refusing to be diverted from his question.

China quailed before the murderous fury in his glittering green eyes. She believed with all her heart that if she answered yes, Gabriel would leave the room, seek out Ian Leyton, and murder him without blinking an eye. She trembled in the crushing grip of his hands.

"No," she whispered, unable to lie to him. "He is not my lover." She saw the glimmer of triumph in Gabriel's eyes, and defiance flared inside her. "But he kissed me, in the forest," she revealed, refusing to let Gabriel's victory be unqualified. "He kissed me, Gabriel, and the memory still lingers in my heart."

A hard stillness came over his face. It was a look China recognized. It was Gabriel Fortune, the pirate, master of the sea, uncompromising, determined to take what he wanted and willing to accept nothing less.

"Then let's burn it out," he muttered.

He took her lips fiercely, crushing her in his arms, curving his body over hers. China struggled but she knew it was useless. Soon, too soon, came the heat, the hot, sweet melting sensation that signaled the surrender of her senses, the yielding of her will to his, the defeat she found so maddening.

When Gabriel released her she nearly stumbled. His strength had become her strength, her legs felt weak and unsteady beneath her. Staggering, she was forced to grip the back of a chair to keep from falling. Her eyes, reproachful, tearful, raised to Gabriel's face.

"Why can't you leave me alone?" she hissed, trembling with anger and frustration. "Haven't you done enough damage? Why can't you get out of my life?"

"I am your life," he breathed, so softly China scarcely heard him. "You belong to me. I claimed you that night aboard Le Corbeau's *Black Pearl*. I made you mine aboard the *Golden Fortune*. You ran away. I thought I'd lost you, but Providence has given you back to me. And I'll be damned if I'll lose you again. You'll always be mine, China. I'll keep you if it kills me . . . or you."

With a last hard look, with a last warning glare of those grass green eyes, Gabriel turned and was gone, leaving China to slip, weeping, to the floor of the dimly lit, ominously silent room.

Ten

Bramblewood plantation straddled a pretty creek that fed into the York River some six miles away from Montcalm. It was the home of John and Philippa Southworth, who were known for the elegance of their entertainments, the beauty of their home, and their fondness for their only child, their son, Cameron. It was only to be expected that the ball to celebrate the return of their son and his bride from their wedding trip abroad would be the most glittering social event of the season.

But as China rode toward Bramblewood, sharing a coach with Ian, Rebecca, and Gabriel, she wished she had stayed home. A quiet evening in her own room would have been far preferable to listening to Rebecca prattle, wondering aloud where she and Gabriel would go on their wedding trip.

China glared at Gabriel who sat opposite her in the darkened coach. He had not broken his betrothal to Rebecca as he'd sworn he would a week before. She thought he had no intention of doing so. But if he thought to stall her until the wedding was a *fait accompli* he was going to be disappointed. If he did not act soon, she had promised herself, she would take matters into her own hands. And she intended to tell him so at the first opportunity.

Still, she was forced to listen while Rebecca mused wistfully:

"Cameron Southworth took Justine to Paris!" Her eyes sparkled as she gazed up at Gabriel. "Will you take me to Paris after we're married?"

China's eyes narrowed. She saw Gabriel glance toward her before he replied.

"We'll have to talk about it," he said vaguely.

"You're no fun at all," Rebecca pouted, but seemed to think there was nothing unusual in his answer. Turning her attention to China, Rebecca said: "You know Justine Southworth, don't you? I think her parents came to Gabriel's and my engagement ball. They are the Wards, you know, of Wards'

Creek on the James River."

China shrugged, shaking her head. She'd been introduced to many people on that night but she remembered few of them. The shock of finding Gabriel Fortune—magically transformed into Gabriel St. Jon—at her uncle's plantation had been too great to let her make much sense of anything or anyone else.

Rebecca chattered on, but China heard none of it. She felt sorry that the marriage plans that obviously meant so much to Rebecca were doomed to come to nothing, and did not care to listen to her cousin plan a life that was ultimately not to be. Nor did she pay much attention to Ian's attempts to make conversation. Instead she simply gazed out the window and wished for them to arrive at Bramblewood. After all, she reasoned wearily, the sooner they arrived, the sooner the evening would end and they could leave.

The long green and gold salon of Bramblewood was lit with what seemed like a thousand candles burning in chandeliers of gleaming brass and sparkling crystal. The beautiful French carpets that normally covered the floors had been taken out, revealing a shining floor polished until it was almost too slippery for dancing.

Candlelight glittered on the jewels adorning the ladies and sparkled in the embroidery of the men's coats and waistcoats. It was an elegant assembly gathered especially to welcome home a couple who represented the merging of two of the greatest landowning families in Virginia.

Cameron and Justine Southworth, married three months, never strayed far from one another's side. They were the very picture of wedded bliss, and China cringed at the sight of Rebecca, her pale blonde head close to Justine's chestnut one, discussing Justine's happiness and Rebecca's dreams of the future.

Glancing about the ballroom, China saw Gabriel in a corner, glass in hand, laughing with a pair of men China recognized from the betrothal ball at Montcalm. Both were from Williamsburg, both were close friends of the fierce pirate hunter, the Royal Governor.

How bold Gabriel was, China thought, torn between amazed disapproval and grudging admiration. He knew full well that his life would not be worth tuppence if the Royal Governor heard that the infamous pirate Gabriel Fortune was in Virginia. And yet here he stood, the fiancé of a prominent Virginian, received in the finest homes, drinking French champagne, behaving as if he had not a care in the world.

"Champagne?"

China did not hear Ian at first. It was not until he stepped closer and spoke louder that her attention was torn away from the tall, sable-haired man in scarlet and black at the far end of the room.

"Thank you," she replied, taking the glass he held out to her.

"Are you enjoying yourself?" he asked, his dark eyes following the direction of her gaze and finding Gabriel. "Would you like to dance?"

China sipped her wine. "No, thank you," she answered absently. "I don't feel like dancing tonight."

Unbidden, her eyes drifted back to Gabriel. A hot flush rose into her cheeks when her eyes met his and he winked over the rim of his raised glass.

Ian noticed her reaction. Glancing toward Gabriel, he found the black-haired man watching them with an intent, curiously irritated look.

Not for the first time Ian wondered what there was between his host's future son-in-law and the girl Ian had decided to make his own. Though China tended to snarl at Gabriel St. Jon and he seemed to view her with sardonic amusement, they were anything but indifferent to one another. Ian knew it would be useless to question either of them. China would be evasive, and St. Jon was almost certain to tell him to mind his own bloody business. Still, if there was anything brewing between China and Gabriel—and Ian was increasingly convinced there was—it would behoove him to know it as soon as possible. If he meant to make China his wife, he had to know if there were any other men in her life.

He frowned, troubled, as he looked at Gabriel. With his looks, his connections, his wealth and prospects, the man could be a formidable opponent in a contest for a lady's affections. But surely St. Jon would not cast a covetous eye toward his fiancée's cousin. It was obvious that Rebecca Clairmont was busily planning her wedding—she, apparently, knew of nothing that might thwart her plans to become mistress of Fox Meadow.

Ian sighed. Surely it was all in his imagination. China was a beautiful woman; in any gathering, she was the focus of many pairs of admiring masculine eyes. And St. Jon, for all that he was betrothed, was a healthy, virile man who appreciated a beautiful woman. That was all it amounted to. Ian need have no fears in that direction.

Having reassured himself, Ian smiled down at China, who had drained her glass. "Let me get you another," he offered, taking the empty glass from her.

With a wan smile as empty as the champagne glass she held out to him, China obeyed. She did not care one way or another if he brought her another glass of wine. But with him dispatched on his errand, she would not be forced to make conversation.

Even as that thought crossed her mind, China wished suddenly Ian were still beside her. His hovering presence might have deterred Gabriel, who was leaving his companions and making his way around the crowded ballroom to join her.

"Leave me alone!" she snarled as he came to her. With a flick of her hand she drew aside her amethyst silk skirts as if afraid of soiling them by contact with him. "Go dance with your fiancée."

"I want to talk to you, China," he said softly, smiling brightly at Rebecca as she sailed past in the arms of Cameron Southworth.

"I'm not interested in hearing any more of your lies and excuses," China retorted. "I've heard them all, and they are worth as much as your promises—nothing."

"I can explain," he persisted. "I know you're angry about Rebecca—"

"Gabriel," China interrupted, glaring up at him, not caring if anyone noticed and wondered at the heated emotion in her eyes, "how can I not be angry about Rebecca? And how can you think I'd believe any explanation you cared to offer? I've no doubt you've thought of yet another excuse, when in reality—"

"Please," he cut in, "come out to the garden. I want—"

"Hah!" China's bark of laughter drew several curious glances. Blushing, she lowered her eyes and snapped open her lilac lace fan. "I know what you want in the garden," she hissed. "The same thing you wanted aboard the *Golden Fortune* and in my room and the library at Montcalm and—"

"Enough!" he muttered. "I'm serious, damnit! If you want to know my reasons for delaying the end of this betrothal, come out into the garden. If you are not there in ten minutes, I'll know you don't care about them."

"But I . . ." China began. But it was too late. Gabriel had left her side and disappeared from the salon, leaving China to wrestle with her indecision.

By the time Ian returned from the small antechamber where bottles of French champagne brought back by the newlyweds rested in tubs of ice from the plantation icehouse, China was gone. His dark eyes scanned the salon; he wondered if some would-be suitor had managed to persuade her to take a turn on the dance floor.

He could not find her there among the dancing couples. She seemed to have vanished. But then . . . He scowled as he noticed her, framed for a moment in a doorway at the far end of the room. In a moment she had disappeared around the corner.

Ian handed the glasses of champagne to a passing servant. His eyes swept the room, searching for the tall, broad-shouldered figure of Gabriel St. Jon. He was not particularly surprised to find him missing as well. He hesitated only a moment before setting off toward the door where he'd last seen China.

"A young woman," he said to a gray-clad house slave he found in the next room, "with silver-blonde hair, wearing a gown of violet silk with orchid bows, did you see her?"

The young man nodded gravely. "She went out," he replied. "Out there."

The door the slave indicated took Ian out of the house and into the moonlit solitude of the Southworth gardens. Though splendor itself, the gardens were unlit. The evening sky had been dark with the threat of rain, so the lanterns that might have illuminated the beds and walks had not been lit.

Ian followed the uneven brick path, pausing every few steps to listen for voices. He had just begun to think he'd been sent on a wild goose chase when he heard the soft tones of China's voice coming from the darkness to his left.

Moving as swiftly as the darkness allowed, he crept close and crouched behind a tall hedge. Scowling, he strained to hear the quiet yet urgent words China was saying.

"You lied to me from the beginning," China was accusing. "Every time you promised you would break with my cousin, it was a lie!"

Behind the hedge, Ian's brows shot up and his jaw sagged in surprise. He'd wanted to discover what was between Gabriel St. Jon and China, but this! St. Jon had promised to leave Rebecca? Could it be they were conducting an *affaire de coeur* beneath his fiancée's very nose? Beneath Lord Clairmont's own roof? Small wonder China had seemed indifferent to his courting!

"How can you do this to her?" China was continuing. "Have you no conscience at all? Are you so lost to all human decency . . ."

"It was not a lie," Gabriel broke in. "It's only that I don't know how to tell her. I don't want to hurt her."

"Hurt her!" China's eyes blazed. "Prolonging this masquerade is what will hurt her most of all! The longer it goes on, Gabriel, the more she will be hurt in the end."

Gabriel stared at her. How could he tell her what he felt? How could he tell her that he intended to break his betrothal to Rebecca in order to be free to court China herself? Rebecca's pain over the broken engagement would be magnified beyond endurance when she realized he wished to be free of her in order to pursue her more beautiful cousin. He dreaded the prospect.

He could not bring himself to tell China that he had fallen in love with her in those days after he had taken her from Le Corbeau. He had vowed to make her his own. But every time she looked at him he saw the loathing in her eyes and could not bring himself to risk her derision, her rejection, by revealing his feelings to her.

It would be laughable, he reflected, if it did not seem so tragic. He, Gabriel Fortune, pirate, brigand, so fearless in battle, quailed before the glimmering blue glare of a woman whose head barely reached his shoulder, a woman he could lift with one hand. Still, he reasoned, perhaps if he told her how he felt, she would be more understanding. Perhaps she would help him prepare Rebecca for the pain that was untimately going to befall her.

"China," he said solemnly, "you must listen to me. I have to tell you that I—"

"I've listened to quite enough of your lies!" China interrupted, not realizing what he'd been about to say, little suspecting the nature of the words that would not now be said. "I can see it all now. You mean to marry Rebecca, to marry the respectability, the protection her father can offer you. You think if you can delay long enough, you can marry her over my objections."

"China, no," Gabriel began.

"Stop lying!" she cried, not caring now if

she was overheard. "How do you think Rebecca will feel when she discovers the truth, when she learns that, rather than being Mrs. Gabriel St. Jon, wife of a gentleman planter, she is Mrs. Gabriel Fortune, wife of a pirate! What will you tell her when it's time for you to go to sea?"

China's voice dropped, imitating Gabriel's far lower tones:

" 'Beg pardon, m'dear, but our funds are a bit low. I shall have to go out for a spot of plundering, a touch of pillaging, but have no fear, I will ravish no maidens unless it proves absolutely necessary!' "

Gabriel's low rumble of laughter rolled across the flower beds surrounding them. It was quickly followed by the sharp *thwack* of China's fist striking his chest.

"Damn you!" she growled. "Don't laugh at me! I tell you right now, if you don't tell Rebecca the truth, I will! Tell her how you took me from Le Corbeau, took me as the prize in a card game! Tell her how you forced me . . . ruined me! How you took me to Fox Meadow intending to keep me as your mistress! Tell her! Because I swear I won't stand by and watch my cousin unwittingly marry Gabriel Fortune!" Her eyes glittered. "Remember, damn your eyes, you've been warned!"

Her heels clicked on the brick path as she stormed off into the darkness. In his hiding place, Ian sagged, mind reeling, astonished by what he'd heard. He waited until he heard Gabriel pass, following China back to the house, and then he, too, left the dark gardens and returned to the ball.

The carriage that brought Gabriel, China, Rebecca, and Ian to Bramblewood rolled back through the darkness toward Montcalm. Silence reigned within. Rebecca slept, her head cradled on Gabriel's shoulder, blissfully unaware of the scalding glare China fixed on Gabriel or of his impatient, defiant, occasionally searching glances in return.

For Ian's part, his attention was focused on the impenetrable darkness outside the carriage window. His thoughts were a swirling eddy of information, realizations, and plans. That China had been Gabriel's captive, that he had taken her into his bed, did nothing to hinder Ian's determination to have her. The thought of all that stubborn, imperious, exquisite pride being forced to a pirate's will only whetted his appetite for her.

And Ian, his head clearer now, his senses less muddied with shock and disbelief, had heard something else in China's words, her voice, during that heated exchange in the garden—something Gabriel had missed, something Gabriel would have loved to know. Despite her anger, despite her accusations and threats, despite the fact that she, herself, would have vehemently denied it, China was in love with the man who had captured her, taken her, mastered her. It was a valuable piece of information, and one Ian thought he could turn to his own advantage.

Grateful to be home, determined to put the troubling scene in the garden at Bramblewood out of her mind for the night, China retired to her room the moment she descended from the coach in front of Montcalm. Her maid undressed her and helped her into her nightdress, but when she would have taken up the ivory-backed brush to brush China's hair, China waved her away, dismissing her for the night.

Seated before her looking glass, China drew the soft-bristled brush through the long, shimmering curls that, unpinned, poured in a silken cascade to her waist. She tried not to think of Gabriel, but his face appeared again and again in her mind's eye. She heard again his voice when he told her he did not wish to hurt Rebecca.

Against her will, she had to acknowledge the twinge of jealousy, of envy, she felt at the memory. How concerned he was for Rebecca's feelings. And yet he did not seem to spare a thought for her—for the way she felt when she saw him and Rebecca together, heard them planning their future life together.

"He cares nothing for me," she told the sad-eyed girl in the mirror. "Nothing. I was merely a prize won at sea. The only thing that was hurt when I ran away from Fox Meadow was his pride. Even now, when he comes to me, when he kisses me, tries to bed me, it is nothing but lust. He has no finer feelings, no higher emotions toward me."

Closing her eyes, China willed away the hot tears that made the flames of the candles burning on her dressing table blur before her. She swallowed hard against the lump in her throat—the sobs she choked back. Her hand, fingers still loosely clasping the ivory brush, fell to her lap and she sat, head bowed, hating Gabriel and loving him, and hating herself for being torn between the two emotions.

The click of the doorlatch jerked her back to her senses. Her heart thudded in her breast. It was Gabriel, she thought, come to try and exercise his power over her senses, come to try and prove to himself and to her that however much she might storm and threaten, her body, her will, were his to command.

China steeled herself, determined not to allow him to triumph over her yet again. Swiveling on the brocaded bench, she rose, lifting her chin.

"Damn you, Gabriel," she began, "how do you dare to come here after . . ."

But it was Ian, not Gabriel, who stood there. He wore a banyan of embroidered silk in an Oriental design and his auburn hair had been brushed and tied at the nape of his neck. His hand rested on the latch of the partially open door.

"What are you doing here?" China demanded, bewildered by the unexpected sight of him where she had thought to find Gabriel.

An enigmatic smile played about Ian's lips as he pushed the door closed behind him. His dark eyes roved over China—the candles burning on the table behind her cast her body into silhouette through the gossamer lawn of her nightdress.

"I want to talk to you, China," he said quietly, advancing into the room.

"But surely we can talk tomorrow," she reasoned, an inexplicable feeling of dread lying heavy in her breast. "I'm certain whatever it is can wait—"

The shake of Ian's head cut her off. "This can't wait," he said. "Not another moment."

Eleven

Curious, confused, China pulled a linen combing mantle over her nightdress for modesty's sake. Sitting down on the dressing table bench, she fixed Ian with a look of grim impatience.

"Very well, sir," she said coolly, "say what you will."

Brushing a speck of lint from his embroidered silk waistcoat, Ian clasped his hands behind him and strolled nonchalantly to the windows. He stood for a long, silent moment gazing out into the darkness, knowing all the while China was growing more and more impatient. He relished the fact that he, for once, had the upper hand with the imperious beauty.

"It's really quite simple," he said at last, swinging toward her. "You cannot be unaware of my feelings for you. From the first, from the earliest days of our acquaintance, my feelings toward you have been quite beyond what I have ever felt for any other woman."

"You flatter me, sir—" China began to protest.

"Not at all," Ian interrupted, silencing her. "I was hesitant to speak because I knew nothing of the depth of your feelings toward me. I hope I am not mistaken when I assume that you are at least not indifferent toward me."

China fidgeted on the bench. She knew he was thinking of that day in the forest when she had let him kiss her and fondle her in order to test her own reactions and to place a buffer between herself and Gabriel. Though she had not meant for Ian to think she returned whatever affections he felt for her, that, apparently, was what he thought, and this awkward interview was the result.

"Sir," she ventured, flustered, "it is true I am fond of you, but that is not enough to—"

"It is a beginning," he persisted. "A base upon which might be built—"

"Please." She tried again. She had hoped he would eventually be bored and leave Montcalm of his own accord. But it looked as though she would not be spared the unpleasant task of rejecting him bluntly and finally.

"You must listen to me, Ian," she pleaded. "I cannot let you go on with this. I would not make you unhappy for all the world—"

"Then do not," he broke in, driving China mad with frustration at his continued interruptions. "You have it within your power to make me the happiest of men. I have searched my heart, dear China, and I cannot be happy until you are mine."

China sighed, her heart sinking. For once she wished Gabriel would make one of his midnight visits, but that seemed unlikely. No convenient rescue was at hand. She would have to deal with the situation herself.

Rising from her bench, she moved toward the door. If only she could discourage him, she could send him on his way and be done with it. But a voice of caution told her to be careful with him.

"Dr. Leyton," she said quietly.

"Ian," he corrected.

China's eyes flashed. She bit back a sharp retort and took a deep breath to calm herself. "Ian," she complied with exaggerated patience, "I am sorry if I have somehow led you to believe there might be a future for us together. While I am grateful, of course, to you for rescuing me from Gab . . ." She caught herself. "From my captor, my feelings for you do not go beyond gratitude and fondness. I hope we will always be friends, but as to anything more, it is impossible."

A little of the saccharine sweetness faded from Ian's face. He drew himself up and eyed her with a hint of smug certainty.

"Then I assume you never intend to marry?" he asked, his voice cool, his tone heavily tinged with sarcasm.

China stared at him. He had always been so gallant, so amenable and accommodating. This was a side of him she had not suspected, a side that was unpredictable, intimidating. Still, she was not one to be easily cowed. Lifting her chin, she returned his haughty stare.

"Without meaning to offend, sir," she said, "my matrimonial ambitions do not begin and end with you."

"Do they not?" Ian questioned. "I wonder."

China bridled. "See here, Dr. Leyton, I am not so disagreeable a prospect as all that!" She moved to the door and laid a hand on the latch. "I think you should leave now."

Ignoring her, Ian sat down in the chair near the window. "Certainly you are a beautiful and desirable young woman," he allowed, showing not the slightest inclination to leave her bedchamber as she had asked. "And your breeding as well as your relationship to Lord and Lady Clairmont would make you a fine match for any young man in Virginia. But there is one rather large point against you."

"And that is?" China snarled, crossing her arms and scowling at her unwelcome visitor.

"Feeling against pirates runs rife in Virginia. Not many families hereabouts would welcome to their hearth and home a woman known to have been held captive by not one but two pirates. I fear assumptions would be made—assumptions that a woman as lovely as yourself would never have escaped their clutches without having been, shall we say, hopelessly compromised?"

A dull flush pinkened China's cheeks. She wondered how he could know that she had been the prisoner of not only Gabriel Fortune but of Le Corbeau as well. Gossip, she supposed. Someone's maid had overheard something and confided it to someone else's valet who in turn used it to impress some reluctant chambermaid.

She decided her wisest course lay in trying to bluff it out. "No one outside Montcalm knows about that," she told him. "Do you intend to tell everyone? Is that your game, sir? Will you use my misfortune against me?"

"Not at all," Ian assured her. "I would not wish to have my wife's shame exposed before all the world."

"Your wife!" China's lip curled with disdain. "I am not going to be your wife. Of that, at least, we can be sure."

"I think you are mistaken," he disagreed calmly.

"If you think I will marry you to save my reputation, sir, then you are the one who is mistaken."

"Oh no." Ian shook his head. "Not to save your reputation."

"Then what?" she demanded impatiently. "My family's honor? Our good name?"

A slow smile, sly and smug, crept over Ian's face. "Your lover," he said quietly. His smile broadened at the astonishment on China's face. "Gabriel St. Jon. Or should I say, Gabriel Fortune."

China felt the floor rock beneath her feet. The room seemed suddenly hazy and blurred before her eyes. She thought she was about to faint and would have welcomed the sweet oblivion, but it was denied her.

Seeing the shock on her starkly pale face, Ian knew his words had struck to the heart of her. Gesturing toward a chair near his own, he invited:

"Come, sit down, my dear. We have a great deal to discuss."

Weak, fearful, China stumbled across the room and sank wordlessly into the chair.

* * *

At mid-morning the next day China and Ian emerged from Lord Clairmont's library after announcing their betrothal to China's aunt and uncle.

Since Ian had expressed his desire to leave Virginia for England as soon as possible, Lord Clairmont had offered to try to have the publishing of the banns waived. The marriage could take place almost immediately.

China felt trapped, caught in the jaws of a wolf who had masqueraded as a lamb until his prey was ensnared. As she had sat listening to Ian in her room the night before, she knew there was no hope of escape. If she refused his proposal, Ian would have Gabriel arrested. He would be tried for piracy, condemned, and hanged, and she, without doubt, would be compelled to testify against him. Gabriel could not hope to escape by fleeing to Fox Meadow, for the Royal Governor of Virginia was no respecter of boundaries. It would not be the first time he had entered another colony to capture one of the pirates who were his especial targets.

She had wondered, as she sat there with Ian droning on and on, why she did not simply do as he threatened. Had she not vowed to destroy Gabriel Fortune? Had she not sworn vengeance on him? She had railed at him to break his engagement to Rebecca. Arrest would surely put an end to the farce that was their betrothal.

But she could not. The thought of Gabriel standing trial, of herself being instrumental in putting the noose around his neck, of his body hanging in chains as a warning to others, sickened her. She agreed to marry Ian to save a man she swore she hated. Not until that moment had she understood how tenuous was the boundary between hate and love. Not until that moment had she finally admitted to herself that she loved Gabriel St. Jon, loved him enough to sacrifice herself to a man she cared nothing for in order to save his life.

Now, in the glare of the morning sunshine, China stiffened as Rebecca ran to embrace her. Her cousin's pale blue eyes were shining with a joy so genuine that it nearly broke China's steely reserve. She blinked furiously to hold back the tears.

"I'm so happy for you," Rebecca sighed. "Mama told me you two are to be married." She seized Ian's hand too. "It's wonderful!" Her smile faltered. "But you are to leave for England directly after the marriage. If only you could stay long enough for my wedding."

"Ian says we must sail immediately after our wedding," China told her in a weak voice.

"I know." Rebecca's eyes were full of fond sympathy. "But perhaps Gabriel and I might come to visit on our wedding trip. You must write the moment you are settled in England. Send me your address so we can come and visit you."

"I will," China promised softly. She glanced around the hallway. "Where is Gabriel?"

"He had to leave."

"Leave?" China wondered if she could somehow get a warning to him so he would know he should not return to Montcalm. Perhaps he could take the *Golden Fortune* and set sail from Fox Meadow. At sea he would be safe from—

"He'll be back tonight," Rebecca was going on. "He only went to Williamsburg. He went to see someone he met at Bramblewood. Business, I suppose."

China's hopes fell. "I see," she murmured. Gently she removed her hand from Rebecca's. "I feel a little giddy," she said, stepping back. "If you'll excuse me, I think I'll go up and lie down for a while."

"I hope you're not ill," Ian said. "I wouldn't want anything to delay our departure. Perhaps I should give you something—"

"I'm all right!" China snapped. Seeing the warning flash in his eyes, she lowered her angry glare. "I'm fine," she assured him meekly. "It's nothing."

"Then I'll look in on you later. We have plans to make, my dear."

"Just as you wish," she acquiesced, turning away. Leaving them there to watch her, she climbed the stairs to her room.

Ian's dark eyes glittered as he watched until she had disappeared around the corner of the corridor at the head of the stairs. Then he smiled down at Rebecca who stood at his side.

"Well, my dear cousin-to-be," he murmured, "what do you say to a stroll in the garden? It's a perfect day."

Rebecca smiled. In fact, it was chilly, overcast and gray. But, she supposed, to one as happy as Ian every day was a perfect day. She slipped her arm through his and let him lead her out into the gardens.

There was a new spring in Ian's step as they went. He was about to set the next phase of his plan into motion. Rebecca Clairmont was about to learn the truth about her fiancé and the cousin she had come to love.

China retired early that night pleading fatigue. Her aunt expressed concern that something served at dinner might have been spoiled, for Rebecca had also retired early looking pale and drawn. But China knew that, in her own case at least, dinner was not to blame. She felt exhausted, though she knew well that it was more emotional than physical. And another pressing reason was that she wanted to avoid a meeting with

Gabriel—a meeting she knew was inevitable but one she longed to delay as long as possible.

He still had not returned from Williamsburg by the time she blew out the last candle and lay back against her pillows in the gathering darkness of her bedchamber. She was a mass of conflicting emotions. She feared Gabriel might have taken too foolish a risk by going to Williamsburg. He might be locked in irons at that very moment. Or he might have somehow sensed danger and fled to Fox Meadow. In either case she would never see him again, and she dreaded that prospect even more than she hated the thought of confronting him once he learned of her engagement.

Her exhausted emotions, her troubled mind, took refuge in sleep. It crept over her softly, took her unawares. And when she awakened she felt confused, dazed. When she remembered that her betrothal to Ian, and the wedding her aunt was no doubt even then planning, was no mere bad dream, she felt worse.

She squinted, glancing around the shadowy room. The house was silent. The hour, she imagined, was late. What then had jolted her awake? There were no sounds; no one lurked in the darkness.

Pushing herself up in the bed, China

rubbed the last clinging vestiges of sleep from her eyes. Her thoughts immediately turned to Gabriel. Had he returned? If so, had someone told him the news? China could not imagine her aunt hesitating a second. But perhaps he had not returned. She sighed. Perhaps he had, but saw no reason to confront her.

Though she thought she knew better, she hoped fervently that was the case. There was nothing to be done. She could not tell him of Ian's blackmail—that had been a part of the bargain to save Gabriel's life. If only Gabriel would stay away, leave her alone, until she and Ian were safely gone . . .

The click of the doorlatch sent a jolt of fear shooting through her. She did not know which she feared more: that it might be Gabriel come to demand an explanation or Ian come to claim the conjugal rights that would be his all too soon.

A single glance at the figure framed for a moment in the doorway told her it was Gabriel. Her stomach lurched. There was no avoiding it. He had come to confront her.

"China?" His voice was little more than a ripple in the silence hanging heavy in the room.

"I'm awake," she replied.

Coming to the bedside, he stepped up onto the mahogany steps and sat on the edge of the wide bed. "What is this nonsense about you and Leyton?" he demanded without preamble.

"It's not nonsense," she replied. "Ian proposed last night, and I accepted."

"Proposed? When? You went straight to bed after we got back from Bramblewood."

China's cheeks flushed. "He came here. It was late."

"Is he in the habit of paying midnight calls to your bedchamber?" Gabriel demanded tightly.

"Gabriel, please," China murmured. "I am going to marry him. Just leave me alone."

Thrusting himself to his feet, Gabriel paced the floor. "When did all this come about?" he snapped, agitated and angry. "Were you intriguing with that bastard from the start?"

China felt the tightness in her throat. Her emotions threatened to betray her. "I love him," she lied, grateful for the darkness that concealed her expression.

"The hell you do!" Gabriel growled.

"Gabriel . . ." China murmured tremulously.

"Do you know where I went today?" he broke in.

"Rebecca said you went to Williamsburg."

"Aye. I went to Bruton Parish Church.

Lady Clairmont bespoke the church for the wedding. I went to tell the reverend there would be no wedding."

"You told him . . ." China felt sick to her stomach.

"I did," he confirmed. "I was going to tell Rebecca tonight, but she went to bed before I got here. And the moment I walked through the door, Lady Clairmont told me about you and Leyton."

"Will you go through with the wedding now?" she could not help asking.

"How can you think I would?" he countered. "I don't love Rebecca. You know that. I never did. I am fond of her. I knew she cared for me. I believed she would be a good wife, a good mother for the children I hoped to have. But love, no. I thought myself incapable of love." His grass green eyes lingered on China's face. "Then I met you."

"Don't say any more," China begged, on the verge of tears.

"Don't marry Leyton," Gabriel asked simply. "It would be a mistake."

"I will marry him," China vowed, wishing desperately she could tell Gabriel the truth . . . tell him she was sacrificing herself to save his life. But she could not. "We are to be married in two days' time. We're sailing for England immediately after the ceremony. Don't try to interfere in this, Gabriel. I promise you will regret it if you do."

"Is that a threat?" he asked ominously.

"This is what I want," she lied. "I am going to marry Ian. If you try to stop me, I'll see you hanged for piracy."

Gabriel's eyes blazed. His body trembled with rage. "Damn you for a scheming bitch!" he snarled. "Marry your precious Leyton, then, and little joy may he bring you! And be damned to all you Clairmonts!"

Storming out of the room, Gabriel slammed the door, not caring if the noise roused anyone else in the house.

China sank into the deep, yielding softness of her pillows. She wept, great gulping sobs, her tears soaking through the lacy pillowcases. She wept for Gabriel, for what might have been between them and now would never be. She wept for Rebecca, whose dreams of a future with the man she loved were to be dashed before her eyes. And she wept for herself, trapped into a marriage she did not want with a man she could not love.

Lost in her misery, awash in her tears, China did not hear the muffled sobs that were a muted accompaniment to her own. Rebecca had hidden herself in China's armoire.

During their walk in the garden, Ian had told Rebecca everything he knew about Gabriel and China. He told her Gabriel's secret, he told her it had been Gabriel who had taken China from the clutches of her first pirate captor, Le Corbeau. He told her that Gabriel had taken China to Fox Meadow, that he had seduced her, and that they had continued their affair after Gabriel had come to Montcalm and been reunited with his erstwhile captive. Finally, Ian had promised Rebecca that, were she to hide herself in China's room, she would hear the truth from Gabriel's own lips.

Rebecca had not wanted to believe him. Still, she could not stop herself from going to China's room and hiding in the stifling folds of the gowns in China's armoire. She'd expected to be discovered at any moment—now she almost wished she had been.

Gabriel. Rebecca's hands curled into fists as she remembered what she'd heard him say. He did not love her. He never had. Damn him. Damn him! Even if China married Ian tomorrow, there would be no wedding for Rebecca, no Fox Meadow, no Gabriel St. Jon.

So be it, she told herself, waiting impatiently for China to cry herself to sleep so she could creep from her hiding place. If she could not have her wedding, if she could not have Fox Meadow and Gabriel St. Jon, the man she loved, she would have the next best thing—revenge on Gabriel Fortune, the God-cursed pirate who had taken her heart and torn it to shreds!

Twelve

The soft night breeze blowing through China's bedchamber window ruffled her loose, tumbling silver curls as she sat gazing out toward the moonlit gardens behind the house. The night was warm, the moon was full and glowing, high in a sky scattered with glittering stars.

Sighing, she drew her lacy shawl over shoulders left bare by her thin-strapped nightdress. Her last night in Virginia. In the morning she would go with Ian to Yorktown, to Grace Episcopal Church where they would be married in the presence of Lord and Lady Clairmont and Rebecca. There would be no reception, no dinner or ball to celebrate their marriage. They would say farewell at the church, and she and Ian would drive directly to the docks where they would embark for England aboard the *Adventure*.

Her brow creased, her lip curled with distaste at the thought of marrying Ian Leyton and leaving with him. How strangely things work out, she mused. She had hated the thought of leaving England for America, and now she loathed the thought of returning to her homeland. But then, she reasoned, it was not the voyage but the circumstances she objected to.

The preparations had been made with astonishing speed. She, Ian, and Lord and Lady Clairmont had driven into Yorktown that day to speak with the minister at the church, to set the time for the ceremony, and to speak with the captain of the ship that would take the bride and groom away. Though China wished some obstacle might arise necessitating a delay, both the reverend and the ship's captain had been only too happy to accommodate them. It was as if some cruel fate had lent a helping hand to Ian Leyton, though why he should deserve such favors was quite beyond China's understanding.

She wondered idly if Rebecca would agree to be her witness at the ceremony. She had not had a chance to ask her, for Rebecca had kept quite to herself all day. Now that she thought of it, Rebecca had been acting very mysteriously.

China could have sworn she had seen her cousin in Yorktown. A carriage had passed as they had left the church, and China believed she had recognized Rebecca inside. But Rebecca had been at home by the time they returned, and when China had questioned her she had vehemently denied ever having left.

"It was she," China murmured to herself as she sat framed in the open window. "I know it! Why would she deny . . ." But she let the thought die. Speculation was useless, and after tomorrow Rebecca and her moods would be nothing more than a fondly recalled memory like Virginia and Montcalm and Gabriel.

"Gabriel," China breathed.

He seemed to have disappeared. Neither Lord nor Lady Clairmont mentioned him, and China thought better of asking Rebecca about it. Still, she supposed it was just as well that he was gone. She could not have faced him knowing that in the morning she would be irrevocably bound to someone else.

China shuddered at the thought. She did not want to think of the future just then. This was her last night of freedom, these few fleeting hours were all that remained to her of the liberty that seemed doubly precious now that they were dwindling away.

Rising from her chair, she left her room and made her way out through the silent house to the gardens where the soft, scented breezes that whispered in the treetops beckoned so irresistibly.

Walking along the flagstone path that led toward the gleaming silver ribbon in the distance that was the York, her way lit by the pale glow of the moon filtered through the moss-hung trees, China savored the solitude, the peace, of the gardens. There in the darkness, with the breezes dancing in the branches and the bushes, she could pretend that tomorrow would never come. That the ceremony she so dreaded would never happen, that the words binding her to Ian, making her his chattel to do with as he would, would never be spoken.

China shivered as the breeze molded the diaphanous fabric of her nightdress against her legs. The sensation was delicious, at once arousing and scandalous. With only the gossamer nightdress and the lacy shawl between her and the caressing breeze, she felt as though she were bathing in the warm, rippling air blowing through the garden.

She turned down a narrow path that branched off from the main walk toward the river. Here the bushes grew thicker, the interlaced branches of the trees all but blocking out the glow of the great, silver moon. China picked her way carefully through the darkness, concentrating on the uneven flagstones that made up the path beneath her feet. And so she did not see the figure standing in the path just ahead until she had nearly reached him.

A sharp, hissing gasp escaped her. Poised to flee, she suddenly realized who it was who stood there before her.

"Gabriel," she breathed, trembling with the shock of finding him there.

"What are you doing out here?" he asked, his voice breathy and soft, a husky accompaniment to the ripple of the breeze around them.

"Walking," she replied. "Thinking . . . or rather, trying not to think about . . ."

"Tomorrow," he finished for her.

Wordlessly China gazed at him, her eyes, her body filled with painful longing. When he held out a hand to her, she went to him willingly, eagerly, molding her body to his, sinking with him onto the soft grass beside the path.

China felt the thin straps of her nightdress give beneath Gabriel's hands even as her own fingers clutched at the buttons of his waistcoat, the fastenings of his shirt. She shuddered, gasping, as he drew her over him, astride him. She knelt there, trembling violently, feeling his hands caressing her, feeling his body beneath her, knowing nothing except that she hungered for him, that she could wait no longer for him.

Gabriel guided her, watched her as she took him, possessed him as completely as he had ever possessed her. His hands on her hips taught her the motion, showed her the rhythm, urged her on as she loved him.

Borne along on a surging tide of emotions, of purest sensation, China moved above him, giving him a pleasure as intense, as breath-taking, as the sensations he was giving her.

China's head fell back, her lips parted. Her hunger for him was glowing and growing inside her until it seemed a thing far too great to contain. She quivered, gasping, poised on the brink of ecstasy, small, whimpering moans escaping her—bliss was but a heartbeat away.

Gabriel, his pleasure, his passion rising apace with hers, drew her down to him and raised his head to kiss the taut, trembling tips of her breasts. He felt the violent shuddering that coursed through her at the touch of his lips, heard her soft, wordless cries, and surrendered his own will, giving himself up to the pleasure, joining her in the throes of their mutual rapture.

In the sweet, drowsy aftermath of their lovemaking, Gabriel held China close and drew his coat over her to protect her from the chilling night air. Tenderly he lifted back a curl.

"China," he breathed, his tone entreating, "come away with me. We'll go to Fox Meadow. We can leave tonight. By the time they discover you're gone, we can be miles and miles from here."

"I can't," she whispered, knowing Ian would make good on his threat—knowing that to run away with Gabriel would be to condemn them both to a life of being hunted like animals, of being exiles from the home he loved so well.

"There's no reason—" he protested. "China—"

Pushing away from him, she picked up the tattered remnants of her nightdress and pulled her lacy shawl over her nudity. "Please, Gabriel," she begged tearfully, "I can't. Believe me. I have to marry Ian. I have no choice. You'll understand one day, I promise you, you'll realize what this was all about."

He stood and reached for her, but she held up a hand to ward him off. Backing away, she whispered a broken "good-bye" before fleeing through the night-shrouded gardens toward the dark house in the distance.

"Will you stop that noise!" China snarled as her maid bustled about weaving ribbons and pearls through her upswept curls.

The maid, young and pretty, an indentured servant from Scotland, exchanged a knowing glance with the older Irish maid who fussed with the cloak China would wear over her gown. China noticed the exchange in the looking glass and gritted her teeth. She knew what they were thinking, they thought her snappishness was simply a case of bridal nerves. Little did they know it was loathing for what lay ahead, dislike for the man forcing her to play her role in this farce, and heartsick longing for the man who had loved her with such fevered passion in the garden the night before.

Rising from her dressing table, she brushed out the creases in her embroidered silk skirts. The wide oval hoops beneath her skirts swayed as she walked; the pearls centered in the embroidered flowers of her oyster silk stomacher glittered in the sunshine streaming through her windows.

There was a knock at the door and Lady Clairmont, the rich scarlet brocade of her gown overpowering her faded beauty, bustled in.

"Ah, good," she approved, coming to rearrange the fall of a curl over China's shoulder. "You're nearly ready. Arthur and Ian are already waiting downstairs."

"I was hoping Rebecca would be my witness," China told her aunt. "But I haven't had a chance to ask her."

Lady Clairmont's expression closed, her mouth tightened. "I'm afraid Rebecca won't be coming, my dear. She didn't get up this morning."

"She isn't sick?" China asked, alarmed.

"I don't know what it—" Lady Clairmont hesitated, then dismissed the two maids with a wave of her hands. When she and China were alone, she spoke in a low, secretive tone.

"Gabriel has left Montcalm," she said quietly, her eyes not meeting China's. "He has broken their engagement. I'm afraid that is all I know about it. Rebecca will not tell me anything more. But I don't think she is quite up to witnessing anyone else's wedding just now, you understand."

"Of course," China murmured, averting her face. She understood only too well Rebecca's heartbreak, for she, too, knew what it was to love Gabriel St. Jon and lose him.

Lady Clairmont sighed. "I fear she will be a long time in getting over this. I can only hope she will soon meet another man who will take her mind off Gabriel. If only there was another such as your Ian for Rebecca."

China rolled her eyes. The last thing the world needed was another Ian Leyton! And as far as Rebecca finding one, she was more than welcome to the original!

China sighed. If only Ian would marry Rebecca. If only Ian would marry anyone else! But it was hopeless; she could delay no longer. Standing still as her aunt laid the pale blue cloak that matched her gown over her shoulders, China steeled herself to go downstairs where her uncle and her bridegroom awaited her.

The sunlight slanting through the windows of the church in Yorktown shimmered on the gold band Ian slid onto China's finger as they stood together at the altar. Lord Clairmont was Ian's witness and Lady Clairmont was China's as the minister pronounced them man and wife.

"Lord Ian and Lady China Leyton," he announced, beaming.

China saw the delight on her aunt's face. Titles meant so much to her. And though Ian called himself "Dr. Leyton," as the son of the Earl of Denniston he was, properly, Lord Ian Leyton. And though he had an older brother who would inherit their father's titles and estates, even the title "Lady China Leyton" was enough for Emily Clairmont.

Forcing a wan smile onto her lips, China accepted the well-intentioned congratulations of the minister. She was embraced in turn by her aunt and uncle, then suffered Ian's mercifully brief kiss as they turned away from the altar.

"It is such a pity you can't stay long enough for us to hold a ball at Montcalm,"

Emily Clairmont sighed. "It would be such a success. Only to think . . ."

China scarcely heard her aunt. She could well imagine that Lady Clairmont would love to invite all the local gentry to a ball to fete her niece, the newly minted Lady China Leyton, and particularly now that her own daughter was not to be mistress of Fox Meadow. Though she would not have thought it possible, China was grateful that they had to leave directly from the church. It was hard enough to look convincingly cheerful over this farce even for the few minutes between the ceremony and their departure. The thought of maintaining the charade for an entire evening was beyond imagining.

She let Ian take her hand as they climbed into the coach that would take them the few blocks to the dock where the merchant ship *Adventurer* awaited only their arrival to weigh anchor and depart.

"Good-bye, my dear," Arthur Clairmont said, clasping China's hand through the open window. His dark eyes searched her face, and China smiled to allay his fears. "Write to me as soon as you reach England."

"I will," China promised. "Good-bye, and thank you for everything."

Emily Clairmont sniffled, lifting a lacy handkerchief to her eyes as the carriage lurched and rolled away. China waved, her own eyes blurred with tears though for a far different reason than any of the casual onlookers might think. She settled back in the seat, her face carefully averted from . . . she hesitated, then forced herself to face the fact . . . her husband sitting beside her.

"You carried that off very well," Ian said. "I almost expected you to bolt halfway through the ceremony."

"Would that have done me any good?" she snapped, still gazing out the window at the passing scenery.

"I would not have forced you to come back," he told her. "I would simply have gone to the authorities."

"And Gabriel would have paid the price for my freedom," she murmured wearily.

"Indeed he would. And that little scene in the garden last night would have taken on a great deal more significance."

China glared at him. "You weren't . . . you didn't . . ." she breathed, appalled that this monster might have witnessed those precious, intimate moments she had shared with Gabriel.

"I saw you leave the house," he revealed. "And I saw you return wrapped in your shawl with your torn nightdress in your hand. It was not hard to deduce the rest."

China felt a maddening flush pinken her cheeks. "Do you intend to punish me?" she demanded, knowing that as her husband he literally held the power of life and death over her.

"Not at all," he assured her. "I do not begrudge you a last night with your pirate lover. Particularly as I know you will never see him again."

China said nothing; she could not have even if she had wanted to, for her throat was tight with emotion, her eyes were flooded with tears. She was scarcely aware that the coach was stopping. She had to let Ian lift her down and lead her aboard.

Even as the captain showed them to their cabin, then left to give the orders that would start them on their voyage, China gazed out the porthole toward the shore and wondered where, oh, where, Gabriel might be at that moment.

As the *Adventurer*'s anchor splashed free of the York, as the wind filled the sails of the three-masted, square-rigged ship, driving it out into the Chesapeake Bay, Gabriel St. Jon was awakening from unconsciousness to find himself in a dark, windowless room furnished only with a matted pallet of straw and a bucket that served as a chamber pot.

He groaned and probed the swelling on his head with tender fingers. The last thing he remembered was returning to the Swan

Tavern. He had climbed the stairs to his room and opened his door to find three men in his room.

"Gabriel St. Jon?" the shortest, best-dressed of the trio had asked.

"I am," he remembered replying. "Who the hell are—"

That was where his memories ended. The room exploded as pain shot through his head. Darkness descended, and he knew nothing until he'd awakened with a headache that would drive a mule to its knees.

Slowly, carefully, he pushed himself to his feet. Taking small, tentative steps, he crossed the tiny cell to the door of heavy wood bound with iron.

Though the impact of his fist on the door seemed to reverberate through his head, he pounded to gain the attention of whomever might be outside.

"What de ye want?" a gruff voice demanded as a small window in the door was thrown open.

Gabriel blinked. The light streaming through the window blinded him. "Where am I?" he asked.

"Williamsburg. The public gaol," was the answer.

"What am I charged with?"

The man smirked and swung the window shut. Gabriel heard his footsteps growing fainter as he walked away. Then, a few minutes later, he returned accompanied by another man. When the window was again opened, Gabriel recognized the second man as the one who had spoken to him at the Swan Tavern the night before.

"Why am I here?" Gabriel demanded, his eyes slitted against the light that seemed to bore into his aching brain.

"I think you know," the man replied, his lip curling with distaste. "The charge, Mr. St. Jon or Mr. Fortune, or whatever you care to call yourself, is piracy. Men have been sent by the Royal Governor to your plantation to arrest your crew. Once they are here, you will all be put on trial, and I assure you you will hang. Make your peace with God and your conscience, if you can. You haven't long to live."

"Wait!" Gabriel barked as the window started to close on him. "Who made the charge?"

"A lady," was the reply. "A lady you kidnapped and abused. She came to the magistrate in Yorktown and gave a deposition that will be used in evidence at your trial."

"And her name?" Gabriel persisted, though he was not at all certain he could bear to hear his worst fears confirmed.

The man arched a brow as though wondering that his prisoner might not know who would make the charge against him. He consulted the signed, sealed deposition he held in his hand.

"Her name," he read, as the prisoner held his breath and hoped against hope that he would be proven wrong, "was Miss China Clairmont. And very lovely I'm told she was. She said she wished to give the deposition as she would not be here for your trial. She was leaving today for England, apparently, with her new husband, Lord Ian Leyton."

Eyes closed, the pain of China's betrayal even worse than the pain of his throbbing head, Gabriel turned away from his gaolers and stumbled blindly across the cell.

Thirteen

The verdict of the trial was a foregone conclusion. As he stood before the "supreme tribunal," the justices appointed by the Royal Governor, Gabriel knew that he, like his crewmen, would be sentenced to pay the ultimate penalty for his crimes.

The long, paneled courtroom was stiflingly hot despite the open sash windows. The curious thronged the benches, jostling one another for a look at the notorious Gabriel Fortune. The gentlemen, feeling triumphant and self-righteous in the knowledge that their Governor Spotswood had brought yet another buccaneer to justice, viewed the scene with satisfaction. The ladies, secretly admiring the dangerous, infamous, and oh so handsome man standing to receive his sentence, shivered with vicarious pleasure at the thought of being kidnapped by such a dashing villain. The deposition given by his victim had been read aloud at the trial. The name of the lady was discreetly omitted, she being identified only as "a young lady of noble lineage." Her testimony of having been kidnapped by one pirate, won in a game of chance by Gabriel Fortune, and taken to his ship where she was "forced to his will," had caused more than one feminine heart to flutter.

Whatever the opinion of the spectators, whatever their lascivious speculations, Gabriel was unaware of them. He cared little for the scowls of his judges or their condemnation of his actions. All he heard was China's voice when she'd vowed revenge on him, all he remembered was her telling him that one day he would understand why she had to marry Ian Leyton. All he could think of was the softness, the fragrance of her skin as she lay in his arms on that last night at Montcalm. She had been eager, passionate, and all the time she knew the authorities were going to be waiting for him when he returned to the Swan Tavern. She had lain in his arms, made love with him, knowing full well she had that very day given testimony that would send him and his men to the gallows. With her words she had signed their death warrants—she had uttered their death sentences with the same lips that murmured words of love. The hand that caressed him so lovingly had signed the document that sealed his fate and that of his crew.

It was deception, treachery, betrayal on a scale that staggered the imagination. He felt numbed; the trial seemed little but a tableau unfolding before him, a play in which he was an unwilling actor. But the last scene, the scene that would take place on the public gallows, would be all too real.

China's face lingered in his mind's eye. Those eyes, bright blue and shimmering, must have gleamed with satisfaction at the thought of what she was doing to him. Those lips, so sweet, so soft, must have curved in a sly smile as she knew she had her revenge.

Gabriel's eyes closed but the image remained, taunting, mocking, once so precious and now so hateful to him. If he were free, he told himself, if miraculous fate would grant him his life, he would find her, track her to the ends of the earth if he had to, and repay her for her betrayal. He would see the life die in those eyes, he would listen as those lips entreated his forgiveness, begged for a mercy he would not give her. His heart was like a block of ice in his chest, filled with cold, hard, solid hatred for the woman who had lulled him with her lies into trusting her, then cold-bloodedly sealed his fate.

He looked up at the sound of his own name. The court clerk was speaking to him.

"You have been found guilty of the crimes of which you are accused," the white-wigged clerk intoned solemnly. "Have you anything to say before sentence is passed?"

"I have nothing to say to this court," Gabriel declared. It was true. Everything he longed to say was directed toward a topaz-eyed woman who was an ocean away.

The clerk consulted the document before him, then read in a high, ringing voice pronouncing the same sentence against Gabriel he had announced for the crew of the *Golden Fortune:*

"You will be taken from the public gaol to the place of execution and there you will be hanged by the neck until you are dead. The Lord have mercy upon your soul."

A buzz went up from the spectators. Several men loudly condemned the prisoners, several others applauded the justices for their verdict. More than one of the women wept at the thought of the tall, handsome man standing so quietly before them being hanged, dying, buried in unconsecrated ground.

At the back of the long courtroom a hooded figure in black and white rose and made her way out through the nearest door.

She was unnoticed by her neighbors, by the justices, by the prisoner as she'd hoped she would be. For she knew her presence in the courtroom would add to the gossip, the scandal, of the proceedings.

It was not until she was well away from the capitol building that she pushed back the hood of her cloak. Her silvery curls gleamed in the sunshine, her eyes, not as blue as those that shimmered in the condemned man's memory, glimmered with unshed tears.

Rebecca leaned against the thick, gnarled trunk of a tree at the roadside. She had not intended to attend Gabriel's trial. Too many people in Williamsburg knew of her engagement to him; she could not bear the thought of the stares and whispers that would follow her as she walked into the long, paneled courtroom. But she had not been able to help herself.

Lifting a hand, she wiped at the tears overflowing onto her cheeks. When she'd impersonated China and given her deposition to the authorities she'd been filled with bitterness, with hatred, for Gabriel and for China. She'd wanted to make sure that they could never be together—that if she could not have him, neither could China.

But seeing Gabriel there, in chains, listening to his crewmen being tried and condemned to death, had shaken her. She'd separated Gabriel and China forever but she'd also caused the death of nearly a dozen men.

Resolutely she shook herself out of her mire of guilt. Had Gabriel not been a pirate, he need not have been tried, condemned, he need not be facing death. He would have met this fate eventually; it was only coincidence that had made her the agent of his downfall. Had he not betrayed her with her own cousin, he could have lived to enjoy life at his plantation. So it was not her fault at all.

She composed herself quickly as the spectators began spilling out of the capitol. As the milling crowd moved past, Rebecca heard many complaining that an example should be made of this Gabriel Fortune. Had not the infamous Captain Kidd's body been tarred and hung in chains after his execution? That would be a deterrent to others. Fortune should be treated the same—his body, they declared, should be hung at the mouth of the York until it rotted.

Shuddering at the thought, Rebecca hurried away. At least she would be spared the sight of Gabriel's body hung like that other pirate as a warning to others. She could not have borne it. Justice would be done—Gabriel would pay for what he had done. She had done her duty as a respectable Virginian, and she knew that many would have applauded her for her actions.

There remained only one thing left for her to do. That, too, concerned Gabriel. China would have to know what fate had befallen the lover she had stolen from her cousin. As Rebecca made her way across the road and started toward the home of a family friend, she vowed that before night fell a letter would be on its way to China in London.

China sighed, relieved, as she listened to the coach drive away into the rain-soaked night. She was standing in her sitting room upstairs in the house she and Ian had rented in Jermyn Street upon their arrival in London.

It had been a dismal month. She fought every day to keep despair at bay, but it was a losing battle. Her marriage to Ian was a sham. From the first—from the day she had stood at the railing of the *Adventurer* and watched Virginia fade into the distance—she had been living in a nightmare.

Ian, she had discovered, could not consummate the marriage he went to such lengths to achieve. It was not her fault, it was not a condition that was new to him, but it was one that was slowly but surely driving him to madness. His existence had been one of restless wandering. From country to country, ranging over oceans and continents, he had sought a cure. His addiction to absinthe had arisen after he'd been told it was a powerful aphrodisiac.

Nothing had worked. He had nearly lost hope of ever living a normal life. And then he had stumbled upon China. From the moment he'd seen her there in the road near Fox Meadow, she had stirred him in a way he had thought would never happen to him again. He had not dared to try to make love to her, but the mere fact that she could elicit a response in him taught him to hope.

He had become obsessed with possessing her. His every hope for the future was tied up in her. He had vowed she would be his no matter what he had to do to have her. He had cheated, he had lied, he had resorted to blackmail and brought about the downfall of his most dangerous rival—Gabriel St. Jon. And for what?

China's smile was bitterly self-mocking when she thought of the nights of her marriage, the nights she had dreaded aboard ship when Ian had tried desperately to consummate their marriage. It was pathetic and tragic to see his hope, to lie beside him and see the light in his eyes as he fondled her, caressed her. But when he tried to make love to her, when he tried to take her, he failed miserably.

Night after night Ian pursued the pleasure, the sensation that eluded him, and night after night China grew more aware of the price she had paid for Gabriel's life. Not that she longed for a normal marriage with Ian; she blessed whatever had doomed them to a chaste union. But with each failure, she could see the light of resentment glow more brightly in Ian's dark eyes. He had pinned so many hopes on the stirrings she had evoked in him. His failure seemed all the crueler for the possibilities she had awakened in him.

She feared now, after a month and more of marriage, that his resentment, his disappointment, had festered inside him, souring and growing into hatred for her. He spent little time in the house her marriage settlement and his small inheritance afforded them. He immersed himself in the seamy underworld of London—the world of gambling halls and the sly, unwholesome people who frequented them. He left earlier and earlier each night and never returned before morning. He spent his days sunk in gloom and despair, awaiting only the setting of the sun to leave his beautiful young wife alone once more in the great canopied bed in her room upstairs.

Leaving her sitting room, China wandered down the shadowy stairs to the reception rooms below. Few candles were lit. No visitors were expected. That in itself China thought odd. Their marriage and their arrival in London had been duly noted in the papers. Whatever Ian's status, China's late parents had enjoyed a wide and loyal acquaintanceship among London's aristocracy. Surely they would not have forgotten her. Surely her parents' friends would wish to welcome her back, to celebrate her marriage to the son—albeit the younger son—of the Earl of Denniston. China did not know the earl, her father-in-law. He had not been a friend of the late Lord and Lady Clairmont. But she had heard that he was very rich and that he lived primarily at his country estate. She knew nothing more.

It was odd, she reasoned, that she had received no callers, no invitations. But perhaps, with time, that would be remedied. For the present she would wait and try to cope with the role fate had cast her in—the unloved wife of a man obsessed by love.

The sound of coach wheels and horses' hooves on the pavement outside sent her spirits tumbling even lower. Surely Ian was not returning—surely he had not exhausted all the dens of iniquity London had to offer—certainly there were many rakes and roués whose acquaintance he had yet to make.

She started for the stairs, nearly colliding with Yeats, the butler, who was going to answer the door.

"If it is his lordship," she instructed on her

way past, "tell him I have retired and do not wish to be disturbed."

"Very good, milady," the butler acquiesced, his face betraying not the slightest sign of emotion. He was far too well trained to show his feelings, but the marriage of the newlywed Lord and Lady Leyton was a subject of much speculation belowstairs.

China mounted the stairs to her room and twisted the key in the lock lest Ian be drunk enough to insist on trying one more time. She shuddered at the thought. It happened occasionally. Filled with liquor and some strange and exotic aphrodisiac pressed upon him by yet another charlatan, he occasionally came to her room and insisted she try to arouse him. It sickened and saddened her, and she wished he would accept his fate and let them live in some dignity.

The knocking at the door startled her. But she relaxed when she heard Yeats' voice coming through the panels.

"Milady?" His voice was soft, muffled. "It is not milord. It is a lady, a caller for your ladyship."

"A caller?" China pulled open the door. "Who is it?" she asked eagerly.

"Lady Sutton," Yeats told her. "She said she was a friend of your ladyship's late—"

"Lady Sutton!" China remembered her mother's bosom companion, a beautiful red-haired widow whose lovers, so gossip said, were numerous and all of exalted rank. "Show her into the salon, Yeats! Bring some wine!"

Unable to hide his pleasure at her animation, the short, white-wigged butler smiled as he bowed. China, her silver curls flying, her pale yellow skirts rippling, was already on her way down the corridor toward the stairs.

Swathed in a nondescript cloak of dark brown cloth, Sarah, Lady Sutton, stood in the shadowy downstairs parlor waiting for China to arrive. Her long-lashed, almond-shaped eyes scanned the room. It was not at all to her taste, for she liked bright colors and glowing candlelight, but the furnishings of a rented house were not the reason she had sought out the new Lady China Leyton.

China's cheeks were flushed, her eyes sparkling when she appeared in the doorway and saw her visitor. She could not help catching her breath when Lady Sutton threw back her cloak and hood to reveal the emerald-gowned, flaming red-haired, alabaster-skinned beauty. It was her beauty that had taken her from the relative obscurity of the country to the innermost reaches of London society.

She had been the daughter of a country vicar when the aging Lord Sutton had first seen her. He knew that however wealthy, however important he might be, he could not hope to win the love of such a gorgeous creature. In that he had reckoned without the generous heart that beat beneath the beautiful white bosom. Sarah had found him kindly and adoring, and she had agreed to be his wife. Moreover, she had been a faithful wife to him until the day he died. He had left her a wealthy, still young and beautiful widow and she had decided to spurn all other offers of marriage and take the reins of her life into her own hands.

Her life since her husband's death had been filled with gaiety and love—her lovers were rumored to be numerous, though she conducted her affairs with discretion. She had been away at the time of China's parents' deaths; her then-lover, an archduke, had spirited her away to Vienna where she'd spent an idyllic year.

She opened her arms to China, who ran into them and was enveloped in a warm, perfumed embrace.

"My darling," Lady Sutton said, holding China at arm's length. "I'm so pleased to see you. I've wanted to come to you since I heard you'd arrived, but . . ."

China stepped back, frowning. "No one's come," she confessed to her mother's best friend. "There have been no messages, no visitors, no invitations. I don't understand why."

With a rustle of emerald silk, Lady Sutton sat on the striped silk chair that faced a matching sofa. "It is Ian, my dear," she told China. "You know no one can invite you alone—not when you're so newly married. And Ian is not—well, he is not received."

"I don't understand," China murmured, eyeing her visitor curiously.

"He didn't tell you about . . ." Lady Sutton's dark eyes widened. "He didn't tell you!" she breathed.

"Tell me what?" China questioned, an uneasy feeling stirring inside her.

"About his family? About what happened?"

China shrugged, shaking her head. "I know little of Ian's family. I know his mother is dead, I know he has an older brother, the Viscount Leyton, I know his father, the Earl of Denniston, lives in the country. Beyond that . . ." She shrugged again. "We've heard nothing from Lord Denniston or the viscount since we got to London."

"Nor will you," Sarah Sutton promised. She hesitated, troubled. "I don't know if it is my place to tell you. But then, were your mother alive . . . she would want you to know . . ."

"Know what?" China persisted. "Please, tell me what all this is about."

"Very well," Lady Sutton agreed. "Ian Leyton is not received, China. He dishonored himself; put himself beyond the pale. And I am afraid that by marrying him you have joined him there."

"But why? How?" China wanted to know.

"It happened some years ago. Ian was just rising twenty. He was wild, as so many young men are. Apparently, and this is mostly speculation and gossip, he seduced a young girl . . . a girl of respectable though not noble family. She became pregnant. She went to Ian and told him, thinking he would marry her. He spurned her cruelly. Shamed, desperate, she threw herself into the river that runs through Lord Denniston's estate and drowned."

"Oh, the poor girl," China breathed, tears stinging her eyes. "No wonder his father will not see him."

"It was not only that," Lady Sutton corrected. "The girl's father swore vengeance. He and her brother waylaid Ian one night when he was returning from London to his father's estate. They beat him savagely. They swore he would never again seduce another young innocent. They tried to . . ." Lady Sutton flushed delicately. "They tried to injure him. You understand? Emasculate him."

China felt her cheeks growing hot. They succeeded only too well, she thought.

Lady Sutton was continuing. "The father and brother were brought to trial at Ian's insistence, over his father's objections. They were condemned and hanged. Ian could have saved them. He could have taken their grief into account; he could have accepted their punishment as just, considering what he had done to that girl. But he did not. Lord Denniston disowned him, disinherited him."

China sagged against the back of the sofa. She scarcely heard her guest's next words.

"Ian was left with a small income bequeathed him by his maternal grandmother. He took up the study of medicine, so it was said, to earn a living to supplement that income."

China nodded absently. Ian had taken up the study of medicine, she knew, to try to find a cure for his impotence. As to his refusing to spare the lives of his assailants, he would not have, knowing the private hell they had condemned him to.

"And he and his father are still estranged?" she asked. "He has neither heard from nor seen him since?"

Lady Sutton shook her head. "Neither the earl nor the viscount will receive Ian. He is an outcast from society."

"And so am I," China murmured, seeing before her a bleak, lonely future.

Leaning forward, Lady Sutton pressed China's hand. "There are many who remember you and your parents, my dear. There are many who would wish to see you. But they cannot invite you alone so soon after your marriage, and they cannot come here." She smiled brightly. "I will arrange what I can. You can come to visit me, and I will contrive to have some of the others there."

"I would not wish you to hurt your reputation for my sake," China told her.

"Don't worry for me," Lady Sutton assured her. Rising, she drew her cloak over her shoulders. "But I must be going now."

China walked with her to the door and they embraced. She smiled wanly as Lady Sutton caressed her cheek.

"I will see you again soon," the older woman promised. Kissing China's forehead, she drew her hood up over her flaming red curls and stepped out into the rainy night where her coach waited.

With the sound of the coach wheels and horses' hooves fading away, China walked back to the salon. Sighing, she sank into the chair Lady Sutton had vacated.

She had thought her situation could not get worse. How wrong she had been! Ian was a pariah, an outcast, and her marriage to him had made her the same.

"Milady?" Yeats stood beside her. He held a silver salver out toward her. "A letter was delivered for you."

"Thank you," China said listlessly, taking it

from the tray. She rose. "If anyone else comes to the door," she said, meaning Ian, for apparently no one else was likely to come, "I've retired."

Yeats bowed, and China left him and went up to her bedchamber where a low fire burned to dispel the chill of the rainy night.

Alone in her room, China broke the seal on the letter. It was from Rebecca, she saw. Her eyes scanned the page quickly. Gabriel's name leapt out from the page in several places.

Wearily, China refolded the letter without reading it. She did not want to hear about Gabriel; she did not want to read Rebecca's complaints and misgivings. Rebecca had lost her fiancé. There would be other men for her. What did she know of unhappiness? What did she know of hopelessness? She had a broken engagement. How would she like to be trapped in a loveless marriage in which her only companions would be her servants and a husband not received in polite society—a husband responsible for the deaths of a young, trusting girl, her unborn child, her father, and her brother?

Opening a drawer in her dressing table, China tossed the letter inside. Perhaps she would read it later, perhaps she would not. Rebecca and Gabriel and Virginia were in her past. She could not bear to think of any of them.

Her temples throbbed. She felt a weariness that seemed to sap the strength from her very bones. Ringing for her maid, she was undressed, prepared for bed, and tucked into the silk-hung tester bed she was condemned to occupy alone.

Fourteen

Three weeks had passed since the night when Lady Sutton had braved scandal and come calling on the daughter of her best friend. She had invited China to her home as she'd promised, and China had renewed old acquaintances, but it was difficult. Ian's disgrace was never mentioned, but China knew that her presence made many of Lady Sutton's friends uncomfortable. They could not invite China to their homes without also inviting her husband, and there was no question of their visiting China at the house in Jermyn Street.

It had bothered her at first. She found herself brooding on it. She knew that most of those who shunned Ian thought of him as dishonorable, ruthless. Few realized what his assailants' attack had cost him.

China sighed. Her marriage to Ian meant that she shared his dishonor. Like him she was an outcast. She knew she would seek Lady Sutton out rarely—it was kind of the lady to try to bring China into society, but it was simply too awkward.

But none of that mattered now. For the past weeks she had nurtured a secret, breathing no hint of it to anyone. She spent her days praying it was true and her nights terrified that it might be. As day followed day she grew more and more certain—and more and more frightened. Ian would have to know; there was no hope of deceiving him. How he would take the news she could not guess.

As though by magic, China's husband appeared in her sitting room doorway. He looked older, though not two months had passed since their marriage. His face was lined, his eyes shadowed from lack of sleep. His hair, when not powdered or covered with a wig, showed a surprising number of gray strands for a man who had not yet passed his thirtieth birthday.

China felt a stirring of alarm. Ian's visits to his wife's bed, those humiliating, abortive attempts at consummation, had nearly ceased. China had hoped he had grown resigned to his fate. But now, seeing the enthusiasm that illuminated his face, the excited gleam in his dark eyes, she feared he had been sold yet another "aphrodisiac" and wished to put it to the test.

"Good evening, madam," he said, sweeping aside his elegant damask coat as he sat down to avoid creasing its long, vented skirts.

"My lord," she said softly. "Are you dining at home tonight?"

"I am," he replied, surprising her. His nightly forays into London's underworld generally began much earlier.

"I'm glad to hear it," China murmured, knowing she could delay telling him the truth no longer. "I have some news to tell you."

"Is it important?" he asked without interest, thinking it must be some household matter.

"It is," she admitted.

Ian studied the fall of his shirt ruffle over his beringed hand. He seemed to have become something of a dandy in the past few weeks. China had noticed but cared too little to question him.

"I'm afraid it will have to wait until another time if you don't mind, my dear," he said. "We are to have a guest for dinner tonight."

"A guest?" China was astonished. "Who is it?"

"He is French," Ian revealed. "His name is Damien Dubuisson. He is the Duc de Fonvielle." Ian's eyes scanned China, who wore a simple gown devoid of the ornate embroidery so much the fashion. Her hair was dressed simply in a knot at the back of her head.

"I hope you can be ready to entertain the Duc," he said. "He is to arrive at eight. Can the kitchen provide a decent meal by then?"

China glanced at the clock on the lowboy against the wall. It was nearly six. "I will speak to the cook," she promised. "If nothing else, something can be brought in. I will see that you are not embarrassed before your friend, sir."

Rising, Ian gazed at China for a long moment. Whatever he felt for her, whether good or bad, affection or disdain, he kept well concealed. With a low bow by way of acknowledgment and thanks, he left to begin his own preparations for dinner.

"Ian!" China called as the door closed behind him. But he was gone. What she had to tell him would have to wait for another time.

Resigned to playing the hostess for her husband's guest, China left her sitting room and went downstairs to give orders for the evening.

China disliked the Duc de Fonvielle from the moment she met him. It was not that he was unpleasant—his manners were perfect, he was gracious and charming, and his praise of her home, of the dinner she served him, and of China herself was unstinting. It was not that he was unhandsome—he was neither too tall nor too short, too thin or too stout. His hair was a rich golden brown dressed simply and elegantly. His eyes were a deep amber that lingered on China as though gazing upon some rare work of art. His clothing was fashionable, exquisite, yet not overpowering. The jewels on his hands and the buttons of his coat and waistcoat were of excellent quality but not too ostentatious. In short, there was nothing wrong with him. And yet, China was wary of him from the first instant.

"What can I offer you, my dear Damien?" Ian asked after they'd retired to the sitting room, where the chandeliers blazed for a change and the fire was bright and cheerful in the black marble hearth. "Some wine, perhaps? Liqueur?"

"Absinthe if you please," Damien replied, his English heavily tinged with French.

"Of course." Ian poured the green liqueur into glittering crystal cups. He served his guest, then took a cup for his own refreshment.

"You do not join us, madame?" the duc asked, the movement of his arm making the silver embroidery of his scarlet silk waistcoat glitter.

"I will content myself with this," China replied, lifting her glass of champagne.

"You do not care for absinthe?"

China did not dare look at Ian. She knew the liqueur was his favorite addiction and he would have been pleased had she championed it for him. But she could not, even to flatter their guest.

"I do not," she admitted. "I have heard . . . I have been told . . . it is harmful to the mind."

"Who told you that?" Ian demanded, causing China to wince.

Damien intervened to soothe Ian's ruffled feathers. "Now, now, *mon ami,* you will have heard these libels against our friend here." He held up his cup. Smiling at China, he said: "There are people, my lady, who abuse liqueurs, narcotics. They give everyone who partakes a bad name. Absinthe is harmless, a liqueur like any other. Though, of course, it is reputed to be a powerful aphrodisiac." China blushed and Damien smiled, his amber-gold eyes glittering. "I have discovered, however, that the finest aphrodisiac in the world is a beautiful woman."

China stared at him, wondering if she could have mistaken the silken tone of his voice, the heavy-lidded look in his eyes. Damien gazed back at her. His admiration was plain, and there was something else in his eyes . . . desire. China tore her eyes away from him and decorously sipped her champagne. What kind of man had Ian brought home? A man who would lust for his wife beneath his very nose.

Ian longed to change the conversation. He had no wish to discuss aphrodisiacs nor to watch the duc make love to his wife with his eyes. Damien had impressed him as a man of power, a man who could accomplish anything he wanted and who could help someone else accomplish their goals. Ian had a plan but he needed help, the kind of help he thought Damien could provide. That was why he had invited the Frenchman to dinner. If Damien saw him with a handsome home, serving elegant dinners, living with a beautiful young wife, he might be impressed enough to aid Ian in his scheme. Now he wondered if Damien might not be too impressed with what he had found at the house in Jermyn Street.

Vaguely, wanderingly, he began to speak of America and his travels there. He mentioned Virginia and the fact that he had met China there, and the duc seemed suddenly to take an interest.

"You are from Virginia, madame?" he asked.

"Not at all," she replied. "I was born in Derbyshire. But after my parents' deaths I went to Virginia to live with relatives."

"And you met your husband." Damien

smiled briefly at Ian. "He is a fortunate man to have found such a treasure in the wilderness of the New World."

"Virginia is not a wilderness," China corrected. "There is a burgeoning society there, sir, of great promise."

"But still wild, untamed," Damien persisted. Crossing his legs, he finished his absinthe and set the cup aside before continuing. "There was mention of Virginia in a journal I was reading recently. Apparently there is some scandal. It seems the Royal Governor of Virginia sent his men into a neighboring colony to arrest a band of pirates."

"Pirates?" China's thoughts went to Gabriel, though he was by no means the only pirate in American coastal waters. "What did the article say, sir?"

"I daresay I did not pay it any great attention," Damien admitted. "It seems there was already one pirate in custody in Virginia. The others were the crew of his ship. They are sentenced to hang, if they haven't been hanged already. News travels deucedly slowly from that part of the world."

Ian saw the pallor of China's cheeks and knew what she was thinking. Worried that Damien might notice and wonder at it, he commented quickly:

"My wife told me earlier she had some

news. Important news. Perhaps you would share it now, my dear."

China gaped at him. Recovering herself, she shook her head. "I hardly think this is the time, Ian. I cannot imagine the duc is interested in our household affairs."

"On the contrary," Damien insisted. "I'm certain that anything important to you, my dear madam, will be doubly so to me."

China ground her teeth. Damn Ian! It was hard enough for her to tell him what she had to. But to tell him in front of his fine French friend . . .

"Come, my dear," Ian was prompting. "Tell us your news."

China saw the look on her husband's face. She wondered if, having seen the desire she provoked in his guest, Ian was having some sort of petty revenge by making her appear foolish in front of Damien. She had no doubt he thought her news was the hiring or discharging of some maid or a new recipe for fruit cordial or something equally inane.

She smiled sweetly, her topaz eyes boring into Ian's dark ones with haughty defiance. "If you wish," she acquiesced meekly. She smiled at Damien, then turned her gaze back to her husband's face. "I am with child."

The smile froze on Ian's face. He stared at her, dumbfounded, not even hearing Damien's congratulations and good wishes.

"Are you certain?" he managed at last, his voice muffled, choked.

"As certain as I can be," she replied.

The Duc de Fonvielle insisted on proposing a toast to China and to the child she was carrying. And then, he announced, he had to take his leave.

Ian went to the door to see him to his carriage, and China went up to her room and called for her maid to help her out of the silver-embroidered blue tissue gown she had worn to help Ian impress their guest. When she was clad in her nightdress, her hair brushed until it hung in long, shining silver ringlets, China sat at her dressing table gazing, unseeing, into her looking glass.

It was true. She was going to bear Gabriel's child. There had been certain symptoms before, but she had put them down to an irregularity in her system owing to the trauma of her forced marriage and her parting from Gabriel. But she could no longer lay the blame elsewhere. On that night, that last night at Montcalm when she and Gabriel had made love in the perfumed garden she had conceived his child.

She laid a hand on her belly. Inside her a child was nestled, part of her and part of Gabriel, made from their love.

She thought of what Damien had said earlier. Pirates had been captured, tried in

Virginia, sentenced to hang. She closed her eyes. There were many pirates there. Surely it could not be . . .

She remembered the letter she had received from Rebecca on the day Lady Sutton had first come to visit her. She had seen Gabriel's name mentioned when she'd scanned it. Perhaps there was something in it that could reassure her. If Gabriel had gone back to Fox Meadow, if he was safely at sea there would be no reason to fear for him.

Rummaging in her dressing table drawers, China found the letter. With trembling fingers she unfolded it. With anxious eyes she read it . . . and wished she had not.

The letter was Rebecca's account of Gabriel's capture and trial. Of course she professed herself astonished by the news that her former fiancé was the notorious Gabriel Fortune. Of course she claimed ignorance of how the agents of the Royal Governor had discovered his secret. She recounted the trial, leaving out the deposition by "China Clairmont" that had sealed his fate. The evidence, she would only say, was "overwhelming." Gabriel had been sentenced to hang, with most of his crew, on the twelfth day of October in the "Year of Our Lord 1717."

China felt the breath leave her body. Her heart thudded painfully in her breast. The room seemed to spin lazily around her; the floor tilted beneath the carved paw feet of her dressing table bench.

The letter slipped from her trembling fingers. China stared off into space. She could not comprehend that the man she loved, the man she had sold herself into a loveless marriage to save, the father of the child who slumbered inside her, had been captured, had gone on trial for his life, had been sentenced to die.

The door opened and Ian, having seen Damien into his coach, came in to confront his wife as to the truth of what she had said downstairs.

"Is it true?" he demanded. "Or were you merely trying to embarrass me in front of Damien?"

"What day is this?" China mumbled, her eyes not quite focusing on his face.

"What?" Ian noticed, for the first time, the stark whiteness of her face, the glazed look in her eyes, the trembling of her body beneath the thin silk of her nightdress. "What's wrong?"

China said nothing. Noticing the letter lying near her small bare feet, he bent and retrieved it. His eyes scanned it once, then again, and his expression changed from curiosity to amazement to triumph.

China saw none of it. Instead she listlessly repeated: "What day is today?"

Ian thought a moment. "The thirteenth," he answered. "Today is the thirteenth of October."

"The thirteenth," China whispered. "Then he is dead. Gabriel is dead."

Ian felt a rush of elation. He was dead, that bastard! Gabriel St. Jon had thought himself the equal of any man, a lord, a rich planter. He believed he had the right to do as he pleased, to associate with decent people, to take what he wanted. Well, he had met an ignominious end at the end of a rope. God rot his soul!

Ian looked again at China. She seemed so stunned, so pale, so vulnerable. He supposed he could understand that. She had loved St. Jon, however misplaced that love was. Ian could afford to be kind to her now that his rival was where he could never touch her again.

Summoning China's maid, he helped her get China tucked into bed. He still wanted to know the truth about her pregnancy, but it could wait. He had time now—China was his and his alone.

A new thought struck him as he walked down the corridor toward his own room. If China was with child, as she claimed, everyone would believe he was the child's father. Damien would believe it. And why not? Who in England knew of China's infatuation with the man who had kept her at Fox Meadow, then claimed her at Montcalm? And now, with St. Jon dead, who would know? As China's husband, he was legally the child's father. Who was to say he was not biologically its father? It would mean an end to the leering speculation, the gossip.

Elated, excited at the prospect of squiring his pregnant wife in public and laying to rest all doubt as to his own virility, Ian once more wished Gabriel St. Jon securely in hell and went to his own peaceful, dreamless sleep.

The ship dropped anchor in the Thames even as Ian Leyton was relishing the prospect of fatherhood. As the passengers crowded the rail, gazing toward London, they kept well away from the tall man swathed in black who stared toward the lights through slitted eyes shaded by the brim of a three-cornered hat. His face, his features obscured by a three weeks' growth of black beard, was nearly hidden by the turned-up collar of his greatcoat. But the edge of a scar, half-healed and red, could be seen slashing up his left cheek, puckering the skin.

He was something of an enigma to his fellow passengers. He had boarded alone, and any attempts to engage him in conversation had been brusquely repulsed.

Hour after hour, day after day, he had

stood at the rail gazing out toward the sea as if willing the wind to fill the sails and speed their journey. It was whispered among the passengers that he was a wronged husband in pursuit of a wife who had run off with her lover. And though this was mere speculation, the product of some overromantic lady's imagination, he became a figure of tragic allure to the ladies aboard. Their eyes followed him when he crossed the deck. They caught their breath if they met him in the companionway and had to pass near him. None dared speak to him. And even if they sighed at the sight of him, even if they discussed him with breathless enthusiasm, they all agreed they would not wish to be whatever lady might be the object of such a grim, relentless pursuit.

Fifteen

Damien, Duc de Fonvielle, became a frequent visitor to the house in Jermyn Street, to Ian's delight and China's chagrin. Ian, so long ostracized from polite society, found the duc's attentions flattering, for Damien was well-known in society, infamous rather than famous, as it turned out, but a man to be reckoned with nonetheless. His intimates were many, and most from the highest ranks of the aristocracy. And even if most of them were notorious rakes, roués, and courtesans, their titles were genuine and their fortunes considerable.

For China, Damien's sudden friendship was both a blessing and a curse. It was a blessing in that it occupied Ian at a time when China, still recovering from the news of Gabriel's death, often needed to be alone, often needed time to grieve and weep and console herself with the thought of Gabriel's child inside her. It was a curse in that Damien's visits to Jermyn Street seemed aimed at winning her friendship, at bringing her into his circle of friends. He brought her gifts, simple things at first, a bouquet of flowers, a perfumed sachet, a box of sweets made by his own confectioners. After a while the gifts became more and more costly—a jeweled fan, a gold and enamel box, a pair of exquisite earrings. China tried to refuse them, feeling as if she were being courted by an ardent beau, but Ian always insisted she accept, assuring her Damien would be insulted if she rejected his offerings and promising her that the cost of such gifts was nothing to a man as rich as the duc.

She wore the latest of Damien's gifts, a bracelet of diamonds in a series of wreathed flowers, when she went to visit Lady Sutton at Sutton House in St. Martin's Street where one of her neighbors was Sir Isaac Newton.

Sarah, Lady Sutton, welcomed China, leading her into her salon. It was late, growing dark, but China knew she needn't hurry home. Ian was off to Damien's country house where he would doubtless spend the night.

"How beautiful you look," Sarah cooed, seeming oblivious to her own flame-haired beauty. "You're positively blossoming. London agrees with you, my dear. Or is it marriage that agrees with you?"

China smiled. It was true, she knew, she looked better than she ever had. It seemed perverse to her that though Gabriel's death was ravaging her senses, his child within her was endowing her with a fragile, almost fairylike beauty. She seemed made of porcelain and silk, her skin was flawless, and her hair shone with silvery lights.

"It is neither," she told her hostess. "It is . . ." She blushed, her cheeks rose-hued and her eyes downcast. "I am going to have a child."

Sarah Sutton could not hide her surprise. She knew the gossip about Ian, all London knew it. Apparently it was untrue. How delighted he must be with this proof of his manhood.

"Congratulations," she said genuinely. "Ian must be pleased."

China bit her lip. She supposed it was wrong to let Ian take credit for Gabriel's child. It was a lie and a libel to Gabriel's memory. But an explanation would reveal more than she wished to reveal, and she could not bear to speak of Gabriel yet to anyone, even Sarah whom she knew would sympathize.

"He is very happy," she admitted softly.

Sarah sensed that something was wrong. She sensed also that China did not wish to discuss it. Anxious to change the subject, she turned her attention to the jewels glittering on China's wrist.

"How lovely this is," she said, reaching out to touch the cold, sparkling stones. "A gift to celebrate the child?"

China shook her head. "It was a gift," she admitted, "but not from Ian. A friend of his . . . of ours," she corrected. "He insists upon showering me with such things."

Sarah laughed. "I would I had such generous friends! Pray, tell me his name. I should like to make his acquaintance."

"He is French. The Duc de Fonvielle." China saw the startled dismay on Sarah's face. "What is it?" she asked. "Do you know him?"

Sarah sat back in her chair. Her long-lashed, almond-shaped eyes were clouded with concern. "Everyone in London knows him," she said softly. "Or knows about him, at any rate."

"Ian seems to think he is wonderful," China told her. "He's been very attentive."

Sarah sighed, closing her eyes. "I was afraid of something like this. Ian has fallen in with the worst set in London, my darling. The Duc de Fonvielle is a scandal. His home in London is reputed to be little better than a brothel, a private gaming hell. At his country home, they say, it is worse. There are rumors of orgies, strange rituals . . ." She frowned, lines marring the flawless skin of her forehead. "They say he was driven from France one step ahead of a mob. He was suspected of practicing witchcraft. Black masses. They blamed him for the disappearances of several young girls in the region and a baby."

"A baby?" China said, feeling an uneasy quiver in her stomach. "But why . . ."

"They say in the rituals . . ." Sarah hesitated, wishing she had never begun. ". . . the spells he is said to cast require the blood . . ."

China paled. Rising, she walked away trying to compose herself before she turned back to Sarah. Damien, so charming, so generous, so handsome . . . The thought of him practicing the black arts, casting spells, using the blood of a . . . Surely he could not be as wicked as all that. Rumor often lied. And yet he made her uneasy. There was that strange warning bell inside her when he smiled too intimately, presented her with yet another gift, paid her yet another compliment.

Troubled, she walked to the window and gazed out into the gathering darkness. Across the street, beneath a tree, a man stood, sheltered by the branches. His collar was turned up against the chill of the night, his hat brim cast his face into even darker shade. He stood motionless, staring toward Sutton House.

China stepped back. She'd had the distinct feeling he was staring at her, that beneath that concealing brim burned eyes filled with loathing.

"Sarah?" she said, looking toward her hostess. "Come look here. Do you know this man?"

Sarah joined her at the window. Squinting out into the deepening twilight, she shook her head. "What man?"

"Across the street, under the tree," China told her. "Right over . . ." She stopped, frowning. There was no one there. China looked up and down the street; her eyes swept the square. There was no one in sight.

"He was there," China insisted, leaving the window. "I was sure I saw someone. He was tall, dark." She closed her eyes, feeling suddenly tired. "Will you call my coach, Sarah. I think I should be going."

Driving home, China leaned her head back against the seat. Surely all the talk of witchcraft and sorcerers had made her imagination run wild. Even if there had been a man in the square, what did it signify? It was only her dismay at what Sarah had told her about Damien. It had her seeing danger everywhere.

The coach drove up before the house in

Jermyn Street, and a footman came out to open the door and let down the step. China climbed down and started for the house. But as she turned to watch the coach drive away, she noticed another coach sitting across the street. It was black and bore no coat of arms. Framed in its window was a man, dressed in black. A jolt of fear shook China as she realized it was the same man she had seen standing in the square across from Lady Sutton's home.

She could not see his face, but once more she felt the heated weight of his stare; once more she felt the hostility rolling from him in waves, buffeting her. Shivering, she hurried into the house and ordered the door locked behind her.

"Milady?"

China screamed at the unexpected voice. Whirling, she found an unfamiliar footman standing before her, a silver salver in his hand.

"Who are you?" she demanded.

"Peter, milady." He was very young, red-haired and freckled.

"I haven't seen you here before." It was almost an accusation.

"No, milady. I was hired this morning. By his lordship."

"Ah, well then. This is for me?" She took the letter from the salver.

"It arrived while you were gone."

"Thank you, Peter. That will be all."

China glanced at the letter when the footman had left her alone. It bore nothing saving her name. She broke the wax seal and opened the crisp paper. Her heart leapt when she saw the words written on the page:

"Murderess,
You will pay for what you have done."

China gaped, dumbfounded. What could it possibly mean? Murderess? She examined the paper. There was nothing to identify the sender. No way for her to discover what she was accused of.

A sudden thought occurred to her. The man she'd seen in the square! The man in the coach! Could he be the one?

Running to the window, she cupped her hands against the pane and stared out into the darkness. The street was empty. The coach had gone, the man had gone, vanished as he had outside Sarah Sutton's.

China left the window and sank into a chair. The note trembled between her fingers. Who was he? What did he want of her? Had he sent the note? And where had he gone so swiftly and silently?

The black coach bearing the man who had disembarked from the passenger ship from America, who had striven to discover the whereabouts of Lady Leyton, who had followed her to Lady Sutton's and then home, drove through night-dark London toward that most fashionable and aristocratic of areas, Grosvenor Square. It turned in between ornate iron gates and drew up before an elegant portico.

A footman in black and silver livery hurried out, but before he reached the coach the door opened and the man leapt out in a swirl of enveloping black cloak. He strode up the steps and into the house with the footman scurrying after him.

Divested of his hat and cloak, the man went into the scarlet-walled salon, where a majestic woman whose bearing belied her age sat in a carved and gilded chair so large it was almost a throne.

"Well?" she demanded, her grass green eyes following him as he went to the fireplace and warmed his hands. "Did you see her?"

The man turned. Nodding, he came to sit on a brocade-covered footstool before the old woman. His eyes met hers, green and green. He was silent for a long moment before he spoke.

"I saw her," he admitted, his voice low, husky, little more than a whisper. "She went to the home of a Lady Sutton in St. Martin's Street, Leicester Square."

"Sarah Sutton," the woman informed

him, the pearls hanging in creamy ropes over her black silk gown glowing with a shimmering iridescence in the candlelight. "She is a ravishing beauty. She was, I believe, a close friend of Lady Clairmont, Lady Leyton's mother."

Gabriel gazed up into the grass green eyes so much like his own. The old woman was shrewd, he knew; she could answer his questions before he asked them. She could also divine his thoughts—even those he did not wish to share. He smiled wanly, the scar on his bearded cheek puckering with the movement.

"Is there anything you don't know?" he asked fondly.

The old woman, Anne St. Jon, Marchioness of Wetherford, reached out and touched the half-healed flesh with a gentle finger. "When are you going to shave that beard?" she wanted to know. "You're not a pirate here, you know."

"I don't want her to know me if she happens to see me," Gabriel replied.

The marchioness sighed. "Is she as beautiful as you remember?" she asked.

Gabriel closed his eyes as though the memory pained him. "More so." He heaved a tremulous sigh. "How is it possible? How can she be so lovely and so treacherous? How can such beauty and such heartlessness exist in one person?"

Lady Wetherford's heart ached for him. "Why don't you simply confront the girl? There may be an explanation . . ."

"An explanation?" Gabriel stood and began to prowl the room. "What explanation can there be? She told me she loved me . . . she showed me her love . . . all the while knowing that she had given the authorities evidence to hang me and my men. She knew she was sailing away the next day. She knew she would be safely away before I discovered what she'd done." He balled his fists. "She is responsible for the deaths of ten men. Only myself and one of my crewmen survived." Gabriel's eyes met the marchioness's. "She will pay for what she has done. I promise you, she will pay."

The marchioness's hands tightened on her walking stick. "Don't act too rashly. Confront her, let her tell you her reasons."

"Her reasons?" Gabriel's laugh was harsh, croaking. "For this?" He pulled away the high, wide neckcloth and exposed the raw, burned flesh where the rope had scarred him. "Or this?" He touched his cheek where the knife used to cut the noose had slashed his face. "No, madam, her actions speak for themselves."

"Damnation!" The marchioness rapped her stick on the polished floor. "Why must you be so pigheaded! You are just like your father, God rest him. You are rash! Stubborn!

Why couldn't you be more like your mother?"

"My mother was a trollop," Gabriel snarled.

"She was your father's mistress," the marchioness corrected sharply. "She was sweet, gentle. She loved my son."

"Aye," Gabriel agreed. "She loved him so much it killed her. She died to bring his bastard into the world."

The marchioness's green eyes flashed angrily. "She would not have considered the price too high, sirrah. She does not deserve your disdain."

Gabriel bowed his head. It was true, his father had loved the mistress who had borne him a son. He had given his son his name, a home, everything but the titles a bastard could not inherit. Gabriel had been raised like the son of a lord, but he was, after all, illegitimate. His father had been dead less than a year when Gabriel had gone to sea to prove his own worth to himself and the aristocratic world that had refused to accept him.

"I beg your pardon," he said softly. "But let me deal with China in my own way. Will you do that, Grandmother?"

The marchioness pursed her lips. "I will consider it," she allowed. "Now come and kiss me goodnight, then go summon my maid. It is time these old bones were in bed."

Obediently, Gabriel bent and kissed the soft, powdered cheek of the grandmother who had loved him no matter what, the only child of her only child.

It grieved her that he could never inherit the titles that should have been his but for the circumstances of his birth. But upon the death of Gabriel's father the estate had gone to a cousin whose only claim lay in the validity of his parent's marriage. Still, she vowed, Gabriel would never want for a home or the love of the grandmother who adored him.

She worried about him. She did not want him to be alone when she was dead. She did not want him to live a life devoid of love. It had been her fondest wish that he would find a woman to love. And now what had happened? The one woman who had managed to possess the iron-clad heart he guarded so fiercely had shattered it like crystal. She had betrayed him, nearly killed him. And yet he said she had loved him, lain with him.

The marchioness waved away the helping hands that reached out to her. She gazed at her grandson sitting lost in thought before the fire. There had to be more to it than merely the treachery of a wicked woman. There was something missing, some key that would unlock the mystery.

And though she had promised her beloved grandson she would not interfere, the Marchioness of Wetherford resolved, as she slowly, painfully mounted the stairs to her suite above, to learn more about Lady China Leyton and what lay behind the breaking of Gabriel's unbreakable heart.

Sixteen

Gabriel was far from pleased when he discovered that his grandmother had made discreet inquiries about China. Though the marchioness did not venture into society herself, her contacts were widespread and highly placed. Very little happened in fashionable London without her knowing of it.

As for Gabriel himself, he knew of China's every move. He knew when she left the house in Jermyn Street, where she went, when she returned. He knew when Ian left, how often he stayed away all night. He saw Damien de Fonvielle arrive at the house and noted how long he stayed. The only thing he did not know was what he wanted to do next.

He had to proceed with caution, he knew. But at the same time he was anxious to see China punished for her treachery against him and his men.

"I don't like to see you so troubled," Lady Wetherford told him one morning as she spread jam on a slice of freshly baked bread. "I don't think you truly want to harm her."

Gabriel scowled. He was angry at himself for his own hesitancy. The next logical step, he knew, was to confront China—perhaps to lure her someplace private where he could carry out his revenge. But he could not bring himself to think of actually laying violent hands on her. His anger at her, his outrage at what she'd done, his loathing of her treachery, had not abated. The memory of that day in Williamsburg, of his crewmen on the gallows, the nooses about their necks, of the providential act that had saved his life and that of one of his men, could still rouse him to a murderous fury. But the thought of exacting an eye for an eye—or a life for a life—from China was one he shied away from.

"When the time comes," he vowed, more to himself than to his grandmother, "I will do what I must. The deaths of my crew will not go unavenged."

The marchioness took a sip of honeyed tea. She sighed. There was no arguing with him, she knew. And she was not certain he was wrong. If China was guilty of betraying him and his crew, then she truly deserved to be punished. But it was hard to believe that Gabriel, who was usually such an uncanny judge of character, would have been so blinded by passion that he would have completely overlooked the treacherous side of the girl.

Gabriel saw the look on the marchioness's face. It was one he recognized well. "You have some advice to impart?" he asked.

The marchioness shrugged. "Would you heed it?" she asked doubtfully.

"I would listen to it," Gabriel allowed. "More than that I cannot promise."

Lady Wetherford inclined her head, knowing that, for her headstrong grandson, that was not a small compromise. "I would counsel you to leave it for a time. If the girl did what you say, then I agree she must be called to answer for it. But do not punish the innocent with the guilty."

"I do not understand," Gabriel replied. "The innocent?"

The marchioness averted her eyes. She knew that what she was about to say would have a profound effect on him, though for good or bad she could not guess.

"Young Lady China Leyton," she revealed, "is reported to be with child."

Gabriel stared at her. A dull flush mottled his cheeks. He felt an emptiness, an ache in his very soul at the thought of China bearing Ian Leyton's child.

"Whatever the mother has done," the marchioness went on, "the child is innocent."

Gabriel frowned, his eyes fixed on a point above the marchioness's head. "She is bearing Leyton's child," he said softly.

The marchioness's heart ached for the pain she saw in his face. The more she saw of Gabriel's heartache, the more she wished she had never heard of China Leyton.

"They say—" she began, then hesitated.

"What else do they say?" Gabriel prompted wearily.

"Rumor . . . gossip . . . says that Ian Leyton is not the father."

A little flare of hope, a dream he scarcely dared contemplate, rose inside Gabriel, then fell as quickly, dwindling into nothing. "Why should they say that?" he asked carefully.

Succinctly, the marchioness told him of Ian's past, of the beating and what it had supposedly done to him.

When she had finished, Gabriel found his heart beating faster. If Leyton was incapable, could it be he had never, that his marriage to China was in name only? And if it was, and she were with child . . .

"If Leyton is not her child's father," he said, his voice hushed, "who do they name the father?"

The marchioness loathed having to tell him, but there was no avoiding it. Better to get it over quickly. "Damien de Fonvielle," she blurted.

Gabriel sagged in his chair. He felt as if the breath had been sucked out of his lungs. How many times, he asked himself, had he seen the Duc arriving at the house in Jermyn Street? He had asked questions, had heard what was said of the duc. He had even made a point of meeting him more than once in one or another of the "clubs" about London that the duc and his friends frequented. He had introduced himself as "Edward O'Meara," a tribute to his first mate who had died on the gallows in Williamsburg.

He had found the duc sophisticated, handsome, with a silken charm that drew women to him. Had China also found him handsome? Had he drawn her to him with that cloying charm that seemed so attractive to feminine senses? Had she lain with him, whispered the same words of love to him she had breathed in his ear in the garden at Montcalm?

Shoving back his chair, he rose and stalked across the floor toward the door. Behind him the marchioness watched with sorrowful eyes. He was in such torment, he was filled with such anger, such pain. Much as he swore he hated China Leyton, the marchioness knew better. Only one emotion could inflict such torture on a man's soul. Only love.

Outside the dining room, Gabriel summoned his valet. When the young man stood before him, Gabriel instructed:

"I've been invited to Aldwych Abbey by the Duc de Fonvielle. On the last night, there's to be a masquerade ball. I want a special costume made. Fetch a pen, ink, and paper. I'll sketch it. You're to find a discreet seamstress to make it for me."

The valet hurried to do his bidding, and Gabriel stared thoughtfully after him. Damien had invited him to come to Aldwych Abbey and had promised to introduce him to his friends. Gabriel could only hope those friends would include Lord Ian and Lady China Leyton.

Even as Gabriel was sketching his costume for the ball at Aldwych Abbey, Ian and Damien sat together in the ornate drawing room of the duc's townhouse. Ian leaned toward him, his face flushed and anxious.

"Can you help me?" he asked, his eyes darting to the corners of the room, looking for eavesdroppers.

Damien leaned back in his chair, the picture of cool disdain. He arched a golden brow. "What you ask is serious, my friend.

You desire the deaths of two men. That is no small matter."

"I know," Ian admitted. "But if I inherited the earldom I would be very rich. I would give you whatever you asked."

Damien smiled, but there was no mirth. His look was contemptuous. "You underestimate me," he said patiently. "I have all the money I could ever need."

Ian trembled. The perspiration broke out on his forehead. He rubbed his hot, moist palms together. "I did not mean to insult you," he insisted. "But I would give you anything for your help in this matter. Ask me for anything I possess and it is yours."

"China," Damien said quietly.

Ian was nonplused. "I don't understand," he mumbled.

"I am a connoisseur of beautiful things," Damien told him, making a steeple of his beringed fingers. "Beautiful homes, beautiful furniture, beautiful art, beautiful jewels . . ." He looked hard at Ian. "Beautiful women. And your wife is very, very beautiful."

Ian was silent. He too was stunned by China's beauty every time he saw her. It startled him, awed him. To live with it day after day and not possess it completely tormented him. To know that other men, Gabriel St. Jon and now Damien de Fonvielle, could both admire and possess her was agonizing. Still, he could never dispose of the obstacles in his path—his father and older brother—and obtain the earldom of Denniston and all that entailed without Damien's help. He had no choice, he had to accept Damien's terms or give up his ambitions.

Defeated, he lowered his head. "Very well," he mumbled. "I agree."

Damien bit back the triumphant smile that sprang to his lips. "Good," he said quietly. "You will bring China to Aldwych Abbey at the end of the week. There is to be a masquerade ball. I wish to get to know her a bit better before we begin on our . . . project."

Ian felt uneasy. He knew that China tolerated Damien but did not particularly like him. He knew she sensed there was something unwholesome about Damien de Fonvielle and his cronies. She would not relish the thought of attending a masquerade ball at Aldwych Abbey, where the duc was reputed to practice the rituals that were rumored to have been the cause of his exile from France. But he would get her there; he was certain he could convince her to attend. The rest he would have to leave to Damien.

"We'll be there," he promised. "Not for the house party. But for the ball. I'll see that China is there."

"Bon," Damien said, smiling. "And you, *mon ami,* will not regret it, I promise you."

Aldwych Abbey was a Gothic pile of pale golden stone overgrown with tangled vines. Parts of it had fallen into ruins; the cloister was half destroyed, tumbled stones lay on the overgrown grass. It looked like the perfect setting for a ghostly tale of phantoms and curses—or witches and warlocks.

China shuddered as the coach drew up before the arched doorway where a pair of torches burned in iron sconces. The tall, lancet windows with their delicate tracery were filled with golden candlelight, and the music and laughter from within spilled out to greet them when a footman opened the door.

China hesitated. She did not want to go in. She had not wanted to come. Beyond the fact that she did not like or trust Damien de Fonvielle, she was disturbed by the note she had received earlier. Like the other, it had been delivered by a messenger who had left the moment he'd given the note to the footman. Like the other, it bore no signature, no insignia had been pressed in the wax that sealed it. China's hands had trembled when she opened it. It read:

"You have blood on your hands.
You will pay for what you have done."

She had torn the note into shreds and cast them into the fire, realizing too late it might have been wiser to keep it and show it to Ian. She did not understand why anyone would send her such notes. She could not imagine what she was being accused of. The mystery haunted her. She was becoming obsessed with it and with the thought that it had something to do with the man she saw so often, like a ghost, haunting her days.

She fell into step with Ian as they entered the long, fan-vaulted cloister. She cast a sideward glance toward her husband. In what she thought was monumental bad taste, Ian had chosen to come as a pirate complete with a cutlass in the wide scarlet sash banding his waist, and a bandolier crossing his chest with a brace of pistols. Not only did he look ridiculous, he clanked when he walked and continually pricked his leg with the tip of the long dagger in his belt.

She had come as a Puritan, all in black and white, covered to neck and wrist, her hair tucked into a prim white cap. They both wore masks.

Directed by the footman, they started down the cloister, which was swathed in shadows. It was eerie with the moonlight streaming down, casting tracery shadows on the opposite wall. China watched her feet, stepping carefully on the uneven stones that paved the cloister. They were nearly halfway to the opposite end when she happened to glance up.

She gasped, instinctively stepping closer to Ian. Coming toward them soundlessly, gliding as though floating above the ground, was a monk in flowing black robes. His hands were hidden in the voluminous sleeves of his robe, his face lost in the depths of his cowl.

China shivered. "Ian," she breathed, laying a hand on her husband's arm.

The apparition came toward them slowly, coming closer and closer. When it was a few feet away, it stopped and raised its head. The hood fell back and the moonlight revealed Damien de Fonvielle's smiling face.

"Welcome," he greeted them, obviously delighted by their pale faces. "Aldwych Abbey is reputed to be haunted by a ghostly monk. I thought you might like to meet him."

Ian's laughter was strained. China made no attempt to laugh at all. She did not even smile as Damien stepped forward and raised her hand to his lips.

"I am delighted you agreed to come," he said softly, intimately, seemingly oblivious to her husband standing beside her. "Come. Everyone is in the great hall."

Tucking China's hand into the crook of his

arm, Damien stepped between husband and wife and led them into the huge, barrel-vaulted great hall where a fire blazed in a marble fireplace carved with exquisite flowers.

From the instant she stepped into the room, China wanted only to flee. Everyone was masked, costumed; men and women lolled on sofas and divans placed about the room. Footmen circulated with goblets of wine. The laughter was loud and coarse; many of the guests were visibly drunk. The costumes of most of the women bordered on indecency.

Damien felt the hesitation in China's step. He cast a look toward Ian, who discreetly moved away toward a table where food was offered.

"You are shocked?" Damien asked China, whose cheeks bloomed pink as her eyes seemed to find a new embarrassment wherever she looked.

"I should not have come," China whispered. "I don't know why Ian insisted." She looked for her husband and found him in conversation with a woman whose diaphanous veils concealed nothing.

"I asked him to bring you," Damien admitted. "I insisted upon it."

China looked into his amber-gold eyes. "But why?" she asked. "I don't understand. I know you are a friend of Ian's . . ." Her eyes never leaving his, she accepted a glass of wine from a footman's tray.

"I would be your friend as well," Damien told her, watching approvingly as she sipped her wine. "Your very dear, very loving friend."

China blushed, drawing a little away from him. But he held her hand tightly in his, her arm linked through his own. She could not go far.

"Please," she said softly. "You must not . . ."

She drew a sharp breath. The flush faded from her skin. Across the room, near the fireplace, a man stood, garbed in black. His head and face were covered with a black silk cowl. His vest and gauntlets were of black leather. The effect was unmistakable. He had come disguised as a medieval executioner. It would have been alarming at any time, but there, in that bizarre setting, it was frightening. All the more so because the man's height, his build, his stance, the way he watched her, were eerily familiar.

"What is it?" Damien wanted to know.

"That man," China breathed, turning her back toward the fireplace. "Who is he?"

"What man?" Damien scanned the room. "Ah, his name is O'Meara. Edward O'Meara. Do you know him?"

"Aye, no . . ." China drew a slow, uneven breath. The room seemed suddenly stifling, she could not catch her breath. Her head swam, colors melded. A wave of dizziness assailed her.

She sagged, leaning against Damien for support. He slipped an arm about her waist and led her toward a small door almost concealed by a painted screen.

As he led her from the room, Damien handed her nearly empty wine glass to a footman. The wine had been laced with a sweet narcotic, an exotic Oriental compound much prized in the harems of the East. On most of Damien's friends, steeped in the use of such mixtures, it would have had little effect. On China, unused to such things, the effect was profound.

Gabriel, in his guise as Edward O'Meara, the newest of Damien's friends, watched as the Duc and China left the room. Damien's arm was about her waist, his golden-brown head close to her linen-capped one. They looked like nothing so much as two lovers slipping away for an intimate tryst.

He looked at Ian, happily ensconced on a divan with a young viscount widely reputed to have driven himself hopelessly into debt with his vices and a faded beauty who had seen three ancient husbands into their graves. Gabriel's eyes narrowed with distaste. The man was more of a fool than he'd thought. He'd married China knowing he could not be a husband to her, then smiled while she went off to bed with another man.

He looked toward the small, narrow door all but hidden behind the screen. He was drawn to it and repelled by it. If he could find China and the duc, perhaps he would see he'd been wrong. Perhaps they were not lovers, perhaps . . . Then again, he told himself, perhaps all he would discover was just how great a fool he'd been to fall in love with China.

Shaking off a raven-haired woman who wrapped herself about him and suggested they find an empty divan, Gabriel crossed the room and slipped out through the door behind the screen.

He found himself in a long corridor that led off into darkness. Few candles burned along its twisting, narrow length. Doors opened off it, dozens of them, all made of wood bound with great iron hinges. These, then, were the cells where once monks had slept and prayed. Heaven only knew what went on behind those closed doors now. Wondering how he was going to find China in that long maze, Gabriel stalked down the hall toward the darkness.

His footfalls passed the room where Damien had led China. The light of the single candle did not show under the door. There was no sound to be heard as Damien gently helped China to lie down on the narrow bed.

"I feel so dizzy," she whispered, one hand

raised to her head. "I don't know what's wrong."

"Nothing's wrong," Damien told her, bending solicitously over her. "Too much wine. That is all."

"It was only one glass," she protested.

"It was not the amount," the duc assured her. "It was the mixture."

"The mixture . . ." China gazed at him, not comprehending. And then— "What was in the wine?" she asked, trying to push herself up.

"Nothing harmful," he promised, tugging off the cap that concealed her hair, watching as the silvery curls showered over her shoulders. "Something to relax you."

His hand caressed her cheek, her throat, moved to the first of the buttons fastening her high-necked costume. He smiled when China said nothing. Her look was curious, wondering, but she did not protest even as the first of the pearly buttons slipped from its hole.

China gazed at him, mesmerized by those glimmering amber eyes. She could not at first bring herself to believe that he intended to seduce her . . . that he had knowingly, deliberately, given her drugged wine in order to lull her into welcoming his attentions. But when his lips caressed her throat, when his hand slipped into her gown and touched the silken curve of her breast, she pushed away from him.

"You must be mad," she breathed, struggling with him and her own giddiness, trying to rise. "Let me go!"

To her surprise, Damien released her. He smiled as she scrambled past him, climbed to her feet, and stumbled toward the door. "You will be mine," he promised as she staggered toward the door. "Your husband has given you to me."

Horrified, terrified, China flung open the door. The corridor stretched off in both directions, ending in darkness. It was lined with doors, all identical, and she could not imagine which would lead her back to the great hall.

Panicking, she started off, stumbling, wanting only to get away from Damien, from this hideous place. She tried one door, another; they were locked. The corridor seemed to undulate before her dazed eyes; she staggered. The darkness loomed before her, black, impenetrable, but she went toward it, believing that nothing in that darkness could possibly be worse than the horror she'd just escaped.

But then, out of the darkness, a nightmare figure emerged, clothed in black, a headsman's cowl covering his bearded face. China screamed. Stumbling, she tripped on the long, full skirts of her costume, her hands groped at the smooth stone walls.

Gabriel reached toward her as she lurched past him. His fingers brushed hers, skimming them, just missing them.

"China!" he called, seeing the terror in her blue topaz eyes as the darkness enveloped her. He had been into that darkness, he knew what was there. His heart thudded with horror as the darkness swallowed her and she fell down the long, winding stone staircase concealed in the blackness.

Seventeen

China lay in her bed at home in Jermyn Street. She scarcely moved, for her body was covered with bruises. But the pain of her bruises was the least of the torment she suffered. The pain in her heart was far worse, for she had lost Gabriel's child, her last link with the past, with Virginia, with Gabriel, with love.

She remembered little of that night at Aldwych Abbey. There was the sound of Damien's voice, the look in his eyes, the touch of his hand. She remembered escaping him, fleeing from him toward the darkness at the end of the corridor. She shuddered at the memory of the man who had appeared before her, the "executioner" who had sent her stumbling backward into the unknown. And then she was falling, falling, and all she knew then was pain.

No, she thought, frowning, concentrating, there was something else. A dim, confused memory. The man, the executioner . . . When she fell, as she plunged downward into that black, endless stairwell, he had reached out toward her, their fingers had brushed, he had tried to stop her fall. And he had called her name. And there was something else. His eyes. She had noticed his eyes. They were green as freshly sprouted grass, green as the first leaves of spring, a color she had seen only once . . .

Shivering, China cursed herself for a fool. She had imagined it. It was some cruel delusion caused by whatever hellish potion Damien had put into her wine to aid in his seduction of her. That was all.

Wincing, she turned onto her side and snuggled deep beneath the coverlets. She could not bear to think of Damien or Aldwych Abbey or the events leading up to the disastrous fall that had cost her Gabriel's child. Damn Ian! Damn him to hell! If only he had not insisted she accompany him to Aldwych. If only he were not under Damien de Fonvielle's evil spell. What had Damien said? "Your husband has given you to me."

"Given me to him!" she murmured to

herself. "How dare he? Who does he think he is?"

But she knew that, as her husband, Ian had a great deal of power over her. As long as she remained with him, she would be in danger. Ian's grasp on reality, apparently always tenuous, was hanging by a thread. He was in Damien's power. His dependence on absinthe was threatening his sanity. Damien encouraged him to drink it, and heaven only knew what other filthy concoctions he gave him.

A tear slipped from the corner of her eye and fell, dampening the pillowslip beneath her head. She was trapped in their nightmare of a marriage. And for what? She had married Ian to save Gabriel. What good had that done? Gabriel was dead, and because of Ian and his horrible friend, she no longer even had Gabriel's child to comfort her.

Her eyes widened; a sudden realization struck her. She had married Ian to save Gabriel! That had been her only motivation! But Gabriel was gone, beyond any harm Ian could do. There was no threat he could hold over her, no hostage he could keep to imprison her in this hell-born union. She did not have to stay! She could leave Ian, leave England, return to Virginia!

A smile curved China's lips. The dark future before her seemed to lighten a little. There was hope after all. All she had to do was rest and recover. When she was strong again and well, she would leave Jermyn Street, leave Ian, and shake the dust of England from her shoes once and for all.

"But you promised!" Ian was protesting as he stood in the crimson drawing room of Damien's London townhouse. He was petulant as a child. Damien expected him to stamp his foot and pout. "You said you would help me! I did everything you asked! You wanted China, I agreed. It's not my fault she ran away! It's not my fault she fell! It's not my—"

"Enough," Damien sighed. "Spare me any further recitation of what is not your fault. Sit down."

Cowed, Ian sank onto the sofa behind him. He eyed Damien as a child might watch a stern father. He was in awe of the duc and not a little afraid of him. He had been present when Damien cast his spells and performed his eerie and frightening rituals. He had seen tragedy befall people who angered Damien. He believed with all his heart in the power of Damien's sorcery.

Damien let the silence drag on and on, knowing that Ian grew more uneasy and nervous with every tick of the ormolu mantel clock. He had thought Ian might prove useful when first he'd met him; he'd been enthralled with the beauty of Ian's wife and thought to possess her through her husband. But he was weary of Ian's slavish devotion and whining demands. He was confident he could have China without controlling her husband. In fact, he believed it would be easier to possess China if Ian were no longer a part of the bargain. He fixed Ian with a cold, haughty stare.

"How is your wife?" he asked. "Is she recovering?"

Ian nodded. "The doctor you sent examined her. There is no permanent damage. The child was lost."

"So I was told." Damien knew it rankled that he had not trusted Ian's judgment and skill in medicine but had insisted upon sending another doctor to care for China. A tiny smile appeared at the corners of his mouth. "She can have other children." The tightening of Ian's lips, the reddening of his face, told Damien the dart had struck home. Ian knew what Damien meant, that any other children China bore would be fathered by him.

A rebellious light flickered in Ian's eyes, then quickly died. He was entirely Damien's creature. If Damien demanded that he give up China, then give her up he must. But Damien had promised him a reward for his loyalty.

"You did say you would help me," he reminded Damien, his tone meek, supplicating.

"So I did," Damien admitted. "But now I wonder at the wisdom of it." Casually, he examined the glittering ring on his right hand. "I've heard that you have been hinting to people that your situation might soon be changing. They say you have intimated that you might shortly be very rich and very highly placed."

Ian shifted uneasily in his seat. He had not been able to keep from boasting that he would not be living in reduced circumstances for long. Though he had not actually said he would be Earl of Denniston, he had told several acquaintances that he would soon have a fine title and an enviable estate.

"I did not think it would do any harm," he defended. "Your name was not mentioned."

"You are known to associate with me," Damien pointed out. "If your father and your brother, the only people standing between you and your inheritance, were to meet with accidents, what do you think the gossips would say? They would remember having heard your boasts. Do you imagine they would think it all a wild coincidence?"

"Perhaps—" Ian began, feeling perspiration break out.

"Perhaps what?" Damien demanded.

"You're a fool, Leyton, and a dangerous fool at that. I will not be driven out of England for your sake."

"I never intended . . ." Ian protested. "I'm sorry."

"Is that enough, I wonder?" Damien rose and walked away. He was aware that gossip called him an alchemist, a sorcerer, that it was said he cast spells to bring sickness, ruin, and even death on his chosen enemies. It was ridiculous, of course. The only ones he could truly harm were those who believed in his power. Their own beliefs hurt them. He had no doubt that if he told the fool sitting before him that he would cast a spell to kill him, Ian would worry himself to death before the year was out.

Damien never had any intention of harming the Earl of Denniston or the Viscount Leyton. But he knew that if he held out that hope to Ian he could control the man. Ian wanted his father's estate badly enough to give up anything for it—even China, the only thing of his that Damien coveted. Once she was in his clutches, Damien intended to dispose of Ian Leyton. Now, it seemed, he would first have to get rid of Ian—who had become a danger to him—and then possess the beautiful Lady China Leyton. Before Ian had even arrived, Damien had resolved to be rid of him. Now was the time to put his plan into motion.

He painted a smile into his lips as he turned back to his guest.

"It was foolish of you, my friend," he said gently, "very foolish. But we all make mistakes. Now, I want you to go home. Visit with your lovely wife. Comfort her. When the time is right, my plan will go forward."

Ian felt limp with relief. "You'll tell me when the time comes?" he asked anxiously.

"I promise you will be the first to know," Damien purred.

Nearly weeping with relief, Ian took his leave and returned home to Jermyn Street, where he found China in better spirits than she had been in weeks.

As soon as she was well enough to leave the house, China paid a visit to Lady Sutton in St. Martin's Street.

The flamboyantly beautiful Lady Sutton let China into her boudoir where they could be sure of privacy. After tea was brought, they were left alone.

"I must tell you," Lady Sutton said as she poured the tea and handed a cup to China. "Rumors are flying. About you. About Ian. About Damien and what happened at Aldwych Abbey."

China shrugged, a flush rising into her pale cheeks. "I fell down a flight of stairs at the abbey. I lost my child." Her tone was hushed and filled with regret.

"They are saying—" Lady Sutton stopped, wishing she had not begun the thought.

But China would not let it go. "What are they saying?" she insisted on knowing.

Lady Sutton heaved a sigh. "They are saying, my dear, that the child you lost was not Ian's child."

"They're right," China surprised her by saying.

"They're—" Sarah Sutton was plainly startled. "You mean it is all true? You are Damien de Fonvielle's mistress?"

"Damien?" China gaped at her. "Of course not! The child was not Ian's, but it certainly was not Damien's!"

"There's someone else?" Lady Sutton blurted.

China smiled at the astonishment in her friend's beautiful face. "There was," she said wistfully. "In Virginia. The child belonged to him."

"But then why did you marry Ian?"

China looked away toward an arrangement of miniatures on a table near the door. "There were reasons," she said cryptically. "None that matter now." She shook her head to banish the unwelcome memories of Gabriel and of that last night at Montcalm that flooded her mind. That time, those emotions, were gone. It only pained her to remember.

She smiled to banish the awkward air in the room. "Let me tell you the reason I have come. I mean to leave Ian. Our marriage is a sham. I can't live with his madness any longer. And I am afraid, Sarah, truly afraid of Damien de Fonvielle. I believe he has convinced Ian that he has some sort of unearthly powers which he will use on Ian's behalf if he gives me to him. And Ian has agreed! I can't stay there any longer. But I need a place to go. I thought perhaps you . . . if you have reservations, I—"

"Reservations!" Lady Sutton was clearly delighted. "Of course I have no reservations! When are you coming? Why don't we simply send someone to pack for you and bring your things back?"

China laughed, relieved that she had found so eager a welcome. "No," she declined. "I have to go back. But I'll be here soon enough. I've had more than enough of Ian, and certainly more than I can stand of Damien de Fonvielle!"

She took her leave of Lady Sutton, promising it would be only a few days at most before she was back. Filled with confidence and hope for the future, she climbed into her coach and rode back to Jermyn Street.

When she arrived home, she found a strange silence. The servants said nothing, their faces apprehensive, strained. They could not seem to meet China's eyes and they melted away before she could question them.

At last she found Yeats, the butler, in the library. He, too, wore a worried expression, but he seemed relieved that she had returned home.

"What's wrong?" she asked. "Has something happened? Everyone seems frightened."

"It is my lord, milady. A letter arrived for him—I do not know from whom—he read it, burned it, then retired to your bedchamber."

"Mine!" China was astonished. Ian had long since ceased coming to her bedchamber for anything. "He's still there?"

"Aye, milady. The door is locked from within. There's been no sound."

Apprehension filled China. Ian had been quiet lately, withdrawn, anxious. He seldom left the house, and no one, not even Damien, had visited him. He seemed to be waiting, worrying over something, but she had not asked him. Ian and his schemes had ceased to be of interest to her.

Now she wished she had tried to discover what was troubling him. She felt certain it had something to do with Damien—the duc was the driving force in Ian's life. What had the duc done to him now, she wondered. What new plan had he enlisted Ian's help in accomplishing? It must involve her or he would not have gone to her room, locked himself inside. Was he waiting there for her?

She put on a brave face for Yeats, who stood before her awaiting instructions. "I'd better go and see what is wrong, hadn't I?" she asked with a wan smile.

Leaving the butler, China climbed the stairs and went to her bedroom. She rattled the latch. The door was locked. She rapped at the panels and called Ian's name. There was no reply, only an ominous silence.

China looked at the butler and the footmen standing in the hall. Stepping back she told them: "Break it open."

The impact of the footmen's bodies against the door seemed to shake the house. The sound echoed along the hall. They tried once, twice. On the third attempt the wood splintered and the door flew open, crashing against the small table beside it, sending the table and the ornaments on it scattering in fragments over the floor.

The footmen stepped aside. They looked expectantly at China, who hesitated a moment, then entered the room.

She found what she'd known she would find. Ian lay sprawled on her bed. His eyes were open but they stared unseeing at the canopy above. His mouth gaped. His hand hung over the side of the bed. On the floor where it had fallen from his lifeless grasp, a crystal flask lay, the golden cap lost in the rumpled coverlet of the bed.

China turned away from the sight. What could have prompted Ian to do such a terrible thing? What could have driven him to such despair that he no longer wished to live?

"Here now!" Yeats' voice, harsh and disapproving, filled the room.

China turned around and saw the butler snatch a sheet of paper from one of the footmen. He glanced at it, flushed, then handed it to China without a word.

She looked at it. Only a few lines of writing marred its pristine surface. It read:

"I know you mean to leave me for Damien de Fonvielle. I cannot live without you."

China saw the looks the footmen exchanged. They believed what Ian had written. It occurred to her that the note had not been sealed or even folded. Ian had meant for it to be seen by whoever broke into the room for her. It was incomprehensible. She had no intention of leaving Ian for Damien. He knew that. And he could hardly wish to die rather than lose her to the duc. Had not Ian already given her to Damien in exchange for whatever hellish favor Damien had promised him?

It seemed that Ian had meant to create a scandal—he meant, with his dying words, to ruin her. He must have known that, once gossip of this got out as it inevitably would, she would be as much an outcast of society as he had ever been.

"Yeats," she said softly, beckoning the butler to her. "We must make arrangements for my lord's funeral."

"A suicide, milady . . ." the butler breathed.

He knew, as well as she did, that suicides were denied burial in consecrated ground. That the usual custom was burial at a crossroads with a stake through the body to keep the restless spirit from roaming.

"Send a message to the Earl of Denniston," she directed, "or, if he is not in London, to Viscount Leyton. Tell them what has happened. Ask for instructions."

Bowing, Yeats went to do as he'd been told. China gave orders that Ian be taken to his own room and that her own belongings be moved into another bedchamber. She had no intention of sleeping in the bed where her husband had ended his life.

Gabriel stood in the shadow of a building facing the Leytons' house in Jermyn Street. The news of Ian's suicide had raced through London society. The contents of his final letter were repeated and discussed at every ball, every dinner, at the theater, in the taverns.

His body had been taken away, by footmen sent by the Earl of Denniston, to the earl's country estate and buried privately. China had not been invited to accompany it, nor had she asked to. Ian, and the part he had played in her life, was behind her.

Now Gabriel, like the rest of London society, waited and watched to see what she would do next. He longed to go to her, to demand the truth about so many things. He did not want to believe she could have driven a man to kill himself. But then, hadn't she cold-bloodedly betrayed him and his men to the very people she knew would try, condemn, and kill them? What, then, did the life or death of one more man mean to her?

As he watched, Gabriel saw the trunks being brought out and loaded into a wagon. He saw the preparations being made for China's departure. The wagon left, and a coach drew up before the door. Though the driver and the footmen on the back of the coach wore concealing cloaks, Gabriel recognized them. They were not China's servants. They were lackeys of the Duc de Fonvielle.

Gabriel stared, disbelieving, as China left the house and, without looking up, climbed into the coach. Immediately the driver set the horses into motion and the coach rocked as it lurched forward. As it turned the corner, Gabriel caught a glimpse of another occupant of the shining black coach—the Duc de Fonvielle himself, leaning forward, speaking earnestly to China who sat facing him.

"By God!" Gabriel breathed as the coach was lost to his sight. "She did it! Leyton not cold in his grave and she's gone off with that devil Frenchman!"

Any doubts, any softening of feeling he might have had for China, vanished. She had not changed from the scheming bitch who had sent him and his men to the gallows. If anything, she was worse!

Well, he thought as he mounted his horse and rode off in the direction of Grosvenor Square and Wetherford House. Let her enjoy her liaison with de Fonvielle while she could, he thought grimly. Soon she would be called upon to answer for what she had done.

Eighteen

It was not until the coach was in motion that China realized her mistake. Yeats had told her the coach was waiting outside the door. What neither he nor she had realized was that it was not her coach.

She looked up into the smiling amber eyes of Damien de Fonvielle. "What are you . . ." Astonished, she looked about her. The interior of the duc's coach was a deep forest green whereas her own was a rich blue-green. Grasping the window ledge, she looked out at the passing scene. They were not heading toward St. Martin's Street, toward Lady Sutton's. "Where do you think you're taking me?" she demanded.

"Aldwych Abbey," he told her matter-of-factly.

"Oh, no," she snapped. "Stop this coach!"

With her fist, she pounded on the side of the coach to signal the driver to stop. But Damien opened the little door that allowed him to speak with his coachman.

"Drive on!" he ordered. "Do not stop for anything until you reach the abbey!"

The coach lurched as the driver whipped up the horses. Soon they were leaving London, passing through the little villages on the outskirts of the capital. China's impulse was to throw open the door and fling herself out, to escape from him at any cost. But the horses were at a near gallop now. It would be suicide to leap from the coach at that speed.

She shot Damien a venomous glare. "Why are you doing this?" she demanded. "You must know I detest you!"

"I know you believe you do," Damien allowed. "But with time . . ." He shrugged.

"Time will not change my feelings for you," she promised him. "I know the kind of man you are. You drove Ian to his death. I don't know how. The butler said he received a letter from you before he died. What did you tell him?"

"It does not matter now, does it?" Damien asked. He smiled cruelly. "Come, my lovely China, do not pretend you are grief-stricken at your husband's death. You are not so great a hypocrite as that, I think."

"I don't pretend that I loved Ian," China admitted. "I will not tell you his death greatly pains me. But you used his troubles against him. You turned the demons inside him against him. I don't know what you hoped to gain!"

"Don't you?" Damien smiled complacently. "I think you do."

China gazed out the window. "Me?" she said softly. "And what did you promise Ian in exchange for his wife?"

"The earldom of Denniston," Damien said bluntly. He saw China's surprised look. "It's true," he insisted. "Ian wanted me to cast a spell to do away with his father and brother so that he would inherit the earldom."

China shivered. "You can't truly kill people with spells and incantations," she said, adding: "Can you?"

Damien chuckled. "It depends on whom you ask. Some people believe such things are possible. For those people the threat of a spell being cast for their deaths is enough to drive them to madness. They become so certain they are doomed to agonizing deaths that they will do anything to escape it—even end their own lives."

"You don't mean . . ." An awful certainty dawned on China. "The letter you wrote to Ian! You told him you were casting a spell to kill him, and it frightened him into suicide!"

Damien's face was the picture of innocence. "Ian believed very strongly in the power of such spells," he said noncommittally.

"And you prey on such people!" she accused. "You're a fiend!"

"A fiend?" Damien feigned astonishment. "Come now, hardly that. Admit it, my dear, you would have enjoyed it if Ian's plot had succeeded, wouldn't you? Wouldn't you have enjoyed being Countess of Denniston?"

I would rather have been Mrs. Gabriel St. Jon, China thought bleakly. And I could have been, but I gave it up to save Gabriel's life. And what good has it done? She saw Damien watching her, waiting for an answer.

"No, I would not have liked to be Countess of Denniston!" she snapped.

"No?" The duc seemed surprised. "Would you like to be the Duchesse de Fonvielle?"

China gaped at him, appalled. "You cannot mean that!"

"I assure you I do." Damien was perfectly serious. "I would make you my duchesse. You have only to agree."

China's eyes blazed with glittering blue fire as she glared at him across the coach. "Marry you!" she hissed. "I would sooner marry the Devil himself!"

Damien leaned back against the tufted leather seat. His smile was serene, sly, frighteningly confident. "Perhaps that can be arranged," he said softly, then lapsed into an ominous silence that lasted the rest of the way to Aldwych Abbey.

"I don't believe it," Lady Anne Wetherford told her grandson flatly. "I will not believe that she had no more than seen her husband into the grave than she packed her traps and ran off with that notorious Frenchman."

"It's true," Gabriel insisted, turning from the bow window that overlooked Grosvenor Square. "Her trunks were loaded into a wagon. After that left, a coach drew up before the door. China came out and climbed in. When the coach turned the corner, I saw Damien de Fonvielle in it as well."

"Oh, dear." Rising, Lady Wetherford went to stand beside her grandson. "Tell me something, Gabriel, my boy."

"What?" Gabriel asked.

"What the devil did you ever see in that woman?"

Gabriel's laugh was half amused, half self-mocking. "Who can say?" he asked wistfully. "Good judgment, common sense, simple wisdom—it all goes by the wayside when you fall in love."

Lady Wetherford's heart ached for him. The pain in his tone, in his green eyes, was too plain to see. She truly believed that if somehow China Leyton were to appear before her at that moment, she would strangle the faithless little trollop with her bare hands to pay her back for what she'd done to Gabriel.

"What will you do now?" she asked, wishing he would simply leave China to Damien—they seemed like a matched pair—and try to get on with his life.

"Get her back from de Fonvielle," he said simply.

"Is your vengeance worth the pain she is causing you?" his grandmother asked gently.

"My pain," Gabriel told her seriously, "is nothing. At least I am alive. That is more than my crew can say."

Lady Wetherford sighed. "I was so certain she could not be as wicked as gossip painted her. I was sure there must be an explanation for what happened in Virginia—even for what happened to her husband." She frowned. "I suppose it's too late to send a messenger to St. Martin's Street."

"St. Martin's Street?" Gabriel repeated.

"I invited Lady Sutton to tea." Anne St. Jon, Lady Wetherford shook her head. "I know she is a close friend and confidante of China's. I thought she could tell us more."

"When is she to be here?" Gabriel asked, glancing at the tall case clock in the corner.

The sound of carriage wheels echoed in the room. From the drawing room window, they saw a yellow and black coach drawing up before the house.

"If I'm not mistaken," Lady Wetherford said. "That is Lady Sutton now. Will you join us?"

Gabriel scowled as the beautiful, red-haired woman in pearl gray and scarlet stepped down from the coach.

"I think I will," he told her. "But say nothing to her about my going after China. I wouldn't want her to warn China that I'm coming."

Lady Wetherford agreed and, on her grandson's arm, went to greet her guest.

Sarah Sutton tried to hide her fascination with Gabriel St. Jon. She had, of course, heard of the illegitimate son of the late Lord St. Jon, but, like most of London society, she had never met him. There was a rakish, dangerous air about him, whether it came from his reputation—rumor had it the life he led in the colonies was less than respectable—or from the glint in his green eyes above the beard that did not conceal his chiseled good looks or the nearly healed knife slash on his cheek.

Sarah did not quite understand why she had been invited to the home of a woman known to shun most of society. Lady Wetherford's friends were carefully chosen from among the highest strata of society. Most had been friends for years, and the younger set seldom received more than a passing glance from those fascinating green eyes.

"Have you met my grandson, my dear?" Lady Wetherford asked as they retired to the drawing room where tea would be served.

"No, I don't believe so," Lady Sutton said, feeling oddly girlish beneath the heavy-lidded gaze of Gabriel's eyes.

"I'm certain I would have remembered a lady so lovely," Gabriel said, forcing a smile into his lips. "Lady Sutton. I am Gabriel St. Jon."

"Mr. St. Jon," Sarah murmured, grateful to sink into a chair before her trembling betrayed her.

"You might wonder at my inviting you to tea when we are not well acquainted," Lady Wetherford said, seeing no point in belaboring the preliminaries.

"I must admit, I did," Sarah acknowledged.

"I know you were a friend of the late Lady Clairmont. And I believe you are also a friend of her daughter, Lady China Leyton."

"I am," Sarah admitted, puzzled.

Lady Wetherford paused long enough for a servant to serve the tea and retire before she continued. "My grandson," she nodded toward Gabriel, "is also acquainted with Lady China. In fact, he was betrothed to her cousin, daughter of the present Lord Clairmont."

Gabriel glanced at his grandmother in surprise, but then the sense of what she was saying struck him. If he did not wish to reveal to Lady Sutton the truth about their interest in China, how much easier to pretend it was only that she was the relative of a close connection such as a fiancée.

"Was?" Lady Sutton inquired, looking at Gabriel.

"The betrothal was ended," he said simply, knowing she would not be so rude as to question the reason.

"In any case," Lady Wetherford was going on, "we are, naturally, interested in Lady China. We were surprised that she went off so quickly after her husband's death. Gabriel, who knew her in Virginia, thought it quite out of character for her to cast in her lot with the Duc de Fonvielle so hastily and—"

"The Duc de Fonvielle!" Sarah's face was pale. "She can't have gone with him!"

"She did," Gabriel told her. "I, myself, saw her leave the house in Jermyn Street with the duc."

Sarah sat back in her seat. "I don't understand."

"I heard it said," Lady Wetherford said

casually, "that her husband killed himself because she was going to leave him for the Duc de Fonvielle."

"That was not true." Sarah shook her head. "She was going to leave Ian, but *because* of the duc, not *for* the duc."

"What do you mean?" Gabriel asked, leaning toward her.

"She was afraid of the duc. The day Ian died she came to see me. She asked if she could come to stay with me. She was going to leave Ian because he was completely under Damien de Fonvielle's spell. She said . . ." Sarah hesitated, not knowing if she should reveal too much, but then plunged on. "She said Ian had 'given' her to the duc."

Gabriel's face flushed with disgust. "How disappointed the duc must have been when China lost his child."

"It was not Damien's child," Sarah told him.

"But I thought . . ." Lady Wetherford began, casting a bewildered glance toward Gabriel. "They said that Ian Leyton . . . that he could not . . ."

"No, no," Sarah interrupted. "China told me the child's father was a man she knew in Virginia."

Gabriel sagged back in his chair. The child was his. His! Whatever his suspicions about China's character, whatever his anger at her betrayal of him, he did not believe she had been with anyone else in Virginia. If Leyton was incapable of fathering her child, then it must have belonged to him.

His stomach twisted at the memory of that night at Aldwych Abbey when China had fallen. She had been startled—by him! If he had not frightened her, if he had been able to grasp her hand and stop her fall, their child might not have been lost.

But then, he reasoned, sobering, as cold-blooded as China was, what sort of mother would she have been to the child of a man she had given up to his enemies?

He rose. "It was kind of you to come," he said to Lady Sutton. "And kind of you to tell us about China. If you'll excuse me now, ma'am, Grandmother," he nodded to Lady Wetherford, "I have to leave."

He left the room, and Lady Wetherford, excusing herself for a moment, went after him. She stopped him as he was mounting the stairs.

"Are you going after her?" she asked.

"I am," Gabriel admitted. "De Fonvielle's probably taken her to Aldwych. That's where I'll look first."

"You're not going to harm her, are you?"

Gabriel shook his head. "I'm not certain what I'm going to do. But first of all I have to get her away from de Fonvielle. Then I'll decide what to do with her."

He started up the stairs, but his grandmother caught his coattail and stopped him once more.

"The child, Gabriel," she said seriously. "The child she lost. Was it yours?"

"It was," he confirmed. Then, smiling sadly, he bent and kissed his grandmother's cheek before continuing up the stairs.

Evening was falling over Aldwych Abbey and Damien paced before the fire in the great hall, a long letter crumpled in his fist.

"So he is dead," he exulted. "The Marquis de Michelet. At last!"

The young, dissolute Viscount Langon looked up from the divan where he lay sprawled, a goblet of wine clasped loosely in one trembling hand. "Who is the Marquis de . . . de . . ." He scowled, unable to remember what Damien had said.

"De Michelet," the thirty-year-old Lord Robert Weston supplied. A younger son, with no goals, no ambitions, he had embarked on a life of vice and ruin before he'd left school. When he'd met Damien, he, like the Viscount Langon, had become an ardent disciple.

Damien eyed them both disgustedly. They were useless, the pair of them, but he kept them around mostly to run his errands and do those less agreeable tasks that needed doing at the abbey.

"The Marquis de Michelet," he informed

them coldly, "along with the Duc d'Aguesseau, was the prime reason I had to leave France. He spread libels about me, out of jealousy, and whipped up resentment toward me. They have the ear of the regent. They turned him against me. They sent *agents provocateurs* into the region near my *château*, planting suspicions. And why? Jealousy. Resentment. They pretend to be so scandalized, so appalled by what I do. This when they are both practitioners of the black arts. The Duc d'Aguesseau taught me everything I know."

"But one of them is dead now," the viscount reminded him.

Damien nodded, smiling. "And I believe I can convince the other to withdraw his objections to my returning to France."

"How?" Lord Robert wanted to know.

"He knows me. He believes in me. He believes in the powers of darkness. What do you think he would do, my friends, if he knew a spell had been cast to kill him? What if he received proof of the spell? What if the price of removing the spell was my being allowed to go home?"

"But how would you prove it to him?" the viscount asked. "What would you send him?"

"The most powerful charm there is," Damien told him, his mind racing. "A heart. A human heart."

The viscount and Lord Robert exchanged an apprehensive glance. "Whose heart?" they asked simultaneously.

"The heart of a beautiful woman," he told them, thinking to himself: If my fine Lady China will not give her beautiful self to me, I will take what I want from her to buy my way back to France.

Issuing orders, giving directions for the preparation of the ritual, Damien dispatched a servant to the cell where China had been locked. He sent her his compliments along with the dinner she had been denied in an attempt to starve her into submission. He smiled when the servant reported that she had eaten her dinner and drunk the fine French wine served with it. Only he and the servant knew of the drug that had been mixed into the wine—the potion that would render China unconscious and prepare her for the ritual he would soon perform.

By the time Gabriel arrived at Aldwych Abbey, Damien, the viscount, and Lord Robert were garbed in the hooded robes they wore during Damien's revels. An octagonal room in one of the towers had been prepared, the stone table in the center cleared, and China laid across it, unconscious, nude, her hair streaming over the table's edge nearly to the floor.

From his collection, Damien chose a jeweled dagger honed to a razor-sharp edge. Positioning the viscount and Lord Robert on either side of the table, Damien was about to begin his incantation when a servant interrupted to say:

"Your pardon, your grace, but Mr. O'Meara has arrived."

"O'Meara?" Damien remembered the man who had come to his masked ball as an executioner. He'd claimed to be a student of the black arts; he'd expressed a keen interest in learning more. And, most importantly, he did not seem to be a bumbling fool like the two assistants he had now. "Ah, good. Give him a robe and send him in."

When Gabriel, garbed in the long, hooded brown robe, stepped into the room, he was stunned. China lay there, her skin pale and cold. She was motionless; she did not even seem to breathe.

"Is she . . ." he murmured.

"Dead?" Damien interrupted. "No, not yet. But she soon will be. We are sacrificing her to the powers of darkness." He smiled. "Beautiful, is she not?"

The duc slid a hand over China's hip, savoring the pale satin of her skin. "Come," he said to Gabriel, "stand here, by me. When the time comes, you will hold out that bowl."

"What for?" Gabriel wanted to know.

"Her heart," Damien told him. "It is what

we need for our ritual. I am going to cut it out."

"The hell you are!" Gabriel growled.

Taken by surprise, Damien did not react as Gabriel snatched up the dagger and plunged it into his chest. The duc crumpled to the floor, eyes staring, mouth agape.

The Viscount Langon screamed as blood spread over the duc's robe. When Gabriel turned toward him, Langon ran to Lord Robert's side and they huddled together, frightened as children.

"In there," Gabriel told them, motioning toward what he knew to be a tiny, windowless chamber he could lock from the outside. "Get in!"

Herding the two trembling men into the room, Gabriel kicked the door shut and dropped the heavy bar into its iron hooks. There was no way they could break out, and he doubted either of them would be brave enough to try.

Returning to China, Gabriel pulled off the robe he had donned over his clothes. He wrapped it around her and, gathering her limp body into his arms, carried it out of the abbey and into the coach he had brought from London.

He did not know, as he drove away, if Damien de Fonvielle were alive or dead and he did not care. All he knew was that China was alive and with him, and if he recognized the irony in having saved the life of a woman he'd vowed to kill, he ignored it as he rode off into the night.

Nineteen

When China awoke, it was to find herself in a room she'd never seen before. The light was dim—the crewelwork draperies at the window glowed with sunlight, but whether from a rising or setting sun she could not tell.

She pushed herself up in the tester bed, intending to get up, but a wave of dizziness made her sink back into the pillows. Frowning, she looked down at herself. She was lost inside a creamy linen shirt. It was not hers. From the size and style, she assumed it belonged to some man.

But what man? Damien? she asked herself. But this was not Aldwych Abbey. When had she left? She pressed a hand to her forehead.

Her last clear memory was of a servant at Aldwych Abbey bringing her dinner. She remembered nibbling a little of the roast chicken and drinking a goblet of wine. Very soon after, she had grown dizzy, had fainted. Damien, damn him, had slipped one of his filthy potions into her food or wine! He had wanted her unconscious, had wanted her helpless and defenseless. For what? she asked herself angrily. What plan did he have in mind for her that . . .

Another memory, dim, shrouded in mist, came to her. She saw herself half-awake, still under the spell of whatever foul brew Damien had concocted for her. She was lying on the seat of a jolting coach. Naked but for one of Damien's woolen monk's robes, she had fought to regain consciousness but achieved only a groggy kind of half-awareness.

There had been a man there, on the opposite seat, sitting silently, watching her. China concentrated, trying to remember the man's face. But it had been concealed in shadows her unfocused eyes could not penetrate. He had been a large man, dark, his eyes concealed by his hat, the lower half of his face hidden by a thick growth of beard that—

China gasped. The beard! It was him! It was the man she'd seen outside Lady Sutton's house, outside the house in Jermyn Street! He had been at Aldwych Abbey as well on the night of the masquerade ball. The executioner! He had frightened her by stepping out of the shadows just before she fell down the stairs.

But what was she doing with him? Where had he taken her and why? Why had Damien relinquished her to him?

Her head swam with the swirl of questions spinning inside it. Pushing back the coverlet, she swung her legs over the side and felt for the bedsteps. The long sleeves of the shirt that was her only garment fell over her hands. Impatiently she pushed them back and tightened the ties that gathered the wrists.

The room was attractive with paneling of a deep golden brown. The furniture, by and large, was of dark walnut in the style of the Restoration. The windows behind the drawn draperies were diamond-paned, fastened from without to prevent their being opened from within.

Outside the window, by the light of a setting sun, China saw rolling countryside, thick green forests, wild hedges thick with vines. The ivy that grew on the sides of the house bordered the windows in frames of deep green.

Letting the drapery fall back into place, China went to the door. She was not surprised to find it locked. Balling her fist, she pounded on the panels. To her surprise, footsteps approached. A key rattled in the lock.

Unsure of who might be on the other side, China backed away. But when the door opened, she found herself face to face with a large-boned, ruddy-faced, flaxen-haired maidservant who carried a candlestick in one hand. She carefully closed the door behind her and locked it before circling the room and lighting candles in brass candlesticks. When she'd finished, she smiled at China as though awaiting instructions.

"Who are you?" China demanded.

"My name is Louise, milady," she replied, bobbing a little curtsy.

"Do you know who I am?"

The girl shook her head. "No, milady, but my master said for me to wait upon your ladyship."

"Who is your master?"

The girl's pale blue eyes looked demurely at the floor. "I am not to tell you, milady."

China was not surprised. "Where are we?" she asked. "What is this place?"

The girl shook her head. "I am not to tell you that either, milady."

"Well, then," China said, knowing the girl was doubtless under orders to tell her very little, "can you bring me some water to bathe?"

"Aye, milady," the girl agreed readily. "I am to bring you food as well."

China waved away the offer, remembering only too well her last meal at Aldwych Abbey. "No food," she demurred. "Just the water, if you please."

Puzzled, the maid could only obey. She left the room and returned a few minutes later with a pitcher of steaming water, a towel, and a cake of rough, homemade soap.

Left alone once more, China pulled off the shirt that fell past her knees and washed her body with the hot water and the harsh, bad-smelling soap. Dried, she put the shirt back on, then wandered around the room hoping to discover something about the inhabitants from the contents.

But there was nothing. The books bore no nameplates, the desk contained nothing that bore a name or coat-of-arms that might hint at the identity of the owner.

China sank into a wing chair in front of the fireplace where a low fire had been kindled to keep back the chill of the late autumn night. Doubts, questions, worries assailed her. Had Damien simply moved her to some other location—had the man in the coach the night before been one of his lackeys—or had he bartered her away to some other fiend like himself? Had he made some hell-spawned bargain with some other villain trading her for something he wanted more? And if he had, what did this man want with her? What would he put her through? Would he harm her, hurt her, even kill her?

China felt a weariness in her very bones. She was tired of fear, of uncertainty. It had been so very long since she'd felt happy—or loved.

A sigh escaped her, wrenched from the deepest depths of her. What would she give, she thought, gazing into the flames in the grate, to be back in Virginia, back at Montcalm, lying in Gabriel's arms in the perfumed night of the gardens? Why couldn't they have stayed together? Why hadn't she run away with him when he'd asked her? They could have gone to Fox Meadow. They could be there now, married, in love, awaiting the birth of their child.

A tear slipped down her cheek unheeded. It had all been for nothing. Gabriel, Ian, her baby . . . all dead. And for what? For . . .

A feeling crept over China, a shiver coursed down her spine. She was not alone in the room. Somehow someone had come in without her hearing.

Thinking it might be the maid, China started to get up. "Louise?" she asked, a nervous tremor in her voice.

"Stay where you are." The voice was low, gravelly, husky.

China froze. Sinking back into her chair, she wrapped her arms about herself, feeling suddenly small and vulnerable. In the curved brass of a pitcher on the table, China saw a reflection of the room. The man stood behind her, not far from her chair, but the reflection was distorted, the light in the room low; she could tell nothing but that he was there, scarcely beyond arm's reach from her.

"Who are you?" she asked softly, unable to raise her voice above a whisper.

There was a moment's silence then the man said: "A ghost. Only a ghost."

China marveled at the tone of the voice; it was filled with regret, with sadness. She couldn't understand.

"Where are we?" she wanted to know, longing to turn around and confront him but not daring to disobey him.

"Sussex," he answered vaguely.

"Is Damien here?"

"No." The voice changed, growing hard, angry, resentful. "You'll never see the Duc de Fonvielle again."

China grasped the arms of the chair. Whatever happened, whatever her captor had in store for her, at least he had taken her away from Damien. "Thank God!" she breathed, too low for Gabriel, who might have been surprised, even moved, by the sentiment, to hear.

"Am I your prisoner here?" she inquired.

"You are," he confirmed.

"Are you the same man I saw outside my house in Jermyn Street and outside Lady

Sutton's in St. Martin's Street?"

"Aye," he admitted. "I was there."

"And you sent those notes to me? The ones accusing me of murder?" China felt her heart beating wildly.

"I did," he confirmed.

"But why? I don't understand. What am I supposed to have done? Of what am I accused?"

"Of murder," he replied. "Of treachery, betrayal."

"I don't know what you're talking about!" China cried. "Please, please, tell me who you are! Tell me how I betrayed you? Tell me who I am supposed to have murdered? Whose blood do you think I have on my hands?"

There was no reply, and China felt the tears start in her eyes, flooding them, blurring her sight, trickling down her cheeks. She was frightened, confused, frustrated at not knowing either her accuser or what she was accused of.

"Tell me," she wept. "Please, why won't you tell me?"

Still her captor said nothing. His footsteps crossed the floor, and China heard the latch of the door click beneath his hand.

"No!" she cried. "Don't go! Please, tell me why you are—"

Pushing herself to her feet, she turned to face her captor. But he had gone, the room was empty, she was alone.

Trembling, weeping, China stumbled back to the chair and sank into it. She could not stop crying; her sobs echoed in the bedchamber and reached the ears of her gaoler outside the door.

Gabriel closed his eyes and sighed, moved by her tears, moved by the sobs he could hear muffled by the door that separated them. She seemed genuinely confused, her protests that she did not know what she had done seemed so real. And yet she had to be guilty. She had to!

Wanting to be shut off from the sound of her weeping, Gabriel crossed the room and went to his own bedchamber on the other side of the cottage. Closing the door, he sank wearily onto the chest at the foot of his bed.

The cottage, the dower house on the estate of the Marquess of Wetherford, belonged to his grandmother. Though the estate had been inherited by a cousin on the death of Gabriel's father, the dower house was Lady Wetherford's for life, and she had loaned it to him so he would have a secluded and private place to take China once he got her away from Damien de Fonvielle.

Gabriel wondered whether Damien had died of the dagger wound he had inflicted on him. He did not really care. He doubted that either the French or English authorities would make a very intensive inquiry into the death of such an undesirable person.

But whatever else was true, he knew the time had come to confront China. He had vowed to avenge the deaths of his crew, to punish her for the betrayal that had cost them their lives and had so nearly cost him his own. He knew he should approach it with the same cold-bloodedness she had shown in turning him over to the authorities.

But to his self-disgust, he found he could not. The thought of going into that room and killing her was suddenly inconceivable to him. He could not bring himself to harm her no matter how much he believed she deserved it.

Looking up, he caught sight of himself in the looking glass on the opposite wall. The bearded face that looked back at him was thinner, paler, etched with lines of anger and grief. He would not have recognized in that stranger the Gabriel Fortune who had sailed the sea with his pirate crew and believed that the world and its treasures were his for the taking. He had known nothing then of love. He had not imagined there could be a pain worse than the slash of a saber or the thrust of a dagger. He had not suspected that the pain of a broken heart was by far the most agonizing pain in the world.

He longed for those old carefree days as he sat in his room in the dower house in the forest. He wished, with all his heart, he could return to that life, without ties, without emotions, without heartbreak.

But he knew he would never be the same. China had changed all that. He would never again be the same man who had seen her, fallen in love with her, in those innocent, unsuspecting days.

Still, he resolved, he would have to try. He would have to finish this distasteful business and return to the sea.

Rising, he rang for Louise and ordered hot water. The first step, he decided, was to shave off the beard he had grown in order to conceal his identity from China while he stalked her and watched her.

Twenty

It was not easy for Gabriel to return to China's room. Her tears, her obvious distress, had affected him more than he cared to remember. He cursed the feelings that still nestled in his heart. He wished they were tangible things that could be torn out like some noxious weed that had taken root in the wrong garden.

Still, he could put it off no longer. He expected her to protest her innocence, perhaps to shed more tears and beg for him to believe her. As best he could, he steeled himself against her, remembering the day in Williamsburg when he had seen his crewmen, loyal men, friends one and all, go to their deaths because of her treachery. He remembered the feel of the noose about his own neck, those last moments before the trap had been sprung beneath his feet. He recalled the scene with agonizing clarity and felt the rage, the cold, hard fury rise inside him as he'd hoped it would. Only then did he feel himself ready to confront her. Only then did he go to her room and let himself in.

China lay on her bed, her head buried in her arms, her cheeks wet with tears. She had cried herself to sleep, worn out by fear, frustration, and confusion.

Gabriel came to stand beside the bed. He gazed down at her, so beautiful, so innocent in slumber, and felt his anger draining away, being replaced by the awe her beauty had always aroused in him. It had to be now, he told himself sternly, now while there still remained the last vestiges of fury inside him, before the sight of her there, her skin like palest porcelain, her hair like silver silk, made him want to make love to her rather than punish her for what she'd done.

"China," he snarled, backing away from the bedside so she was far out of reach. "China!"

On the bed, China stirred. His voice reached some part of her and touched off a memory, a memory of scented gardens, a moonlit night, a lover's caress. Her fingers plucked at the coverlet. Her lips parted, whispered his name.

"Gabriel," she sighed. "Gabriel."

Shaken, Gabriel could not let it go on any longer. "China, wake up, damn you!" he barked.

Startled out of sleep, China rubbed at her eyes with the back of one hand. She saw him standing there, the light of the candles shining in the depths of his sable hair, glimmering on the buttons of his brown brocade waistcoat, and it seemed to her she must still be dreaming.

"Gabriel," she whispered, not daring to believe the evidence of her own eyes. "But it can't . . ."

Stunned, she slipped off the bed and came toward him warily, as though afraid it was all a mirage. Her heart was pounding as she approached him.

"You're alive," she breathed, reaching out but not quite touching him. "You're alive!"

"I am," he agreed coldly. "I'm sorry if that disappoints you."

"Disappoints . . ." She frowned, bewildered. "But Rebecca wrote to me. She said you'd been arrested. She said you and your crew had been captured by Spotswood and had been condemned to hang."

"We were," he confirmed. "Even as you were sailing away with your fine new bridegroom, I was waking up in the public gaol in Williamsburg."

"But how, Gabriel? We were together at Montcalm. Everything was fine. What happened between the time you left and . . ."

"Enough!" he snarled. "I've had enough of this play-acting of yours!"

China fell back a step. "What do you mean? I'm not—"

"When I left Montcalm, I went back to the Swan Tavern. There were men there—men from Williamsburg. They knew I was Gabriel Fortune. They arrested me. Or tried to. The next day I woke up in gaol."

"But how could they know? No one knew who you were except—"

"Stop lying!" Gabriel's voice echoed in the small room. "I was arrested, China! Spotswood sent men to Fox Meadow to arrest my crew!"

"Well, don't shout at me about it!" she cried. "I knew nothing about it!"

"We were tried," Gabriel went on, ignoring her. "We were condemned to die. I watched my crew die, can you imagine what that was like? They were my men! My friends! And I watched them kick away their dying breaths dangling at the end of a rope!" He paused, caught his breath. "Then it was my turn," he went on, his husky voice low, tense. "I mounted the scaffold. They put the noose about my neck and sprang the trap."

China smothered a gasp, but Gabriel did not hear it nor did he notice the pasty pallor or her horrified expression. She took a step toward him, wanting to comfort him. But she did not dare touch him.

"Think of it," he told her, his green eyes glittering. "I fell, the rope snapped taut. Imagine it, China. The burning of the rope on the skin, falling, choking, the pain . . ." He jerked aside the edge of his neck cloth to expose his throat with the dark, healing line that encircled it.

He turned away, shaken by the memory. When he spoke again, his voice trembled noticeably. "Spotswood did not arrest all my men. Some were not at Fox Meadow during the raid. They came to Williamsburg, mingled with the crowd. They created a diversion, a fight. In the confusion, I was cut down. They slit the noose from my neck. The knife slipped . . ." He touched the scar on his cheek.

"You survived," China breathed. "But all the rest of your men . . ."

"One survived," he told her. "A young gunner's mate. They spirited us away from Williamsburg. Le Corbeau had brought the *Black Pearl* up the James. We were taken aboard. He set course for New Providence Island. When I recovered I came back and booked passage out of Charles Town for London. I came to find you."

"And to kill me," China finished for him.

"Aye, to kill you," he agreed. "I came to demand payment for the lives of my crewmen."

China went to the chair before the fire and sank into it. Her legs felt weak; her senses swam. He had followed her, stalked her, all the time planning to murder her.

She gazed into the fire that burned low in the grate. "I did not betray you," she said softly. "I am not to blame for the deaths of your men."

"I don't believe you," he told her flatly.

"I know," she acknowledged. "But it is the truth."

Pushing herself to her feet, she went to face him. "You have told me of the horror you went through. Now let me tell you of mine." Lacing her fingers together, she pressed them to her lips. Taking a deep breath, casting back her memory to Montcalm and what had followed, she began:

"Ian Leyton knew your true identity. I don't know how. I did not tell him. He came to my room at Montcalm. That night after we'd been to Bramblewood—do you remember?" She glanced at him but continued without waiting for a response. "He told me he knew you were Gabriel Fortune. He knew that we were lovers. He told me he wanted me to marry him. I refused. He said if I did not agree to marry him and leave for England, he would turn you over to the authorities. He said you would be tried and hanged. I knew it was true. So I agreed to marry him."

Gabriel's expression was one of blatant skepticism. "Why didn't you come to me?" he asked. "I could have taken care of Ian Leyton."

"I was afraid to," she insisted. "It would have been so simple for him to alert Spotswood, set him on you." She sighed, looked away. "He did it anyway, despite my agreeing to marry him."

"He did not!" Gabriel snapped. "Damnit, China, will you listen to me! The deposition was given by 'China Clairmont.' The woman was described to me—it was you!"

"It was not me!" she shouted. "Why won't you believe me? I'm telling you, it was Ian!"

"It's convenient to blame Leyton," Gabriel remarked snidely. "After all, he's dead. He can't contradict you."

"Oh!" China wanted to scream with frustration. There was no way to convince him. He was like the tribunal in Williamsburg—his mind was made up, she was tried and condemned—before she had ever had an opportunity to defend herself.

"The deposition was signed by you," he went on, unmoved by her distress.

"Then it was a forgery," she snapped. "My God, Gabriel, do you think I could have met you in the gardens of Montcalm, made love to you, told you how I loved you, all the while knowing I had betrayed you? Do you think I could have lain with you knowing that Spotswood's men would be waiting for you when you got back to the Swan Tavern?"

Gabriel said nothing. His eyes were like shards of cold green ice as he gazed at her, stony-faced.

China took a deep, shaky breath. "You do believe that, don't you? Good Lord."

"It was all there, China," Gabriel told her. "The way we met, our going to Fox Meadow, your escape, Leyton's rescue, everything from the very beginning. Who else knew about it all? Who did you tell about us?"

"No one," China admitted. "But someone must have found out somehow."

"How?"

China clenched her fists. "I don't know! What must I do to convince you?" Looking up at him, she could find not the slightest sign that she'd made the smallest impression on him. His belief that she had been to blame for the deaths of his men, for his own near-death, was as strong as it had been the moment he'd boarded ship in pursuit of her.

Trembling, China made her slow, halting way to the chair and sank into it. It was hopeless, she thought. There was nothing she could do. He despised her; in his heart he longed for vengeance against her. There was nothing left inside him of the love they had felt for one another. That inevitable, irresistible attraction they had felt from the beginning, that desire that had drawn them to each other no matter how they had tried to fight it, was gone now. His loathing for her had burned it out of his heart, his mind.

Suddenly it seemed as if there was no hope for the future, no purpose to life. She had lost Gabriel, then lost his child. Now he had been restored to her, but he bore no feeling for her save resentment, disgust, mistrust.

Pushing herself to her feet, China walked slowly past him to the bedchamber door. Gabriel watched as she opened it and left the room. He followed her and from the doorway saw her hesitate, glancing around the small cottage.

"Where is your room?" she asked, not turning toward him.

"Why?" he asked, wondering at her reasons.

She glanced over her shoulder at him. "Which?"

"Over there," he replied, indicating a door on the opposite side of the cottage's great room.

China went to it and let herself inside. She rummaged among his things until she found what she sought.

Gabriel waited, curious. When she returned, when he saw the pistol cradled in her hands, he stepped forward, alarmed.

"China, what do you think you're doing?" he demanded.

Her face devoid of expression, China came to him and held the pistol out to him.

"Take it," she said softly. He made no move and she held it higher. "Go on," she urged. "Take it."

Nonplused, he lifted the heavy gun out of her hands. "What is this about?" he asked when she stood silently before him.

"You came to England to find me," she said. "You came here to kill me, didn't you?"

Gabriel looked away from her. He said nothing for a moment but finally admitted: "I did."

"Well, then, go ahead."

"China," Gabriel began softly.

"No," she interrupted. "You've tried and condemned me in your own mind. I've told you I did not betray you. I've sworn to you I am not to blame for the deaths of your men, but you don't believe me. If you still think I deserve to die for the crimes I'm accused of, then go on, exact your revenge."

The gun lay in Gabriel's hand, the smooth wood of the butt and the cold hard metal of the barrel feeling foreign to him. He looked at her, saw the hopelessness in those topaz blue eyes, saw the willingness in her eyes to lay her fate in his hands.

Her forlorn despondency was painful for

Gabriel to see. Turning away, he laid the pistol on the table.

"Go to bed, China," he said dully. "Tomorrow we will leave this place."

"And go where?" she wanted to know.

"Home." He looked back at her where she still stood, small, trembling, dwarfed in his shirt. "Tomorrow we will take ship for North Carolina. We will go to Fox Meadow." He saw the concern in her eyes and assured her: "It will be safe there. There was a great scandal over Spotswood's sending men into another colony to arrest my crew. We won't be troubled."

"Why do you want to take me there?" she wanted to know. "Why don't you simply take your revenge and be done with it? Wouldn't that make you happy? Isn't that what you want?"

Gabriel shook his head, feeling weary, uncertain. It was as if her defeat, her meek acceptance of his accusations, had robbed him of all the cold loathing he had harbored for her. He'd been so sure that she'd betrayed him, so certain that she'd lied every time she said she loved him, so confident that when the time came he'd demand payment for the lives her treachery had cost.

He'd believed that the moment she was in his clutches he would be able to take his revenge with no compunction. But now . . .

"Go to bed, China," he repeated. "I've

always done as I pleased. I've lived on whichever side of the law I wanted. But I've never, to my knowledge, harmed an innocent person. You claim you are not to blame for what happened to me and my men."

"And you don't believe me," she reminded him.

"It doesn't matter if I believe you or not. I'll take you to Fox Meadow. I'll give you the chance to try and prove your innocence. But be warned, if you turn out to be guilty after all, I will have revenge."

China nodded and left him to return to her bedchamber. But as she lay there with only the flickering light of the fire lighting the room, she felt the dismal gloom in her heart lift, if only a little. If Gabriel still did not believe in her innocence, at least there was a shred of doubt in his mind. He was willing to admit there might be a possibility she was telling the truth. And that small concession, that little admission, was enough to kindle the embers of hope in China's heart, warming her, raising her from the black depths of despair that had taken hold of her. Only a few minutes before, she had been willing to stand silently while Gabriel fired a shot that would end her life. Now she felt reborn, invigorated. The future which had stretched before her bleak and empty was now alight with the precious glow of rekindled hope.

Outside, in the great room, Gabriel sat in a

wing chair, the darkness gathering around him as the candles in their brass candlesticks burned down. The pistol lay at his fingertips on the table beside his chair.

China's willingness to accept death at his hands had shaken him. He had followed her halfway around the world to kill her but he could not. He found himself wanting to believe her protestations of innocence. He had thought his heart hardened against her, believed his hatred was impervious to her beauty, to the love they had once shared. But deep in his heart the embers of their love still burned, and now he felt them bursting into flame again. He closed his eyes, wishing he could feel again the cold abhorrence he'd felt for her before. It had been so much easier then. There were no questions in his mind, no doubts. Now he found himself wanting desperately to believe in her innocence.

He wanted to believe she had not betrayed him—that she, like himself, had been the victim of someone else. He wanted to trust her again, even to love her, but he did not quite dare, and that uncertainty, that doubt, tormented him.

Twenty-One

The next morning Gabriel and China—dressed in one of Louise's linsey-woolsey gowns—left the dower house and started out for London and Wetherford House.

"Wetherford?" China had said when Gabriel revealed their destination. "The Marquess of Wetherford's townhouse in Greville Street?"

"No, the marchioness's—the dowager marchioness's—in Grosvenor Square. Do you know her?"

China shook her head. "I've heard of her, but she and my parents were not friends. How do you know her?"

Gabriel gazed out at the passing scenery, the lush, incredible green of the English countryside with the morning sun glistening on the dew. "She is my grandmother," he said softly.

"She's what!" China cried.

As they rode toward London, Gabriel told her what he'd told few others—the story of his father's ill-starred love for his mistress, her death in childbirth, his father's melancholy existence and early death. By the time he finished, he found China gazing at him with sympathetic eyes.

"It must have been hard for you, to see your father's titles and estates going to someone else."

Gabriel shrugged. "I never longed to be called 'milord' and to be bowed and scraped to. I made a life for myself, an estate of my own."

"What of Fox Meadow?" China asked, wondering what might have become of Gabriel's home now that he was under a sentence of death for piracy.

"Charles Eden, the governor of North Carolina, is a friend of mine. He'll grant me a pardon. With my whereabouts unknown, Fox Meadow will be held in abeyance. It will be there for me when I return. It's quite beautiful. The house is nearly finished."

They lapsed into silence then—the subject of Gabriel's "hanging" in Williamsburg threw up the barriers of his suspicion between them—and rode into London, where they stopped at Wetherford House long enough for Gabriel to retrieve his belongings while China waited, at his request, in the coach. They then drove on to St. Martin's Street, where China's belongings had been taken on the night Damien de Fonvielle had abducted her from Jermyn Street.

Lady Sutton drew China aside out of Gabriel's earshot as they waited for China's trunks to be loaded onto the wagon with Gabriel's own.

"What is this about?" she wanted to know. "I was summoned to Lady Wetherford's and questioned about you and Damien and Ian. "Now you are with Gabriel St. Jon. Taking ship for America with him? I don't understand."

"I can't explain it all," China told her. "Suffice it to say that he is the man I loved in Virginia. He was the father of the child I lost."

"But you married Ian," Sarah Sutton reminded her.

China smiled kindly at her bewilderment. "I told you I can't explain. It would take far too long."

"Well," Sarah said, tidying the ribbons on the cherry silk gown China had changed into when she'd arrived at Sutton House. "It doesn't matter. You're together now. I know you love him, and he must love you as well, to follow you all this way."

"He followed me here to . . ." China hesitated, loath to reveal too much. "I'm not certain how he feels about me, Sarah. I think he loves me, but it's buried beneath so much mistrust, so much resentment. I don't know if it will ever again surface."

"Be patient," Sarah counseled. "Give it time. I wish you all the best, you know that."

"I know," China acknowledged, hugging her friend.

"China?" Gabriel appeared in the doorway. "We have to go."

"I'm coming," she promised softly. She smiled reassuringly at Lady Sutton. "I'll write when we reach America."

Without daring to look back, China accompanied Gabriel out to the coach and climbed in. As they rolled away down St. Martin's Street, China wondered if she would ever see the beautiful, flame-haired Lady Sutton again. If she could not convince Gabriel of her innocence . . .

She forced that thought from her mind as they drove to the docks and boarded the *Castlegate* outward bound for Charles Town.

"Why Charles Town?" China wanted to know when they were in the cabin allotted to them as "Mr. and Mrs. Edward O'Meara."

"This was the first boat going to America. The next was bound for Yorktown and, if you don't mind, I'd rather stay out of Virginia."

China busied herself unpacking the one trunk she had had brought to the small cabin she would share with Gabriel. The others, along with most of his baggage, were stored in the hold of the ship. She looked around—the cabin was scarcely big enough for a bunk built into one corner, a table with a lamp swinging in its gimbal, and a worn armchair. A cabinet built into the opposite corner from the door held a basin and pitcher and a chamber pot.

"Couldn't you have booked two cabins?" China asked him when they bumped into one another the third time. "Are there so many people sailing for Charles Town that there was only one cabin available?"

"I'd rather stay here," he told her. "I prefer to keep you where I can see you."

"And where do you think I'm going to go?" she challenged. "Do you imagine I'm going to jump overboard and swim for England?"

Gabriel gave her a long, steady look before leaving the cabin to go up on deck. His look, to China, seemed to say he would not put anything past her. It was clear that, despite his postponement of her punishment and his willingness to look deeper into the matter of her guilt and innocence, he still did not trust her out of his sight.

Sinking onto the edge of the bunk, China sighed wearily. It was going to be a long, long voyage.

Gabriel, wrapped in a blanket, tried without success to sleep in the armchair, his feet propped on the foot of China's bunk. They were ten days out from London and the voyage had become a torment for him.

He gazed at her now in the dim, silvery light of the moon shining through the cabin window. Her face, relaxed in sleep, was flawless; her lips, pale pink and pouting, tempted him; his fingers itched to touch her soft, curving cheek, to feel the weight of that cascading pale blonde hair between his fingers.

Her body was a long, undulating curve beneath the quilt on the bunk. Gabriel remembered the feel of her body against his, recalled with painful clarity the satiny skin of her legs against his own. He could almost feel the beating of her heart beneath her breasts as she had arched against him in the cool, scented darkness.

With a muffled groan, Gabriel threw off his blanket and stalked out of the cabin seeking the calming chill of the ocean air on deck.

By the time China awoke, the moonlight that had so bewitched Gabriel was gone, obscured by gathering stormclouds that filled the midnight sky. The wind had risen, the sea tossed the ship like a child's toy, the salt water lashing at the sides, washing the decks.

Sitting up, she caught at the side of the bunk as the ship rolled. "Gabriel?" she said, squinting into the darkness. "Gabriel?"

There was no reply. China's heart contracted with fear at the thought that he might have gone on deck to offer his help to the crew.

Throwing back her quilt, China swung her legs over the side of the bunk. She should be glad, she thought wryly, that he was gone. The past week had been a nightmare. The tension inside the tiny cabin had been like a weight pressing down on them. It lightened a little when they were apart, when he or she took a turn on the deck. And yet, even with the strain between them that resulted more often than not in frazzled nerves and petty quarreling, China missed him when he left her alone.

The ship rolled as a wave crashed against the side. The diamond-paned window was awash, though whether with rain or ocean spray she could not tell. All that was certain was that they were in the midst of a raging storm and Gabriel was not there, safe, with her.

Feeling around in the darkness, China found a pair of slippers and pulled them on. The wet, she knew, would ruin the fine pink damask, but she didn't care. Inching her way across the cabin, she retrieved her camel-colored velvet mantle and pulled it on over her lawn nightdress. She pulled the hood up over her head and left the cabin to go in search of Gabriel.

She did not see him at first when she emerged on the upper deck. The ship rolled, China grabbed at the railing to steady herself. Waves lashed the deck and the rain whipped across the deck in sheets, blinding the crewmen as they stumbled across it.

Step by step, foot by foot, China made her way along the railing. The rain quickly soaked her mantle, and the weight of it dragged at her. Her slippers were sodden, their smooth soles slipped beneath her, making an already treacherous deck that much more hazardous.

And then, at the other end of the ship, China saw Gabriel. Standing near the bow on the fo'c'sle deck, he and two crewmen worked at the rigging.

"Gabriel!" China shouted, but the howling wind and the roar of the ocean swallowed the sound.

She moved forward, inching toward him along a deck that suddenly seemed miles long. Her eyes never left the tall, broad-shouldered figure ahead of her. Again and again she called to him, though she knew he could not hear her.

And then, at last, he turned toward her. His eyes scanned the deck, passing her then stopping and returning, unable to believe what he saw through the lashing sheets of rain.

He started toward her. China saw him and raised an arm to wave. But as her hand released its hold on the slick wooden railing, a wave crashed over the side and caught her, sweeping her along as it rolled across the deck toward the opposite railing.

China screamed, arms flailing, hampered by the weight of her soaked velvet mantle, as she felt herself being hurled against the railing. The ship rolled, the sea reached for her, greedy fingers of icy salt water grasping at her, trying to snatch her from the railing where she clung desperately, frozen with terror.

She felt the hands grasping at her, trying to pry her hands from the balusters of the railing. Looking up through the rain, she saw Gabriel's face above her. The rain dripped from the brim of his hat and from the broad collar of his greatcoat.

Releasing the railing, China clutched at him. She wept as he lifted her into his arms, holding her tightly, and made his careful way back across the deck and down to their cabin.

Kicking the door shut behind them, Gabriel stood China on her feet, but she swayed, nearly falling, and he guided her to the bed and let her sit on the edge.

"What the hell were you doing out there?" he demanded, the horror he'd felt upon seeing her so nearly swept overboard turning to anger now that she was safely back in the cabin.

China lifted her chin like an obedient child while he untied the neck of her mantle. She stood, shakily, while he pulled the dripping cape from beneath her and tossed it into a soaking pile on the other side of the cabin.

"I went looking for you," she told him simply, sinking onto the bunk once more and lifting her feet as he pulled her ruined slippers from them.

"And you nearly got killed!" he reminded her, pulling off his greatcoat and throwing it, with his hat, on top of her mantle.

"I was worried about you," she cried, wiping her face with the backs of her hands. "I woke up and you were gone."

"I've been sailing for years, China," he told her, "I know how to move on a ship in a storm. You shouldn't have worried about me."

"Well, I'm sorry!" she snapped, perilously close to tears. "Next time I'll not give a damn if you fall overboard!"

Gabriel's anger softened at the sight of her quivering chin. "You should not have risked your life, China," he told her, his tone more gentle. "You could have been killed so easily . . ."

"Then why did you save me?" she challenged, pouting prettily. "Why didn't you let me go overboard? Why didn't you—"

"China, don't," he asked quietly.

"You believe I'm such a horrible person. You hate me so, you—"

"I don't hate you," he disagreed, kneeling beside the bunk, his arms on either side of her.

"Don't you?" she asked, her eyes very wide and very blue.

Gabriel noticed suddenly that the dripping wet lawn of her nightdress clung to her skin, the thin, creamy fabric hiding nothing of her from him. The pink tip of her breast quivered with her muffled sobs as she wept, tears mingling with the salty drops on her cheeks and throat.

Gabriel trembled, hanging his head until it nearly rested on her knee. His desire for her raged like the storm that lashed at the ship. It was a mindless, fierce need as wild as the winds that buffeted them. It was like a force of nature, undeniable, unquenchable.

Uncertain, China laid a trembling hand on his wet sable hair. She was not sure of his emotion; he seemed to shiver though his skin was hot to the touch.

"Gabriel," she breathed, her hand slipping

beneath his chin to raise his face to hers. "Gabriel?"

He looked up at her, his grass green eyes meeting her topaz blue gaze. His eyes fell to her lips where a single droplet of sea water clung to the outer corner.

Slowly he rose, his arms bracketing her. He leaned toward her, his face above hers, and China stretched up to meet him, her lips trembling, her eyes on his mouth.

Together they lay back on the bunk. Their hands, trembling, their fingers, fumbling, peeled away the layers of sodden fabric that separated their skin. China gasped as their bodies touched, his skin and hers, the moisture of the clothes making their flesh cling to one another.

China shuddered, opening herself to him, her arms encircling him, drawing him against her as she arched to meet him. She wanted no preliminaries, no sweet sentiments breathed in her ear, no coy kisses teasing tender lips and lobes. She wanted nothing more than the joining of her flesh and his, the aching, agonizing, exquisite thrusting of his body against hers, inside hers.

She stirred restlessly beneath him as he kissed her throat, her shoulder, her breasts, his hands caressing her, relearning the contours of her body, rediscovering the silken flesh that had haunted his dreams.

"Gabriel," she breathed, driven to tears by the need of him.

Poised above her, Gabriel gazed down at her, watching her face, her eyes, as he took her slowly . . . slowly . . . burying himself in the moist, welcoming depths of her.

China moaned, moving against him, her legs banding his, holding him, urging him wordlessly to love her, unable to bear the thought of parting from him.

The storm that howled outside the ship was no more furious, no more turbulent, than the tempest raging in that narrow bunk as the two of them, filled with the ravening hunger of lovers too long parted, at long last found their way home to one another's arms.

It was quiet when China awoke. The storm was past, the morning sun shone outside the window. She was alone, Gabriel had left the cabin.

Lying in the narrow bunk, China thought about what had happened the night before. Gabriel had saved her life, had kept the angry, tossing sea from snatching her off the sea-swept deck. And then . . .

She closed her eyes and remembered what had happened in the bunk. Driven by a passion as wild and uncontrollable as the storm outside, they had loved each other and then, in the sweet aftermath of their love, had lain together wordlessly in one another's arms until mutual exhaustion had overtaken them.

China knew that the matter of Gabriel's suspicions still lay between them. Even last night, awesome as it had been, could not banish the questions that plagued him and separated them. But she was more certain now that despite his doubts and suspicions, he still cared for her, still desired her, could not bear to lose her.

That knowledge, that certainty, was enough to sustain her and fan the flames of hope in her heart.

Twenty-Two

As the coach that had brought them north from Charles Town turned into the long, curving drive that led to the nearly finished mansion of Fox Meadow, China saw the inn that had been her objective on that night when she'd fled from her captor "Gabriel Fortune." What might have happened, she wondered, if she had reached the inn instead of meeting Ian Leyton on the road.

Ian. China reminded herself of her mother's teaching her that she must not speak, or even think, ill of the dead. But considering what she had gone through because of Ian, it was hard to think well of him.

Now she was coming back to Fox Meadow,

willingly. If only things were better between Gabriel and herself she could also say happily.

She glanced askance at Gabriel who leaned forward eager for his first glimpse of Fox Meadow in several months. Since the night of the storm aboard the ship, the night when their mutual desire had overcome any suspicions, any grudges Gabriel held against her, they had not been together. Gabriel held himself away from her, seemed to regard her more warily than ever before. But China had caught him more than once gazing at her with an earnest look in his green eyes. She knew he was fighting his own desire for her—she knew he longed to touch her, to love her as much as she yearned for him. And that knowledge, scant comfort that it was, sustained her. She clung to her belief that, if only she could find the proof she needed to lay his doubts to rest, they could be together with nothing to mar their love.

As the coach reached the clearing, China leaned forward to see the house. Nearly complete now, it was a long two-story frame house, its roof pierced with dormers spaced along its length. A wide, many-pillared veranda ran along the front, and red-brick chimneys rose at either end and in the center of the white-painted house. Behind the house, separate buildings housed the well, the kitchen, and the laundry.

"It's finished," China said, surprised, remembering the skeleton framework she had seen when Gabriel had brought her here before.

"Almost," Gabriel agreed. "Some of the woodwork inside needs to be finished and some of the painting. Some furniture has yet to be delivered. But it should be livable."

Leaving the coach, China followed Gabriel up onto the veranda and into the house. The foyer was pale blue. A twisting staircase of black walnut rose up along one wall, turned, and climbed up to the second floor. A parlor to the left was painted in oyster and slate blue. A dining room to the right was walled with pale gold paneling carved with arches and fluted pilasters. A brass and crystal chandelier hung over a long, gleaming table. The chairs were upholstered with gold damask that matched the draperies at the tall windows.

"It's beautiful," China told Gabriel, following him into other rooms, some unpainted, most largely unfurnished.

Gabriel nodded absently. His eyes seemed fixed on something far away, and China wondered, with a twinge of jealousy, if he were thinking of the life he had planned to live here—with Rebecca and their children.

She forced such thoughts from her mind. They would do nothing but set her to brooding on things she could not change. It would do no good to ask Gabriel his thoughts. Despite the passion they shared for one another, there was a line between them she did not dare step across.

As their baggage was being brought into the house, Gabriel directed the servants to take the bags upstairs, China's to one bedroom, his to another. China looked away, hiding her expression. She had hoped, after the way they had been together aboard the ship, that Gabriel would keep her close to him at Fox Meadow. Apparently that was not to be.

"I'm going to go look around," he told her. "If you need anything, just ask. There aren't many servants, but I'm sure a maid can be found to help you."

China nodded, not trusting herself to speak. She watched as he strode away, then asked a maid to take her to her room where she could have privacy in case her emotions got the better of her.

Gabriel did not return, even as it began to grow dark. China's dinner was brought to her in her room, and water was brought for a bath before the fire in her bedroom fireplace. The scullery maid, Bab, who had been drafted to help China, took away her dinner dishes and later returned to help her out of her clothes and into her nightdress.

"Has Gabriel come back?" China asked.

"Oh aye," the girl assured her. "The master came back hours since. He was in the study last I heard. Should I ask him to come up?"

Unsure of what Gabriel's response would be to such a summons, China declined the girl's offer and dismissed her. Alone in her room, China went to the fireplace and added another small log to the fire. She felt cold, but it had nothing to do with the night air. The chill was in her heart, for she believed that wherever Gabriel was, the sight of Fox Meadow had brought back memories of his crewmen—the friends who had gone to their deaths on the gallows in Williamsburg. And those memories, she feared, had brought back all the suspicions and doubts he harbored against her.

The room Gabriel had allotted her was painted pale blue. The windows and four-poster bed were hung with crewelwork of exquisite roses, leaves, and vines on a rich creamy background. From the windows, China could see the wide sweep of lawn stretching down to the river. The dock was there, but no ship was moored at it. China had noticed it but had not dared to ask Gabriel what had become of the *Golden Fortune*. She feared that Governor Spotswood had confiscated it during his raid on Fox Meadow. If that was the case, then Gabriel could add one more grievance to those he already harbored against her, and she did not care to know about that.

As she stood at the window gazing out while the darkness gathered around the house, obscuring the view, China knew there was nothing for her to do but go to bed and trust that eventually the truth would out and she and Gabriel could be together and happy.

The fire had nearly died when she woke up. It was dark; even the moonlight was obscured by the clouds gathering in the night sky. China felt perilously close to tears. She needed Gabriel's arm around her. She felt so alone, so frightened. The great, unfinished house lay all about her, silent, dark, unfamiliar.

Pushing back the coverlet, China slipped out of bed and pulled her combing mantle over her thin silk nightdress. Leaving her room, she found herself in the upstairs corridor where a candelabrum burned on a table near the head of the stairs, its candles nearly guttered out.

China hesitated outside Gabriel's door. If she knocked, would he turn her away? Would he be cold to her? Would he understand the emotions that had driven her to seek him out?

She knocked softly at the door. There was no reply. Perhaps he, unlike her, had no trouble sleeping. She wondered if he would be angry if she woke him up.

Holding her breath, she pressed down the latch and opened the door. "Gabriel?" she said tentatively as she stepped across the threshold. "I'm sorry to wake you but I—"

She stopped. The room was lit only by the fire burning in the fireplace. The bed had been turned down but it was obviously unslept in.

Frowning, China left the room. Bab had said Gabriel was down in the study. Surely he could not still be there. That was hours before.

China descended the stairs. The study lay at the back of the house, the doorway nestled under the sweep of the walnut staircase. But its door stood open and the room was pitch dark—deserted.

Looking around, China wondered where Gabriel might be. He wasn't in his room, he wasn't in the study. She noticed a candle burning on the table near the front door. If Gabriel was outside, she had no hope of finding him. He—

He appeared suddenly as the front door opened. Framed in the doorway, half-lit by the guttering candle on the table, he leaned against the doorjamb and gazed out at the darkness. His head was bowed; he seemed to China to be bearing the weight of the world on his broad shoulders.

China stepped back into the shadow of the staircase. The moment seemed so private, so intimate, she did not dare interrupt it. She waited, silent, still, until Gabriel closed the door and mounted the stairs, his footsteps echoing over her head as he ascended.

Above, in the hallway, Gabriel looked toward China's door at the end of the hall. His impulse was to go to her. He wanted nothing more than to lie in the darkness with her, hold her, love her, tell her that he loved her. But he could not. Not until he knew the truth. He did not dare let himself love her completely, trust her, believe her. Not yet. He remembered all too well the pain he'd felt when they'd told him she had been the one whose treachery had led to the deaths of his men and very nearly his own. He could not trust her again, love her again, give her his still-mending heart, only to find she was as treacherous as he feared.

Resigned to a long, lonely wait until he knew the truth, Gabriel let himself into his room and prepared for a long night in his cold, unwelcoming bed.

China heard the click of his doorlatch as Gabriel went into his room. She could not go to him now. She knew what troubled him and she knew her presence would do nothing to ease his mind or calm his fears. She could only wait now.

But, she told herself as she climbed the stairs to return to her own room, as long as he kept her there at Fox Meadow, there was hope. And as long as she had hope to cling to, she could bear to wait. Resigned, hopeful, she went back to her room and climbed back into bed.

The situation at Fox Meadow remained the same for the next week. Gabriel was kind, gentle, considerate, but distant. He could not bring himself to abandon his suspicions—the evidence against China was too damning to allow that—nor could he look any deeper into the matter. He was afraid of discovering that she was guilty, because then he would have to punish her for he had sworn to avenge the deaths of his crewmen.

China lay late in bed in the mornings. She preferred to wait until Gabriel had breakfasted and left the house before she came downstairs. Much as she loved Gabriel, much as her eyes hungered for the sight of him, it was far too painful to be near him, see him, speak to him, and not be able to touch him. It was better, she decided, to keep herself apart from him until they could be together completely with no barriers between their hearts, their minds, or their bodies.

"Has your master gone out?" China asked

Bab, who had come to take away the damp towels from China's bath and to help her dress.

"No, milady," Bab replied, for Gabriel had instructed his indentured servants in how to address his guest. "He's below, in the front parlor, with the man from the ship."

"The ship?" China asked, smoothing the skirts of her cherry-colored gown. She picked up her brush and began brushing her freshly washed hair. "What ship?"

"At the dock, milady. She docked in the wee hours of the morning."

Laying aside her brush, China went to the window. Above the tree line at the far end of the lawn, the skeletal masts of a ship rose skyward.

"Whose is she, do you know?" China asked the maid.

"No, milady," the girl replied.

China went and sat before Bab while the girl pinned up her hair, weaving a cherry ribbon through it and leaving tiny curls to frame her face. A hope began inside her, a hope that the ship had brought news that might clear her. If only someone would come forward and tell the truth, admit that the woman who had given the deposition that had damned Gabriel and his men was not her but an impostor.

China closed her eyes, not quite daring to hope and yet praying it would be so. She loved Gabriel. She believed with all her heart that he loved her in return. If only the shadow of his suspicion could be done away with, then nothing would cloud their joy.

Leaving her room, China went down the corridor to the head of the stairs. From there she could see the parlor door. She could hear low, masculine voices speaking earnestly. But she could not make out their words.

She hesitated at the head of the staircase. No doubt Gabriel would come to her if his guest brought any news that concerned her. But she could not stand the suspense, the not knowing. Taking a deep breath, she descended the stairs and went to the parlor doorway.

Gabriel stood halfway across the room facing her. Dressed in tall leather jackboots, brown breeches and waistcoat, a full-sleeved linen shirt, and a lace-edged cravat, he looked very like he had on the night China had met him. The morning sun filled the room with light, glinting in the sable depths of his hair which was brushed back and tied at the nape of his neck with a brown grosgrain ribbon.

He did not at first see China. His attention was fixed on the man who stood before him.

China glanced toward his guest. He was much smaller than Gabriel. His hair was ebony black, and the hand that moved, emphasizing his words, was burned dark by constant exposure to the sun. He was dressed in gaudy colors, his coat trimmed with gold buttons and lavish gold braid, his breeches of bottle green velvet, his cuffs awash with lace, his waistcoat, which showed when he swept up one hand in an expansive gesture, was rich red damask.

China thought she knew him. The sight of him, even from the back, struck a chord of memory. At that moment Gabriel noticed her there. The expression on his face made his guest pause in what he was saying and turn toward the door.

China found herself gazing into the glittering onyx eyes of her first pirate captor, Le Corbeau.

His dark eyes glinted as they swept over her from head to foot. His expression, when his gaze once again rested on her face, was disdainful.

"You will forgive me, madame, if I say I am not pleased to see you again."

He looked back at Gabriel. "I am disappointed in you, *mon ami*. When you left New Providence for London, you vowed to punish this woman for her betrayal. Have you forgotten the feel of the noose about your neck? Have you forgotten the last, gasping breaths of your men? Their souls cry out to you for vengeance, but what do you do instead? You bring this woman back to your home."

"She told me she was innocent," Gabriel

defended. "She swore to me she did not betray me."

"And you believed her!" Le Corbeau's tone was filled with sarcasm. "*Mon Dieu*! Are you so blinded by your lust for her that you accept her lies as truths? What else do you expect her to say?"

"I will not take action against her until I see proof of her guilt," Gabriel vowed stubbornly.

"Proof!" The swarthy pirate swore under his breath. "Look in your looking glass. Look at the scar on your face where the knife slipped when the noose was cut from your neck. Look at the unmarked graves in Williamsburg where your men lie buried, the hemp still about their throats. There is your proof!"

"It's a lie!" China cried, entering the room to confront him. "I do not know who betrayed Gabriel, but I swear to you I did not."

"Then who did?" Le Corbeau challenged.

"I don't know!" China felt a desperate need to make Gabriel believe her but knew there was no way she could. "I don't know."

Le Corbeau looked from one of them to the other. His expression did not hide his contempt for China, whom he considered a traitoress, nor his disgust for Gabriel, whose failure to punish her betrayal was a shameful weakness. Had it been up to him, he would have drawn his saber and killed her on the spot, but it was not for him to exact vengeance for the deaths of Gabriel's crewmen. Gabriel had sworn to do it but had fallen under the woman's spell.

"I have brought the goods you wanted," he told Gabriel after a long moment's silence. "I have been to France and to Martinique. The holds of the *Golden Fortune* are filled with furniture, carpets, ornament, fabrics . . . Everything you wanted to finish this house."

"The *Golden Fortune*?" China asked, looking at Gabriel.

He nodded. "Le Corbeau's Black Pearl was sunk in a fight with a British man o' war. I have sold him the *Golden Fortune*. My pirating days are over. That was part of the bargain for my pardon from Charles Eden."

He glanced at Le Corbeau. "How soon can the goods be unloaded?"

"I'll set the men to it right away," the swarthy pirate told him. "But you'd better keep her out of sight." He jerked his head toward China. "Some of the men used to be your men, and some of my men were friends of your dead crewmen. If they discovered she was here, it might not be pleasant—for any of us."

Without a word or a look for China, Le Corbeau turned and left the parlor and the house to return to his ship and set his men to unloading Gabriel's goods.

Twenty-Three

China remained in her room the rest of the day. From her window, she could see the constant stream of men and carts carrying the cargo of the *Golden Fortune* to two storehouses at the forest's edge where it would be stored until the house was ready for it.

Among the men making their way back and forth from the storehouses China recognized one or two from Le Corbeau's Black Pearl and a few from her voyage aboard the *Golden Fortune* when Gabriel had brought her from New Providence to North Carolina.

Watching them, China shuddered. She remembered what Le Corbeau had said in the parlor . . . that the men would not take it well if they knew Gabriel was sheltering a woman they looked upon as a traitoress. In their eyes she had committed the cardinal sin—she had betrayed her lover, their captain, to the authorities. She had been the cause of several of their number going to dance the jig of death on the public gallows. For that, in their eyes, she deserved death.

So rather than risk their discovering her presence, China remained in her room, shut away from prying eyes, trying, without much success, to concentrate on a book. She wondered where Gabriel was, and when Bab came with her lunch she asked her, but the maid did not know.

By dinner time, when Bab brought China's evening meal and lit more candles to dispel the gathering darkness, China asked her again.

"Where is your master? Do you know?"

"Aye, milady," the girl replied, drawing the draperies at the windows. "He's gone to the cottage for supper."

"The cottage?" China remembered the little cottage in the forest where Gabriel had first taken her when they'd reached North Carolina from New Providence. "Why is he eating his supper at the cottage?"

"His friend is there, the small, dark man . . . Le . . . Le . . . " She shrugged. "Whatever his name is."

"Le Corbeau," China supplied. She frowned, thinking of Gabriel there at the cottage, no doubt listening to Le Corbeau harangue him for keeping her with him.

Bab cleared her throat, and China, realizing she was waiting to be dismissed, smiled and told the girl she would ring for her when she was ready to be undressed and prepared for bed.

Ignoring her dinner, China got up and went to the fireplace. It seemed so cold, winter was fast approaching, but China knew the chill she felt had little to do with the season. She was afraid, for she had seen the scorn in Le Corbeau's dark eyes. He hated her for what he believed she'd done. But he was willing to leave the matter alone . . . to leave it to Gabriel's judgment, faulty as he obviously thought that was. But Gabriel's men, those few who had survived Spotswood's raid on Fox Meadow, and the crewmen of Le Corbeau's Black Pearl who now sailed aboard the *Golden Fortune* might not be so willing to leave her fate to their former captain and friend. They might wish to take matters into their own hands.

She rubbed her arms. The empty house seemed cavernous and lonely, filled with danger. She wished Gabriel would come back from the cottage. Only when he was back in the house would she feel some measure of safety, of security.

Returning to the little table Bab had set, she picked at her food but it seemed tasteless, unappetizing. She left the table and took up her book once more, but the words blurred together, the sentences had no meaning.

"Oh Lord," she breathed, staring into the flickering fire, "please let Gabriel come back soon. I don't like being here without him, not when those men are out there, those men who would like to see me dead!"

As she sat there, wishing for Gabriel's return, China heard the front door slam. Bolting out of her chair, she flew out of her room and down the hall to the head of the stairs.

"Gabriel?" she called, leaning over the railing. "Oh, Gabriel, I hoped you would come—"

She stopped, horrified. Below in the entrance hall, a man she recognized as one of the crewmen from the *Golden Fortune* stood looking up at her.

He stared, mouth agape, as though he were seeing a ghost. "You!" he breathed, his dark eyes narrowing. "Hell and damnation!"

China's heart froze inside her. Snatching up her skirts, she fled back up the corridor to her room. She slammed the door behind her and twisted the key in the lock.

Leaning against the door, China tried to

catch her breath. She listened, expecting to hear the pounding of footfalls climbing the stairs, coming down the hall. She waited, terrified, thinking that at any moment she would hear the crash of a shoulder against the door, the splintering of wood.

She waited. The ticking of the mantel clock was like the beating of a heart in the silent room. China pressed her ear to the door. She heard nothing. She longed to look out, to see if the man had gone away, but she feared that he might be lurking outside, waiting for her, dagger in hand, thirsting for her blood.

Trembling, nearly weeping, she sank to the floor and sat there, her weight against the door. Would the nightmare never end? Would she ever manage to prove herself innocent?

"Gabriel," she breathed, her head back, her arms wrapped about herself. "Gabriel, come back, please!"

But it was more than two hours later that Gabriel returned. He was weary, tired in mind and body, worn out by Le Corbeau's grumblings about China. In vain had he tried to defend her, to tell him he had doubts about her guilt. There was no convincing the pirate from Martinique. China's guilt was a foregone conclusion, Le Corbeau declared, and Gabriel's failure to punish her might very well cost him the respect he enjoyed among the pirate fraternity.

Gabriel shrugged out of his greatcoat and tossed it and his tricorne onto the settee in the entrance hall. The house was silent. He imagined China had long since gone to bed.

As he crossed the entrance hall to the staircase, he noticed the muddy footprints on the hall carpet.

They were large, the prints of jackboots, not of the kind of shoes worn by the servants in the house. Gabriel felt a *frisson* of fear. One of the men from the *Golden Fortune* had come into the house. Though their orders had been to carry the goods from the ship to the storehouses, it was clear that someone had disobeyed.

China! Suddenly the silence in the house seemed ominous, threatening. Could they have found out she was there? Could one of the men have come to exact payment for the deaths they blamed on China?

Galvanized into action, Gabriel bounded up the stairs. "China!" he shouted. "China! Where are you?"

China, above in her room, had heard the door open downstairs. She had heard the pounding footfalls mounting the stairs. Her heart pounding, she held her breath believing the end had come.

And then, like the answer to a prayer, she heard Gabriel calling her name. Scrambling to her feet, she twisted the key in the lock and flung wide the door.

Gabriel was there, his chiseled features filled with worry, fear for her safety. He opened his arms to her and she ran to him, throwing herself into his strong, protective embrace.

"Gabriel, oh, Gabriel!" she wept, the tears slipping down her cheeks and staining the dark brown cloth of his coat. "I was so frightened! I wanted you to come back!"

Gabriel held her, his heart pounding. His relief that she was safe overshadowed every other emotion. He had not realized until that moment how frightened he had been for her.

"I saw the footprints in the hall downstairs," he told her, his face against the crown of her head. "I thought . . . I was afraid . . ." He let out his breath in a long, low sigh. "But you're all right." He held her out at arm's length, his green eyes sweeping over her filled with concern. "You are all right, aren't you?"

China nodded. "I'm all right. I'm just frightened. There was a man here. I heard the door slam. I thought you'd come back. I went to the stairs." She shivered and went back into his arms. "There was a man there. I recognized him from the *Golden Fortune*. I don't know his name." She drew a deep, shuddering breath. "Oh, Gabriel! He stared at me with such hatred! I ran back to my room and locked the door. I expected him to come after me, to break down the door and kill me. God! I was so frightened!"

"But he didn't come after you?" Gabriel asked.

China shook her head. "No, he went away." She trembled in Gabriel's arms. "I prayed for you to come back. I felt so alone, so vulnerable, without you."

Gabriel held her close, his arms tight around her. "I'm sorry I stayed away so long," he told her softly. "Le Corbeau will be sailing in the morning."

"He wants you to kill me, doesn't he?" China asked so quietly Gabriel could scarcely hear her.

He hesitated, not wanting to answer her, not wanting to tell her, but knowing she knew the truth only too well.

"Aye," he answered at last. "He believes you betrayed me to Spotswood. He believes you're to blame for the hangings in Williamsburg."

China held her breath. Time seemed to stand still as she asked him breathlessly: "Do you believe that as well?"

Gabriel's arms tightened about her. His lips caressed her hair, his fingers tangled in the silken skeins hanging down her back. "I want to believe you're innocent, China. You cannot imagine how much I want to believe it."

China knew it was true. She knew how he was torn between his doubts and his desires. She knew he could not abandon his vow to avenge the deaths of the loyal crewmen who had died in Williamsburg and yet he could not bring himself to believe that she had betrayed him. It was an unenviable dilemma.

She held him, her arms as tight about him as his were about her. They stood there, in the darkness of the corridor, the only light the dim glow filtering up the staircase and spilling out through China's open doorway. She took strength, security, from him and he held her, suspending for those few precious moments the doubts and suspicions that made his every waking hour a misery.

And then, in the silence, they heard the shouts. China looked up at Gabriel and found him scowling, listening to the sounds from outside.

"Stay here," he told her, releasing her from his embrace.

He strode off down the hall, entering his room only long enough to fetch the long, curving cutlass he had carried aboard the *Golden Fortune*.

China, left behind in the hallway, could

not bear to spend another moment alone, locked in the room where she'd spent that long, frightening day. Lifting the trailing skirts of her gown, she followed him down the corridor and down the stairs.

A shocked gasp escaped her as Gabriel, cutlass in hand, flung open the front door. The crew of the *Golden Fortune*, nearly one hundred strong, thronged the lawn before the mansion. Some carried torches that cast a flickering light over them. Many were armed, some with daggers, some with cutlasses, a few with muskets and boarding axes, the tools of their lethal trade.

"What do you want?" Gabriel shouted. "Go back to the ship!"

"You know what we want!" a one-legged pirate called back, brandishing the ax he held in his hand. "We want your woman! We want justice for the men she killed!"

"Give 'er to us!" another man demanded. "We'll give 'er a taste of the rope!"

"I swore to avenge the deaths of those men," Gabriel reminded them. "And I will!"

"When!" a young, blond gunner asked. "When you're tired of laying with her?"

A chorus of guffaws followed. But then one of the men caught sight of China in the hall behind Gabriel. The laughter turned to muttering, the muttering to cursing. China's cheeks flamed, her ears burned as she was hailed by a hundred voices, reviled, pelted with insults and obscenities.

"Give her to us!" the one-legged pirate repeated. "If you've no stomach for the task, we have! We'll see she pays the price for what she did."

"After we've finished with her, she'll thank us for killing her," a tall, black-haired rigger predicted, smirking.

Gabriel stepped toward them. "I'm telling you all, damn your eyes, that any man who sets foot in this house will go through me! Most of you know me, or know of me. Anyone who feels like fighting me, step forward now."

The men grumbled among themselves, but not one of them cared to put Gabriel's prowess to the test. They glared at him, mumbled, cursed him and threatened, but no one took up his challenge.

"Go back to the ship," he ordered. "You're to sail in the morning. I tell you now, I mean to know the truth of what happened in Williamsburg. And when I know that truth, I will see the traitor punished—whoever he—or she—might be."

There was more grumbling, a few arguments, but after a few moments the men turned back toward the docks. Gabriel watched from the veranda, cutlass in hand, until they were no more than glowing torchlights in the darkness. Only then did he return to the house and lock the door behind him.

He found China crumpled on the settee in the hall, trembling violently. She cried out when he touched her.

"It's over," he told her. "They've gone."

With a cry, China threw herself into his arms. "I can't bear any more of it," she told him. "The hatred, the threats. I can't bear it, Gabriel!"

"In the morning they'll be gone," he promised. "Now go up to your room. I'll send Bab up to help you to bed."

"No," she whispered, her arms tight about his neck. "I don't want to be alone."

"I won't be far away. Go up, now."

Reluctantly, China obeyed. But she ordered Bab to leave a candle burning—the darkness was too filled with loneliness and fear—and she lay a long time in her bed before finally falling asleep.

Dawn was still several hours away when China cried out. Caught up in the horror of a nightmare, she felt herself seized by dozens of hands, borne to the ground, beaten, ravished, abused in a hundred ways. And then she was lifted, half-carried, half-dragged to a tree. She felt the rough hemp of the noose as it was forced over her head. She felt the painful press of the knot against her neck.

She was held up in the air while the rope was thrown over a high limb, and then she fell, her feet dangling inches above the ground. She was choking, choking, her lungs burning, bursting . . .

She screamed, tearing at the bedclothes, pulling at the neck of her silk nightdress that had twisted with her writhings and tightened on her throat.

As her scream echoed in the dark room, the door burst open. Gabriel appeared, cutlass in hand. He had spent the night in a chair dragged to China's door. He could not be certain the men of the *Golden Fortune* would obey him. He was no longer, after all, their captain, and he knew that many believed he had fallen under China's spell and forgotten the men who had lost their lives on the gallows.

To his relief he saw no one in the room. Only China, writhing on her bed, tangled in the bedclothes, clawing at them frantically.

Laying aside his weapon, he went to her, shook her, called her name to awaken her.

China came awake with a shrill scream of pure terror. She stared with horrified eyes at Gabriel. Tears stained her cheeks. She trembled violently, her teeth chattering as she grasped at his arms.

"It was only a dream," Gabriel soothed. "Only a dream. You're safe. China, do you hear me?"

Shuddering, gasping, she stared at him for a long, uncomprehending moment before she finally nodded.

"A dream," she whispered wonderingly. "It was so real. They caught me, those men. They tore at my clothes, they hurt me, they . . ." She raised her eyes to his face. "They hanged me. Oh, Gabriel, I felt the rope. I couldn't breathe. I felt as if my lungs would burst."

Gabriel listened sympathetically. He knew that sensation only too well. Stroking her hair, he held her against him.

"It's over now," he murmured. "All over. Try not to think of it."

China nodded. For the first time, she realized he was still in his clothes. "You haven't been to bed," she said wonderingly.

"I brought a chair out into the hall," he replied. "I was outside your door. Just in case."

She saw the cutlass lying on the carpet beside the bed. "I did not know you were there. Thank you."

"You don't have to thank me," he told her, laying her back against her pillows. "Now try to go back to sleep."

But as he would have left her, China caught at his sleeve.

"Don't go," she begged. "Stay here with me, please, Gabriel. Don't leave me alone."

Gabriel gazed down at her. She was so

frightened, so vulnerable, and so very beautiful. Nodding, he went to the door and closed it, turning the key in the lock. He retrieved his cutlass from the carpet and propped it within easy reach of the bed. Then, with only the glowing embers of the fire lighting the room, he pulled off his clothes and slid into the high bed beside her.

As they lay there together, their arms about each other, Gabriel felt the hot, urgent arousal she had always evoked in him. He stroked a hand along the petal-soft skin of her thigh, caressing her leg, her hip. Slipping a hand into the curve at the back of her knee, he drew her leg over his hip, molding her body to his, feeling the trembling start in her.

Gently, tenderly, he loved her, his mouth moving over her skin, kissing, tasting, arousing her to a fever pitch. By the time he moved above her, by the time their bodies became one and moved together, China was wild with desire for him. Everything, every fear, every worry, every terror, was blotted from her mind. She knew nothing but the heat of him, the warmth of his skin, the hot, electric caress of him, as he brought her to a shattering climax that drove her to the edge of ecstasy—and beyond.

Twenty-Four

The *Golden Fortune* set sail with the dawn, and China stood on the veranda watching its snowy sails take it away down the Neuse in the direction of the Pamlico Sound.

"Relieved?" Gabriel asked, coming up behind China and sliding his arms around her.

China leaned back against him. "Very," she told him. "I hope by the time he comes back . . ." She said no more.

"You hope all this is behind us?" he prompted.

China nodded. "There must be a way, Gabriel, to prove my innocence. I thank you for protecting me last night, for defending me against those men . . ." She shivered at the memory of those weapons brandished in the torchlight, of the insults and epithets and threats. "But I want you to be certain, in your heart, in your mind, that I was never so treacherous, so wicked, that I would lie with you, love you, all the while knowing I had signed your death warrant and that of your men."

Gabriel stepped away. He wished he could tell her he harbored no doubt any longer. He longed to reassure her and tell her he believed in her innocence.

Anxious to change the subject, he told her, "As long as Le Corbeau has taken the *Golden Fortune* and gone, I'm going to Bath to see Charles Eden."

"Must you go now?" China asked. "Can't it wait a few days, or weeks?"

Gabriel smiled, his leaf green eyes fond as they rested on her face. "It could wait, I suppose," he admitted. "But the sooner I see him about my pardon, the sooner I can stop worrying that Spotswood will discover I've come back and send men after me. He still could, you know. But once I've been pardoned I'll be safe—so long as I don't go a'pirating, and so long as I stay out of Virginia."

"Oh, all right," China agreed. "Go then, if you have to. But don't stay away too long."

Gabriel agreed, and early the next morning he rode away leaving China alone, standing in the drive, watching until he'd disappeared from view.

By late afternoon, China was bored—bored and lonely. She wandered from room to room like a lost child, longing for the hours to pass and bring Gabriel's return closer, yet dreading the coming night when she would be there in that great house without him.

Deciding to take a walk before supper, China dispatched Bab to her room for a cloak. The girl returned a few minutes later with a black velvet mantle lined with white satin.

"Is there anything else you need, milady?" the girl asked.

China shook her head. "Nothing. I'm going for a walk."

"Would you want some company?"

"No, thank you, Bab. I feel like being alone."

The maid eyed her uneasily. She doubted that the master would approve of his lady wandering about in the forest alone, but there was little she could do about it. It had been only a few years since the attacks by the Tuscarora Indians on settlements on both the Neuse and Pamlico Rivers. And though Indian attacks were few, they happened, as did confrontations between settlers and black bears in the forests.

Even so, there was nothing she could do.

But she could not help a feeling of foreboding as China walked away up the drive.

China wandered along the drive following the ruts left by wagon and coach wheels. The hoofprints of Gabriel's horse were still clear and distinct, and the sight of them made China long even more for his return.

She walked along, the house disappearing as the forest thickened around her. She was about to turn back when she noticed the cottage half hidden by the trees in front of her.

The sight of it brought back a breathtaking array of memories. She remembered the night Gabriel had first brought her to Fox Meadow, her escape during the storm, her flight through the forest, her meeting with Ian Leyton . . .

Lost in the past, she was nearly upon the little cottage before she noticed the black coach standing behind it, horses hitched and ready.

China stepped back, startled. Gabriel had ridden off on horseback. The coach was not one she had seen in the stables of Fox Meadow. He had said nothing about letting anyone stay in the cottage. Who then could be . . .

She felt the man's presence before she saw him. Whirling about, she found herself face to face with the one-legged pirate who had been among the most vocal in demanding she be punished for the deaths of Gabriel's men.

"So, ye saved us the trouble of comin' to git ya," he grinned, showing her a mouth full of broken and rotted teeth.

Petrified, China stared. She was unable to run, unable to move, unable even to scream.

"What've ye got there, Sylas?" a gruff voice demanded. "That's not the cap'n's bitch, is it?"

"Aye," the first pirate confirmed. "She come to us."

China looked toward the second man. It was the young blond gunner who'd also been among the men mobbing Fox Meadow's lawn the night before.

He smiled slowly, slyly, his dark blue eyes glinting with a light that made China's skin crawl. "Mighty civil," he agreed. Reaching out, he fingered the silvery curl lying over China's shoulder. "Mighty pretty, too."

Eyes flashing, China slapped the hand away. "Don't touch me, damn you!" she snarled.

"Think yer too good fer the likes of me?" he growled. "Think because Fortune's the master of this place that makes him fit to lay with you?" He seized China's wrist and yanked her against him. "Before we're done with you, you won't be fit to lie with a bilge rat!"

Burying his hand in her hair, the pirate

jerked back her head. His lips slanted across hers and he tried in vain to part her clenched teeth with his tongue.

China struggled against him, gagging, feeling the sour bile rising in her throat. She was powerless against him, her strength was nothing against his.

But suddenly he was gone. China stumbled, nearly falling, and saw the blond pirate sprawl on the ground ten feet away.

"I said you were not to touch her," Le Corbeau snarled. "And I mean what I say."

"You only want 'er for yerself!" the blond pirate accused. "Yer as bad as Fortune! You don't want 'er to pay fer what she did. You only want to lie with 'er an'—"

The pistol shot echoed in the forest. The horses hitched to the coach reared and whinnied. The blond gunner jerked as a crimson flower blossomed on the front of his dirty linen shirt.

"My God!" China gasped, stepping back.

Le Corbeau tucked his pistol back into his belt. "The man's been trouble since he signed aboard," he said to no one in particular. "He was a budding mutineer, and I will not have mutineers aboard my ship."

He looked around at the half-dozen pirates who stood staring at the corpse at their feet. "Drag him into the forest and let's be off, *mes amis*. We never know who might have heard that shot."

Three pirates seized their fallen shipmate and hauled him off toward the underbrush. China watched, horrified, until they disappeared, then turned her attention back to the pirate from Martinique.

"Aren't they going to bury him?" she asked.

"We haven't the time," Le Corbeau replied casually. "It doesn't matter, there are scavengers aplenty in these forests—bears, foxes." He shrugged.

China recoiled, repelled by the thought of a man being left that way. But she had other worries just then, more important concerns than the final resting place of a pirate who had just assaulted her.

"What are you doing here?" she demanded of the swarthy pirate.

Le Corbeau smiled unpleasantly. "Come now, *chérie*, false-hearted you might be, but you are not stupid. We have come for you. The *Golden Fortune* is anchored in the Neuse where it cannot be seen from the road. We left it there and came back for you. Since Gabriel Fortune cannot bring himself to deal with you, we must."

"I'm innocent, I tell you!" China cried. "Why won't you believe me?"

"The evidence is against you, I'm afraid. But fear not. We are not barbarians. You will have a trial."

"A trial! With pirates as my judges? What

kind of trial would that be?"

Le Corbeau's black eyes glinted like faceted jet. "The same kind of trial that Gabriel and his men had in Williamsburg, I suppose, a pirate before Spotswood's tribunal."

China stared at him for a moment, two. Then suddenly, without warning, she whirled and in a swirl of black velvet and white satin she ran off toward the mansion that seemed miles away.

She knew it was futile; she'd known that before she began to run, but she had to try. There was always the chance that someone had heard the shot and would come to investigate. If only Bab had heard—if only she had sent men to find China in the forest.

But there was no help for her. She had not gone fifty yards when Le Corbeau, small, wiry, and fleet of foot as he was, caught up with her and, with a blow of one hand, sent her tumbling to the ground in a flurry of velvet and satin and lace-trimmed petticoats.

China lay there, sprawled at his feet. She glared up at him, topaz eyes ablaze, while he regarded her with amusement and not a little admiration.

"Do not think I do not understand what Gabriel sees in you, *chérie*. You are as spirited as you are beautiful. Gabriel will be a long time recovering from losing you. But then, perhaps that does not move you. You are used to leaving a trail of destruction behind you, are you not?"

"I told you," China hissed, "I did not betray Gabriel and his—"

"That is not what I meant," the ebony-eyed pirate interrupted. "I was speaking of London, of your husband and the Duc de Fonvielle."

China felt the blood rush from her face, leaving her deathly pale. "How did you know . . ." she breathed.

"I was in Paris," he told her. "There was talk. They said the Duc de Fonvielle had been murdered in London. He was killed, so they said, over a woman. Rumor had it that he had driven the woman's husband to take his own life so that he might possess her. Then, having gained possession of the woman, the duc himself was killed by a mysterious man who took her away on a ship bound for the New World." Le Corbeau smiled wryly. "They said the woman's name was Leyton. Lady China Leyton, the daughter of the former Baron Clairmont. I must say, I was not particularly surprised to see you causing such mayhem. I remembered well your beauty—Meghan Gordon."

China closed her eyes. She had not known until that moment that Damien was dead. Cold-hearted though it might seem, she could not be sorry.

"Let me go," she asked him softly. "Please. There has been enough misery."

The swarthy pirate chuckled. "Let you go? If I did that, your misery might end but mine would just begin. My men would mutiny." He shook his head. "No, *chérie*, you must come along. It is your fate—and mine."

Pushing herself to her feet, China brushed the dirt and twigs from her gown and mantle. She knew it was futile to try to run away. She was no match for the pirate. Her mantle and the voluminous skirts of her gown and petticoat would make her easy prey for any one of the men who watched her and their captain. And even if she reached the mansion, even if the indentured servants who toiled there defended her, how could she set them to fighting against these savage, well-armed men to whom killing was a way of life? There was no help for it. She would have to go with them and pray for some miracle to deliver her from them.

Laying her hand in the outstretched hand of Le Corbeau, China was led to the coach and bundled inside. As two pirates climbed up onto the box and the others held fast to the back of the coach, China bit her lip to stifle the tears of fear and despair that welled into her eyes. She would not let them see how terrified she was of them, she would not let them know that she feared for her very life. Even if they condemned her to death—

which was what she expected—she would die rather than let them know how their very presence filled her with mortal terror.

As the driver slapped the reins and the coach rocked and turned in a wide arc, China tried not to think of her nightmare of the night before—the nightmare that now showed every sign of coming true.

Gabriel turned his horse into the drive, riding beneath the overhanging branches, feeling filled with confidence and hope. Charles Eden had been perfectly willing to grant him a pardon under the Act of Grace. He was a free man in North Carolina, anything he had done as Gabriel Fortune was forgiven him. And though the governor had warned him that he should stay out of Virginia, for Spotswood, no respecter of colonial boundaries, could not be counted upon to respect the pardon either, Gabriel felt as though he had been reborn into a new life.

He galloped up the drive eager to tell China what had happened in Bath. It had taken less time than he thought—he wondered if she would be surprised to see him back a day after he'd left.

He dismounted in front of the mansion and, fixing his horse's reins to a hitching post, all but ran up the stairs and across the veranda.

"China!" he bellowed as he flung open the door and crossed the entrance hall. "China!"

There was no answer. His voice echoed up the stairwell. The house was silent around him, no servants came to meet him. Gabriel felt the pricklings of foreboding snaking up his spine.

"Bab!" he shouted, his voice impatient, angry. "Bab! Where the hell are you?"

The scullery maid who had been promoted to China's lady's maid appeared reluctantly at the head of the stairs. Her mob-capped head was lowered, her hands were clasped in the skirts of her linsey-woolsey gown. Her eyes, when she dared fix them on her master, were red. It was obvious she had been crying.

"Where is your mistress?" Gabriel demanded. "And where is everyone else?"

"They're hidin', sir," the girl said so softly he could scarcely hear her.

"Your mistress?" he questioned.

"No, sir. The others. They're hidin'. Milady . . ." She twisted at the skirts of her gown, biting her lip. "Milady is . . ."

"Go on," he ordered impatiently. "Milady is what?"

"Gone, sir."

"What!" Gabriel's exclamation made the maidservant cringe. It was all she could do not to bolt and run for cover. "What the hell do you mean, she's gone?"

"She went out yesterday afternoon," Bab told him. "She called for her cloak and went out. I offered to go with her, I did!" the girl insisted, terrified that she would be punished. "But she said no. She went out and did not come back."

"Did anyone look for her?" Gabriel asked, feeling his heart constrict with fear for her.

"Oh aye!" The girl assured him. "When she didn't come back for supper, the men went out to find her. They thought a bear might have chased her, or a . . ."

"What did they find?" Gabriel prompted.

"Coach tracks," Bab told him. "By the little cottage in the wood. Coach wheels' and horses' hoof marks."

Gabriel was stunned. Coach wheels. Who could have taken her away? Who knew she was there?

He looked back up at Bab. "Were there signs of a struggle?"

Bab shrugged. "No, sir. There was nothing. She went away with whoever was in the coach."

"You don't know that!" Gabriel snapped. Then, wearily, he waved a hand at her. "That's all, Bab."

Relieved to be dismissed, Bab disappeared up the corridor, leaving her master alone in the cavernous entrance hall.

Gabriel sank onto the settee. It was incomprehensible. China gone! Where? How? With whom? His brain swam with questions to which he had no answers.

She must have been forced, stolen away from him. But that did not make sense. Why would she have gone into the forest alone? Didn't she know the dangers that lay there? Didn't she realize that the countryside teemed with all sorts of people, good and bad, honest and dishonest? There were men who would not hesitate to prey on a beautiful young woman they came upon alone in the forest.

And yet, beneath his concern for her, another possibility crept slyly into his consciousness. China had written a letter not long after they'd arrived at Fox Meadow. She had said it was to her friend, Lady Sutton, in London. She had sent it off by messenger. Could it have been to someone else? Could it have been addressed to her uncle in Virginia? Perhaps she had written to tell him she was back in America, to plead with him to send someone to take her back to Virginia, to Montcalm.

"Bab!" he roared again bringing the maidservant on a run. "Bab, who took milady's letter to Bath to be posted?"

"Cyril, sir," she told him. "The stableman."

"Fetch him," Gabriel ordered tersely.

Within moments the tall, gangly stableman stood before his master. He shuffled from foot to foot as though afraid his boots would mar the beauty of the entrance hall floor and his Adam's apple bobbed as he swallowed nervously.

"You carried a letter to Bath some time since, didn't you?" Gabriel asked.

Not quite meeting his master's eyes. The boy nodded. "I did," he confirmed.

"Who was the letter addressed to?"

The boy shook his shaggy brown head. "I don't know, sir. The man what took it said he'd put it in the packet on the boat."

"Come now," Gabriel snapped. "You don't have to be afraid. Doubtless you glanced at the address. What was the name."

"I don't know," the boy repeated. His dark eyes flickered to his master's face for a brief instant. "I can't read."

Gabriel ground his teeth in frustration. "Well, then, the boat. The boat that was carrying the mail packet. Where was she bound?"

Cyril screwed up his face in an effort to remember. "The man said," he began slowly, deep in thought, "he said the boat was bound for London."

Gabriel relaxed a little, but then the boy went on:

"The boat," he said, brightening, pleased with himself for remembering, "was bound for London, by way of Yorktown!"

Gabriel trembled. Growling a dismissal, he

sent the servants packing. Yorktown! His rage filled him to bursting. Hell and damnation! The baggage had run back to Montcalm. All the old doubts, all the old suspicions came flooding back, scalding him like boiling oil. Seizing a delicate porcelain statue off a pedestal in the hall, Gabriel dashed it against the wall. But even the rain of fine shards on the polished wood of the floor could not begin to take the edge off his boundless fury.

Twenty-Five

Gabriel knew he was risking his life by entering Virginia. He knew full well that, were he caught in Alexander Spotswood's colony, he could not hope to escape the noose that he had eluded once.

But he did not care about the risk to himself. He was filled with self-loathing. He believed that China had lied to him all along—that she had played her part so well, played upon the feelings she knew he had for her, to save her own life. She had used his own emotions against him to keep him from carrying out the vengeance he had sworn to have. She had used the attraction he felt for her to convince him to take her away from Damien de Fonvielle and bring her back to

America where she could go back to the life of a pampered beauty on a fine Virginia plantation.

He ground his teeth in disgust when he remembered how he had protected her from the pirates at Fox Meadow. He had slept outside her door that night to guard her. He would have killed anyone who had tried to harm her.

Fool! he cursed himself. Stupid, credulous fool! She had known he would protect her! She had known she could depend on him to keep her safe until she found a way to escape back to Virginia and her uncle's plantation.

As he entered Virginia and rode for Yorktown and Montcalm, Gabriel told himself that China's flight proved her guilt. All those suspicions, all those doubts that had haunted him for so long were well-founded. He felt certain of that now, and it was time for her to pay the price for what she'd done to him and to his men.

The air was cold; winter had come to Virginia. But Gabriel, hunched in the folds of his greatcoat, the broad collar pulled up, his hat pulled low, barely noticed the chill or the frosting of snow that crunched beneath his horse's hooves and sparkled on the ground and the branches of trees and bushes along the way. He was intent upon his goal; Yorktown, Montcalm, China, and nothing else mattered to him, nothing else touched him. There was no room in his mind for anything but thoughts of vengeance too long postponed, of punishment richly deserved finally to be meted out.

Gabriel skirted Yorktown lest he be recognized by one of the ghoulish spectators who had flocked to Williamsburg to see his execution. He rode through the forest, avoiding the roads, toward Montcalm.

The gardens of Montcalm, empty, bare, frosted with a glittering sprinkling of snow, were in sight when Gabriel dismounted and tied his horse to a tree. Cursing the snow that crunched beneath his jackboots, he crept toward the garden, wishing the overcast day would soon give way to an early night so that he could enter the house and confront the betraying vixen he hated as much as he loved.

Hiding behind a hedge, fortified by the brandy he'd carried in a flask, Gabriel waited and watched. Night was falling, the darkness was gathering about the house he remembered so well. The glow of candlelight lit the windows. He watched the windows of the room that had been China's. They remained dark, but that meant little. She could have been given a different room upon her return. Montcalm was a large house—there was more than one guest room available.

Still, that presented a problem. He would have to be careful if he was to search the house. He knew which room had been Lord Clairmont's, which belonged to Lady Clairmont, and which was Rebecca's. Those he would have to avoid. All the others, he would watch to see if candles were lit, if there were some sign that his prey was there, unsuspecting.

It was dark, overcast, cold, when Gabriel left his hiding place and made his stealthy way through the garden to the house. The small door at the back that he knew was seldom locked provided him with an entrance.

He took up the night candle left burning on the hall table. It was a risk, he knew, but an unavoidable one. He had to see China before he could confront her—he had to be certain he had found her before he could punish her.

He climbed the stairs, his footfalls muffled by the heavy carpet. Stealthily, silently, he made his way along the corridor, avoiding Lord and Lady Clairmont's rooms and Rebecca's. But in all the other rooms he found nothing. There was no sign that anyone occupied them. They had that empty, sterile look of guest rooms unused.

Disappointed, Gabriel made his way back

downstairs. Was it possible that China had not come to Montcalm? Could he have mistaken her motive in fleeing Fox Meadow?

He was puzzled and thoughtful as he replaced the candle on the hall table and returned to the little door through which he'd entered. He let himself back out into the gardens. It was then that he heard the crunch, crunch of footsteps in the snow.

Crouching behind a hedge, Gabriel watched as two shadows appeared at the corner of the mansion. The shadows parted and melded as they moved along the snowy paths. A man and a woman.

As Gabriel watched, they paused near the back of the house. The man pulled off his gold-braided tricorne and the woman tilted her face up, lips pursed, inviting a kiss. As the man bent toward her, his hand cupping her delicate chin, the woman's hood fell back, and in the glow of the hall candle shining through the window, Gabriel saw a glint of silvery-pale hair.

The scene seemed to take on a red tinge as Gabriel's temples throbbed with the hot blood of fury and jealousy. The faithless trollop! Not only had she betrayed him, lied to him, used him and duped him, she had had a man waiting for her the moment she returned to Virginia! No doubt she'd had him all along! He'd probably gone with her to the authorities when she'd given the fatal deposition that had so nearly cost him his life.

Another thought occurred to him. This man, whoever the hell he might be, could be the father of the child China had lost. He remembered Lady Sutton saying China had told her the father had been a man she had loved in Virginia. Christ! What a stupid, credulous fool he had been!

He watched, eyes narrowed, as the man and woman kissed again, embraced long and lingeringly, then parted. The woman stood watching as the man left her, disappearing around the corner of the mansion, leaving the way he had come.

Reluctantly, the woman turned toward the house. It was then that Gabriel made his move.

Darting out from his hiding place, Gabriel was upon her before she knew he was coming. He wrapped her voluminous mantle about her, pinning her arms to her sides and covering her mouth with one snowy edge. Lifting her off her feet, Gabriel carried her back to where his horse stood tethered.

With one hand he held the woman while with the other he released the horse's reins and swung himself up into the saddle. Kicking the horse into a gallop, he rode off into the forest, far enough from Montcalm's great house that no screams for help would awaken Lord or Lady Clairmont.

By the time he reined in his mount and dropped to the ground, his captive held immobile in his arms, they were well away from Montcalm, in a copse atop a bluff overlooking the York. Gabriel tossed the horses's reins over a tree branch and turned his attention to his squirming prisoner.

"If you scream," he told her, his voice low and growling, "no one will hear you. If you run, I will be forced to shoot you. That would not make me unhappy, so do not test me. Do you understand?"

The woman in his arms nodded, and Gabriel warily, slowly loosened his hold on her.

Stepping out of his grasp, she pushed back the stifling green velvet, fur-lined hood that had fallen over her face and nearly smothered her.

"Who the hell are you!" Rebecca Clairmont snapped, shoving back the hood that covered her pale blonde hair, so like her cousin China's.

"Rebecca!" Gabriel exclaimed, stunned.

Rebecca fell back a step, her face pale in the dim light of the moon that was peeking through a break in the clouds. Her eyes were wide and staring.

"Gabriel," she breathed. "I can't believe it. But . . . but . . ."

"Surely you heard I escaped the gallows," he said grimly. "I was certain it would be all the talk."

"There was talk," Rebecca agreed, "but no one knew the truth. Some said you were alive. Others said your men had merely stolen your body in order to spare you the kind of burial your crewmen had."

"I was alive," he told her, scowling at the memory. "Barely."

"And you've come back to me," Rebecca murmured, moving closer to him.

Gabriel eluded the hand that would have risen to caress his cheek. "What would your beau say to this, Rebecca?" he asked wryly.

"My . . ." She had the grace to blush. "The man in the garden. That was Joshua Sayer from Silver Creek. He is a friend, no more."

"A friend?" Gabriel arched a skeptical brow. "That was a mighty 'friendly' kiss he gave you."

Rebecca bridled, pleased. "Are you jealous, Gabriel?" she purred.

"No," he replied flatly. "I did not come back to Virginia to see you."

The simpering smile left Rebecca's face. "Then why did you come back?" she asked. "If you were discovered your life wouldn't be worth tuppence."

"I know. But I thought the risk worth my while." His eyes glinted beneath the brim of his black hat. "Where is she, Rebecca?" he demanded.

"Who?" Rebecca frowned, genuinely confused.

"China." He scowled. "Don't play games. I'm in no mood. Just tell me where she is."

"China!" Rebecca stared at him as if he were mad. "China's in England with her husband. You know that. She and Ian Leyton—"

"Leyton's dead," Gabriel snarled. "I brought China back from England with me. Now I'll ask you once more. Where is she?"

"How should I know?" Rebecca glared at him. China! It was always China with him. Damn him! "You brought her back! Why don't you know where she is?"

"Rebecca . . ." Gabriel snarled, his nerves and patience frayed to the breaking point.

"I didn't even know she was back from England!" Rebecca leaned closer. "What happened to Ian?"

Gabriel's mind was racing. Rebecca seemed genuinely surprised that China had returned. But if China hadn't fled to Montcalm . . . He realized Rebecca was saying something to him. "What?"

"I said, what happened to Ian Leyton?" Rebecca repeated.

"He killed himself," Gabriel told her. "A French duc, the Duc de Fonvielle, drove him to it. He wanted China for himself."

"Why didn't she stay with him?" Rebecca asked.

"Because I killed him," Gabriel replied matter-of-factly.

Rebecca felt confused. "Why did you do that?"

"He was an evil son-of-a-bitch," Gabriel said casually. "And I wanted China."

"China!" Rebecca snapped. "Everybody wants China!"

But Gabriel did not hear the venom in her tone. His thoughts were elsewhere, immersed in the question of where China could have gone . . . and why. If she hadn't come to Montcalm, where else could she have gone? She had no other relations, she knew few people . . .

Rebecca, still piqued, mumbled on. "If China runs back to England, she'd better be careful," she said. "If pirates attack her ship, she'll be back where she began in all this."

Gabriel's leaf green eyes flickered over her face. "What did you say?"

Rebecca shook her head. "Never mind. You're so damned concerned over—"

"What did you say!" he barked.

"I said," she repeated sarcastically, "that if pirates captured China, she'd be back where she began in this affair."

"Pirates . . ." Images flickered in Gabriel's mind, images of the pirates from the *Golden*

Fortune thronging the lawn of Fox Meadow. Images of Le Corbeau, disdainful, disgusted, telling Gabriel he was weak and foolish to keep China alive. He remembered speaking to Charles Eden in Bath. The governor had said he'd heard that the *Golden Fortune* had been seen in the Pamlico Sound entering the Neuse River. But though *Le Corbeau* had said he intended to sail into the Pamlico River to meet with Edward Teach, also known as Blackbeard, who was fast becoming the pirate king of the American coast, no mention had been made of the *Golden Fortune* being sighted anywhere near the mouth of the Pamlico.

"Le Corbeau," Gabriel groaned. "Damn his black soul to hell!"

"Why do you say that?" Rebecca wanted to know. She remembered that Le Corbeau had been the first pirate to capture China. "What has he to do with—"

"He's taken her, don't you see?" Gabriel snapped. "He berated me for not killing her for betraying me to Spotswood. His crew wanted to kill her. He bowed to their wishes and abducted her." Gabriel closed his eyes, horrified at the thought of China in the clutches of that mob. "God in heaven!" he breathed.

"The pirates have her?" Rebecca murmured. "What do you think they will do to her?"

"They'll kill her," he answered shortly. "But first . . ." He drew a ragged breath. "First they'll make certain she suffers."

He looked at Rebecca, his face suddenly haggard and drawn. "Come along, Rebecca. I'll take you home."

"You don't have to go so soon, do you?" she cooed. "It's been so long since I've seen you."

"I've got to go after her," Gabriel replied, shuddering with thoughts of China and the horror she must be enduring.

"Gabriel . . ." Coming to him, Rebecca wound her arms about his neck. "Forget China. Stay with me. We can go to—"

"I've got to go," Gabriel repeated, extracting himself from Rebecca's clinging embrace. "Come on, now, I'll take you home."

"Gabriel . . ."

"Come on!" he ordered. "Or I'll leave you here!"

Annoyed, Rebecca planted her hands on her hip. "Why should you rescue her?" she demanded, pouting. "After all, she betrayed you, didn't she? She caused your men to die. She nearly cost you your life!"

But Gabriel merely glared at her. He mounted his horse and held out a hand to her. Rebecca knew, from the hard glint in his eyes, that neither tears nor pleas could move him. Since it was a long, cold walk home, she went to him and let him swing her up into the saddle before him.

As they rode back through the cold night, the long plumes of breath from the horse's nostrils trailing back along his glossy sides, Rebecca laid another grievance at China's door.

Anchored off Ocracoke Island, the *Golden Fortune* rode gently on the calm sea. The windows of the master cabin were aglow, shining like beacons in the darkness.

Inside the cabin, China stood, her wrists bound with rough hemp, facing a long table. Behind it, their eyes glinting with triumph and loathing, sat Le Corbeau, his first mate, and four crewmen who had served under Gabriel aboard the *Golden Fortune*.

China faced them with a calm that was only partly bravado. She believed with all her heart that she was about to die. She knew they hated her, she knew, without being told, what their verdict would be. The only irony, as she saw it, was that her trial was being conducted, and her fate being decreed, in the very cabin where she'd first gotten to know Gabriel, where they'd first lain together, where the seeds of love had been sown in their hearts.

She forced herself not to think of Gabriel. He was the chink in her armor, and she would not allow these men to see any of the weakness that threatened at every moment to betray her.

She faced them squarely as Le Corbeau said gravely:

"You have been accused of betraying Gabriel Fortune and the men of his crew. You are accused of causing their deaths. Such treachery cannot be forgiven. The evidence . . ."

"Evidence!" China snarled. "What evidence? That damned deposition? A piece of paper! Produce one man who saw me sign it! Show me one witness who heard me say those things!"

"Enough!" the pirate from Martinique snapped, his voice loud and echoing in the low-ceilinged cabin. "We have reached our decisions. What say you?" he asked, looking to his left.

The hulking, brown-haired pirate at the end of the table glared at China. "Guilty," he snarled.

"Guilty," the man next to him agreed.

It went down the table, unanimous. Guilty, guilty, guilty.

Le Corbeau stared at China for a long time before he, too, agreed. "Guilty." He glanced again at the men who sat on either side of him. "And the sentence?" he asked.

They replied as one: "Death."

China swayed, her eyes closing. She had

expected it. It came as no surprise. But that did not lessen the shock of hearing her worst fears put into words.

Their heads close together, the pirates conversed in low, urgent tones. Le Corbeau spoke quickly, tersely, apparently arguing with the others.

China watched them, her stomach aquiver. It was obvious that Le Corbeau disagreed with the method the others had chosen. It was equally obvious that they were unwilling to compromise.

Beaten, unable to move them, Le Corbeau turned back to China. Seeing the grudging sympathy in his ebony eyes, China feared the worst.

"You will be taken to an island," he told her softly, obviously reluctant, "and you will be left there, alone, with neither food nor water nor weapon."

"Marooned," China breathed. Left to die of hunger and thirst on some desolate patch of land in the middle of the sea. It was the worst, the cruelest, punishment the pirates could devise.

Without another word, without a tremble or a tear, China slid to the floor in a faint.

Twenty-Six

Gabriel!" Rebecca called when he left her near the back door of the great house at Montcalm.

He looked down impatiently. He had wasted precious time in coming to Virginia, taken needless risks. He was exhausted and worried. He wanted only to find some place to rest for an hour or two before setting off again in search of Le Corbeau, who, he was convinced, had China in his clutches.

"What is it?" he demanded tersely. "I have to be on my way, Rebecca."

"Why?" she demanded. She clutched at the stirrup of his saddle. "Let the pirates do what they will with China."

Gabriel glared at her. "You don't know what you're talking about."

"Please, Gabriel," she persisted. "I love you! I've always loved you! China doesn't deserve you. Don't go after her. Don't risk your life for her!"

"I have to," he said softly, seriously. "I can't help myself. I love her."

"No!" Rebecca's wail was one of pure agony. "I don't believe you!"

"It's true," he assured her. "Good-bye, Rebecca."

"Damn you!" she hissed as he wheeled his horse to ride away. "Damn you to hell! You promised to marry me! You promised! You're mine."

Gabriel drew in his reins. "Rebecca," he soothed, "I can't help what I feel. I never meant to make you unhappy."

"Will you never learn?" she demanded bitterly. "When will you realize that you cannot leave me? I can't lose you. I won't! If I can't have you, neither will China!"

"There's nothing you can do," Gabriel told her. "Nothing."

"You think not?" Rebecca snarled. "You're a fool, Gabriel St. Jon. Go on, go after China. Enjoy her while you can! It won't last long, and you won't escape this time!"

Mind dulled by fatigue, Gabriel paid little attention to her mutterings. Kicking his horse into a gallop, he rode into the forest, looking for a tumbledown cottage built by some forgotten settler, where he intended to sleep for a few hours before setting out in search of China.

It was growing light when Gabriel awoke. He cursed himself for sleeping so long. He had been bone-weary, but even so, China was depending upon him and he had to do everything humanly possible to save her.

His horse whinnied softly as Gabriel saddled him and swung himself up. His stomach growled with hunger but he had no intention of stopping, even to eat, until he had left Virginia and was safely back in North Carolina.

As he had the day before, he skirted the edges of Montcalm plantation. He was nearing the clearing where he had taken Rebecca the night before—when he had thought she was China—when he saw the couple standing in the fast-melting snow. A horse was tethered to a tree nearby. The man and woman were speaking earnestly together.

Gabriel felt a moment's excitement. He thought it was China standing there, but then he realized it was Rebecca. Slowing his horse to a walk, he studied the scene. Something about it troubled him . . . Rebecca's resemblance to China, something familiar about the man she was speaking with.

As he rode around the clearing, Gabriel

saw the man's face. With a sudden shock of recognition, he remembered the man. He had seen him before . . . on the night at the Swan Tavern when he had been arrested. The man was from Williamsburg. He had brought the warrant, signed by the Royal Governor, that charged Gabriel with piracy.

In that moment, it seemed, Gabriel's eyes were opened. He felt as if he had emerged from a long dark night into the brilliant light of day. It had been Rebecca. Rebecca! She was the one who had betrayed him. She had pretended to be China and given the deposition that had been so damning at the trial. The description given of "China Clairmont" could have been a description of either woman. The treachery that had cost his men their lives had not been China's, but Rebecca's!

He felt sick, stunned, appalled. He had pursued China to England, fully intending to kill her, for something she had not done. She'd pleaded her innocence again and again but he had not listened. He had decided she was guilty and her protestations fell on deaf ears. And now . . . He closed his eyes, despairing . . . now she was in the clutches of Le Corbeau and his men, desperate men filled with hatred, lusting for vengeance. Even now it could be too late. China might already have paid with her life for a crime she did not commit.

Behind him, in the clearing he had just

passed, Gabriel heard Rebecca's voice, shrill with excitement.

"There he goes!" she cried. "That's him! That's Gabriel Fortune!"

"You there!" the man shouted. "Fortune! Stop where you are!"

Glancing back, Gabriel saw the man untying his horse's reins and leaping into the saddle. Spurring his horse to a gallop, Gabriel rode away. He wanted no part of Governor Spotswood's representatives—or Governor Spotswood's nooses!

But the man was after him, a pistol waving in his outstretched hand. "Stop!" he ordered. "Stop, I say, in the King's name!"

Gabriel spurred his horse, outdistancing the man. Doubtless, he thought, he could have shot him—the pistol tucked into his belt was loaded and he was a fine shot. But he was not about to add murder to the charges Spotswood could bring against him—not unless it became a case of his life or his pursuer's.

They were coming to a creek; it was narrow but the banks were steep and rocky. Gabriel saw it and prepared himself for the jump. But even as his horse's hooves left the ground, the crack of a pistol shot rang out. Gabriel felt the impact, the burning as the ball tore through his clothing and grazed the flesh of his upper arm.

He heard a cry behind him and looked

back to see his pursuer falling, his horse's hooves failing to find a purchase on the rocky bank of the creek. As they fell, the horse neighing, the rider cursing, Gabriel rode on, ignoring the pain of his wound, the warm, sticky flow of blood down his arm.

He vowed, as he rode away, that one day he would deal with Rebecca. She had caused the deaths of his crewmen, very nearly caused his own death, and, if he could not find her in time, would have caused China's death as well. He had been blind, so very blind, to it all. He could only hope now that Providence would guide him, would somehow keep China safe until he managed to find her and save her.

While Gabriel searched, pausing only long enough to eat when he had to and sleep when he could drive himself no further, China was locked in the master cabin of the *Golden Fortune*.

There had been much discussion of their proposed destination. The pirates had spent hours poring over charts and logs searching for an island that would meet their needs. More than once, Le Corbeau tried to persuade them to abandon their plans. He thought that, with time, cooler heads would prevail. But it was useless. The men were determined to leave China to die on some barren speck of land. It was the ultimate punishment, and they meant to mete it out to her. Le Corbeau knew that if he tried to keep them from marooning China his crew was likely to mutiny. His choice was between watching China be left to die an agonizing death and losing his ship and, possibly, his own life. There was nothing he could do.

The island they chose was a small, completely uninhabited rock, bare save for some straggly shrubs and jagged coral. It lay in the Atlantic some three days sailing from New Providence. Le Corbeau remembered seeing it and thinking it a lonely, desolate place.

The pirate captain stood at the rail as the ship sailed past New Providence Island. He knew his crew would want to come back to the pirate refuge once their prisoner had been left on her island. He did not relish the prospect . . . he wanted nothing more than to sail off to his native Martinique and see the wife and family few of his comrades knew existed. He felt suddenly as though he'd lost the edge that had made him a fine captain, a successful member of the pirate brotherhood. He found he had no taste for what they were doing, and that puzzled him, for China richly deserved death for her treachery.

Ah well, he thought to himself as he left the rail and went to check the ship's heading. It would soon be over and he could forget he had ever seen the beautiful woman he was taking to her death.

He took the helm himself and guided the *Golden Fortune* to anchor off the speck of land that was to be China's living tomb. As the jeering crew stood at the rail, China and Le Corbeau were rowed ashore. The sailor who rowed the tender boat stayed with it while China and the black-eyed pirate splashed through the last few feet of water and up onto the rough, rocky shore.

Glancing over his shoulder at the pirate standing near the boat, *Le Corbeau* took China's arm and drew her further up the shoreline.

"There is nothing I can do to save you," he told her softly.

"I did not expect help from you," China retorted coldly.

"But I would help you if I could," he assured her. He glanced around the barren scrap of land that offered no food or water or shelter. "I would not wish this on any man, let alone a woman."

"Even though you, too, condemned me to die?"

Le Corbeau nodded. "Even so. I still believe you are guilty of what you were accused of. And I believe you deserve to die for it. But like this—?" He looked around once more. "Not like this. Were it up to me, I would choose a quicker death."

"How kind you are," China sneered.

He gazed at her, understanding her feelings. She was about to be left to die of thirst and hunger and exposure to the broiling sun. He could not but admire her bravado. Many men, he knew, would be on their knees begging for mercy. But not this woman. She was too proud to show him the terror she must be feeling. And for that, he decided, she should be shown a leniency he might not otherwise have granted her.

From his belt he drew a long dagger. Its hilt was worn smooth from use, its blade was long and narrow, curving to a lethal point.

"Take this," Le Corbeau said.

China laughed bitterly. "To defend myself?" she asked. "Or to hunt the teeming game hereabouts?" She looked behind her. Through the scrubby brush covering the craggy ground she could see the blue of the sea on the opposite side of the tiny isle.

"I mean it," the pirate captain said. "Do you know what is before you? Hunger, thirst. The sun will bake and blister your skin." He shook his head. "Take the knife."

"To kill myself?" China asked incredulously. "My God!"

"Take it," he urged. "Use it or not, as you please. But if you find you can no longer bear the hunger, the thirst, the pain of your burned flesh, you will at least have the means to end your suffering."

For the first time, Le Corbeau saw the flickering of fear China could not hide. He held out the knife to her and she took it, her hand trembling, her face pale.

"Thank you," she breathed, her eyes averted. She tucked the knife into the bodice of her gown where it would not be seen by the sailor in the boat.

The crewmen aboard the *Golden Fortune* shouted to their captain. They were eager to be away, on their way to New Providence and the gambling, liquor, and women who waited there for them.

Le Corbeau glanced toward them, then looked back at China. "It is time," he told her. "*Adieu.*" He gazed at her for a long moment. "If it becomes too much for you . . ." he said softly.

China nodded. "I have the knife."

The pirate captain turned and left her, returning to the tender boat that would take him back to the *Golden Fortune*. Behind him on the shore, China watched, oblivious to the jeers and catcalls of the pirates aboard the ship, feeling only the profound hopelessness of her situation.

As the anchor of the pirate ship was hauled up and the sails filled with the wind that would take them away, China felt the heat of the blade tucked into the bodice of her gown. How long would it be, she wondered, before desperation drove her to use the knife the pirate captain had left for her? How many endless, agonizing days would pass before she would embrace death as her only hope of relief from her torment?

As the ship grew smaller and smaller, disappearing into the distance, China turned away. She already felt the first pangs of hunger, her throat was dry, her skin was pinkening with the glare of the sun . . . what would it be like in an hour? A day? Two days? Without water she could not expect to last more than a few days.

Moving to the scant shelter of one of the scraggly bushes, China sank onto the rocky ground. There was nowhere to go, nothing to see, nothing to do but sit and wait while every passing hour brought her closer to the inevitable outcome of her ordeal—death. Her only option, the only choice that was hers to make, was between a slow, tormenting, and painful death from exposure and thirst, or a swift death from the blade of Le Corbeau's dagger, her blood spilling onto the craggy soil of an insignificant island that had not even a name.

Twenty-Seven

"It was damnably foolish for you to go to Virginia," Tobias Knight told Gabriel, pouring another tankard of Jamaican rum and setting it before him.

"It was worth it," Gabriel declared. "I discovered the truth about what happened to me and my men there. I had accused the wrong person." His face clouded. "She may die because of it."

"And you nearly died to discover the truth," the other man reminded him.

Gabriel shook his head. "This?" he asked, pointing to the arm that was sore and bandaged beneath his clothes. "It's nothing. A graze. The ball was nearly spent when it hit me, and the sleeves of my greatcoat, coat, and shirt slowed it even more."

Tobias Knight, Governor Eden's collector of customs, took a long draught of his ale. He, like the governor, was rumored to have an "understanding" with the pirates who plied the American coast. He was an especial friend, so they said, of Blackbeard, but he knew most of the captains and kept abreast of their comings and goings. It was said he offered them the hospitality of the colony—and the protection of the governor's pardon—in exchange for a share of the rich bounty they harvested in coastal waters.

It was for that reason that Gabriel had sought him out. If anyone knew when the *Golden Fortune* had sailed and where she was bound, it would be Tobias Knight.

"Le Corbeau took her out three days since," the customs collector told him.

"Where was she bound?" Gabriel asked eagerly.

"I don't know." The man shook his head. Looking up, he saw Gabriel's green eyes on him. "My word, Fortune, I don't know. But I heard they were going to put in at New Providence on the way back."

"They could be there today," Gabriel observed, "or a week from today, or a month . . ."

"Or not at all," Tobias finished for him.

"Or not at all," Gabriel agreed. "I suppose all I can do is get to New Providence and hope they are there."

"If I hear anything in the meanwhile . . ." the customs collector began.

"Thank you, Tobias," Gabriel told him, leaving the table. He clapped the man on the shoulder and left the tavern to try to find a ship bound for New Providence.

On her small, tropical prison, China lay in the shade. Using Le Corbeau's dagger, she had cut the billowing skirt from her silk gown. Driving sticks into the rocky soil, she had draped the yards of fabric over them and made herself a makeshift shelter that kept the sun off at least part of her red, blistered flesh.

Dipping her fingers in the tiny pool of water, she gently wetted her cracked lips. The moisture was like paradise, but she resisted the temptation to dip her hands into her meager store of water.

It had rained on the second night of her imprisonment. China had stood there with the rain pouring over her, feeling as if heaven itself had opened its gates to her. Tilting back her head, she had let the cool, fresh water run down her throat until she choked and coughed.

Then, suddenly, she realized the waste of it

all. Scrabbling out a little hole in the ground, she had lined it with rocks and leaves and a piece of ragged silk. The water had gathered there and, miraculously, had not drained away into the soil.

It would, she knew, drain away too soon. But for now she could feel it, cool and wet. She could wet her painful lips, soothe her parched throat, dampen her raw and aching face.

As she lay in the shade of her makeshift tent, she gazed out over the endless expanse of blue ocean. The rain, she thought, it was a miracle, heaven-sent. It was . . .

Painfully, she saw how foolish she was. She was only prolonging her pain. The few precious ounces of water she hoarded like priceless treasure might refresh her, but the end was inevitable. The drops of water she felt sliding down her throat were only postponing the end that would surely come under the hot, merciless sun.

How much better, she thought, fingering the dagger that was never far from her fingertips, it would be to end it now and hope for better things when she was past her pain.

Lying there, her body blistered and burning, she drifted off into the semiconscious stupor that passed for sleep. When she awoke, the sun rested on the horizon, a giant orange ball that dominated her every waking hour. She watched, longing, for it to disappear. The night would bring a drop in temperature, the cooler air a balm to her baked flesh. It was . . .

China squinted toward the horizon. There was a ship, a proud, beautiful ship, its snowy sails filled with wind. It was sailing toward her, its bow slicing through the waves. It was coming to save her, to rescue her, to take her away from this—

It was gone. Frantically, China scanned the line where the sea met the sky. It was empty. There was nothing, no ship, no rescue, only the endless sea. She had imagined it all.

Resting her cheek on the piece of lacy petticoat that served as her bed, China lay, quiet, bereft. She could not cry, there were no tears. She felt nothing, nothing. All she wanted was to sleep in the cool darkness and never have to feel the scorching heat of the tropical sun again.

As night fell she dozed off. In her dreams, she saw herself again at Fox Meadow. Gabriel was there. Gabriel. So strong, so handsome, desiring her, loving her in spite of the suspicions that had led to all their troubles. She felt his arms around her, felt his lips on hers. He kissed her, gently, tenderly, then savagely with all the passion they felt for one another.

In her dream, China lay, spent and trembling in Gabriel's arms. But then they were torn apart, Damien de Fonvielle and Ian Leyton were there, pulling them away from one another. Le Corbeau stood in the shadows watching. His black eyes seemed sympathetic, but he made no move to help them. And through it all there were the voices, the mocking glares, the obscenities and epithets screamed from a hundred throats.

A scream tore its way out of China's parched throat. Her body jerking, she awoke. There was nothing, no one, no pirates, no ghosts, no Gabriel.

"Gabriel," she whispered, unable to raise her voice above a harsh croak. "Oh, Gabriel, I need you so much. Where are you? Oh, God, please come find me. Please, come save me . . ."

But as she lay there, weeping without tears, without sound, she believed in her heart that she would never see Gabriel again, that she would die there alone on that desolate flyspeck of an island.

Gabriel stood at the railing of the *Queen Anne's Revenge* as she sailed into the harbor of New Providence Island. He scanned the ship-choked harbor looking for the sleek, familiar lines of the *Golden Fortune*.

"D'ye see 'er then, Fortune?" the captain of the *Queen Anne's Revenge*, Blackbeard, asked as they sailed into the harbor.

Gabriel shook his head. "Not yet. Christ! If she's not here . . ."

Blackbeard scratched at the chest-length thatch of matted hair that gave him his name. "All this over a woman?" he said wonderingly. "Go ashore. If it's a woman ye want, there's scores of 'em there."

"She's not just any woman," Gabriel insisted. "You don't understand, Teach, what it is to love a woman."

Blackbeard guffawed. "The hell you say!" he barked. "I've loved hundreds of the wenches and I'll tell you this, Fortune, they're all alike when it's said and done."

"I want her for my wife," Gabriel said wistfully, unwilling to believe it was too late for such hopes and dreams.

"Ah, a wife," Blackbeard said solemnly. "That's a different breed of beast. I ought to know. I've had fourteen of 'em." He chuckled at the look Gabriel gave him. "And I loved 'em all dearly," he vowed. "Right up to the day I threw 'em to my crew."

Gabriel might have risked Blackbeard's wrath to give him his opinion on the subject of matrimony, but just then he spotted the ship he'd been looking for.

"There she is!" he cried, relieved and apprehensive. "The *Golden Fortune*!"

"So it is," Blackbeard agreed, shading his eyes to look off across the harbor. "Well, my friend, fortune has brought you this far. May she take you all the way to your heart's desire. Come along, I'll get some one of the God-cursed lazy wretches to row you over."

"Where is she!" Gabriel demanded less than an hour later when he stood in the master cabin of the *Golden Fortune*.

Le Corbeau did not meet his eyes. "Forget her, my friend. Sit down, join me in a drink."

"Answer me," Gabriel persisted. "You had her, didn't you? You took her from Fox Meadow after I had gone to Bath?"

"Aye," the swarthy pirate captain admitted. "The men demanded it. They were on the point of mutiny. I had no choice but to give in to their demands and take her from you."

"Can't you discipline your men, Le Corbeau?" Gabriel asked, the hint of a sneer in his voice. "Who is the captain aboard this ship?"

"Take care, *mon ami*," the smaller man warned. "The *Golden Fortune* is mine now. Remember you are a guest aboard my ship."

Gabriel scowled as he sank into a chair opposite the small, swarthy pirate. He fixed Le Corbeau with a hard, uncompromising glare.

"What did you do with her?" he demanded, his tone brooking no further evasion.

Le Corbeau sighed. "The men wanted her

tried on charges of—well, you know why."

"And did you?" Gabriel prompted.

"Aye. I sat in judgment along with my first mate and some of your old crewmen. Naturally she was found guilty."

"Naturally," Gabriel agreed sarcastically. "And then?"

The black-haired pirate pinched the bridge of his aquiline nose. "*Mon Dieu*, Fortune! I wish you would forget the girl. There was nothing I could do. The men decreed the punishment. I argued against it, but they would hear none of it." He heaved a heavy, troubled sigh. "She must be dead by now," he finished softly.

"By now?" Gabriel's brows shot up. "What the holy hell do you mean, 'by now'? What did you . . ."

The truth, the horrible, incomprehensible truth dawned on him. "You didn't," he muttered. "You couldn't . . ." But he saw the confirmation of his fears in the other man's face.

"Marooned!" he whispered. "You marooned her, didn't you!"

Shamefaced, Le Corbeau nodded. "Aye," he admitted. "The men—"

"You bastard!" Gabriel snarled, lunging for the other man. "You God-cursed, black-hearted son of a whore!"

Knocking the smaller man out of his chair, Gabriel rolled with him across the cabin floor, knocking tables and chairs aside, smashing glasses and bottles.

Le Corbeau gasped for breath as Gabriel's powerful hands closed about his throat. "I tried to talk them out of it," he defended. "I did try!"

"Do you know what you did?" Gabriel demanded, throttling the man who had been his friend. "You left her there to die! You left her there to starve, to die of thirst!"

"For what she did!" the other man defended frantically. "For what she did to you! To—"

The door burst open and a half-dozen crewmen, having heard the commotion, pulled the two men apart. Le Corbeau, his face red, his breath coming in short, harsh gasps, rubbed at his throat.

"For what she did in Virginia," the pirate captain finished softly. "The deaths of the men hanged in Williamsburg had to be avenged."

Calmer now, Gabriel slumped into a chair one of the men had set back on its feet. "But she didn't do it," he told the pirates dully. "She was telling the truth when she said she was innocent."

Rising, Le Corbeau went to Gabriel's side and laid a hand on his shoulder. "I know you loved her, *mon ami*, and I know you do not want to believe she could have betrayed your love, but—"

"Damn you!" Gabriel snarled, slapping away the hand that was meant to comfort him. "Will you listen to me? I'm telling you she was innocent! I know that now. I know it's true. Not because that's what I want to believe but because I've seen the truth for myself."

"What d'ye mean, cap'n?" asked one of the pirates who had served under Gabriel's command.

Gabriel took a deep, shuddering breath. "I went back to Virginia." He nodded, silencing the surprised murmurs of the crewmen crowding into the small cabin. "I went back to the plantation where China lived with her relatives. Her cousin was there. I knew her before I met China. I was going to marry her." His green eyes swept the panorama of surprised faces around him. "But then I met China. After that, Rebecca did not exist for me. When I broke with her, when she discovered China and I were lovers, she went to the authorities. She pretended to be China. *She* gave them the evidence that was used at the trial. And China got the blame."

Looking around, he saw the expressions on the pirates' faces. Some seemed shocked, some sheepish, some blatantly skeptical.

"Take me to her," Gabriel asked Le Corbeau. "Even if we're too late to save her, we can give her a decent burial."

The onyx-eyed pirate from Martinique

shook his head sadly. "I gave her a dagger," he told Gabriel. "In case the pain was too much for her to bear. I thought . . ." He let the sentence trail off.

Gabriel closed his eyes. The thought of China in agony, dying by her own hand, drove him very near the breaking point. By sheer force of will, he remained calm.

"Take me to her," he asked again.

"Wait, cap'n." A hulking crewman, a known rabble-rouser, stepped forward. "I ain't callin' you a liar, but we all know this woman's got 'er hooks into you right and proper. I don't know 'bout anybody else, but I'd like to see this other wench. The one you say really betrayed our men."

There was a murmur of agreement among the men, and Gabriel mentally cursed the man who, with those well-chosen words, might have doomed any tenuous chances of getting to China before the terror and pain of her predicament was too much for her.

Gabriel glared at the man. "If it's proof that you need," he snarled, "then haul that flyblown carcass of yours on deck and drag up that anchor. We'll set sail for Virginia and I'll get you your damned proof."

The pirate turned to leave, but Gabriel called him back.

"I'll tell you something right now, Murphy," he growled. "I'll take you to Virginia.

I'll bring Rebecca to you and prove to you that I'm telling you the truth. But if this delay costs China her life, I swear before God that you'll pay for it. Do you hear me?"

Murphy's dark eyes met and held the resentful stare of his former captain. After a long, tense silence, he nodded.

"Aye, cap'n," he agreed at last. "I hear ye."

"Then get above and put your back to it!" Gabriel snarled.

As the crewmen filed out of the master cabin, pushing and shoving to obey Gabriel's orders, Le Corbeau looked at him with a mixture of amusement and respect.

"I know you love that woman, *mon ami*," he said quietly. "And I pray we may reach her while there is yet time to save her."

"Thank you," Gabriel replied, knowing the swarthy pirate was sincere.

The sound of the anchor being hauled up out of the bay and the thudding of scores of feet on the deck above sounded like thunder. The ship lurched, rocking, as the sails filled with wind and drove her forward. She turned as the pilot steered out of New Providence harbor.

"I have only one question," Le Corbeau said as the two men walked toward the door.

"What is that?" Gabriel asked.

"Why don't those scurvy ship rats jump to obey my orders like that?"

Gabriel chuckled wanly as he and the smaller man left the master cabin and went up to the quarterdeck.

From there, standing at the railing near the huge ship's lantern, Gabriel watched as New Providence was left behind in the wake of the ship he'd always loved.

He'd given up the sea for China. He'd sacrificed his life aboard ship willingly, determined to make a life for himself and for the woman he'd fallen in love with. Now all his hopes, all his ambitions, all his dreams hung in the balance.

If only China could survive, he wished fervently. If only she could hang on just a little longer. If only he could reach her in time to save her, he would make amends for all the pain he'd caused her, for doubting her, accusing her, leaving her open to the horrendous pain she must be suffering. He would take her to Fox Meadow and make a life for her filled with peace and beauty and love.

As the bow of the *Golden Fortune* cut through the waves, throwing back cold salt spray to wash across the decks, Gabriel willed the wind to fill the sails and carry him to Virginia so he would then be free to go to China's side.

Twenty-Eight

The *Golden Fortune* entered the Chesapeake Bay and anchored in a secluded cove known well to the pirates plying the coastal waters. Gabriel, Le Corbeau, and the pirate Murphy rowed ashore. At a coaching inn they secured horses and rode north, heading for Yorktown.

"We can't go to Montcalm," Gabriel told them. "After Rebecca called in the authorities, the plantation might be being watched."

"How can we get to her, then?" Le Corbeau wanted to know.

"We'll have to lure her out." Gabriel smiled grimly. "I think I know how."

He took them to the burnt-out ruins of

what had once been a prosperous farm. The house was little more than a shell. The chimneys of the fireplaces jutted up from the crumbled foundations and charred timbers that were all that remained of a once fine home. In one of the storehouses, Gabriel sat on a broken barrel. He took out the cheese and bread he had bought at the inn and broke off a piece of each. Passing them on to Le Corbeau, he said:

"I sent a messenger from the inn to Montcalm. He's to tell Rebecca he's from Joshua Sayer."

"Who might he be?" Murphy demanded as he chewed on the cheese his captain had given him.

"His parents own Silver Creek—a plantation that lies not far from here. He is Rebecca's beau. I told the messenger to say Joshua wanted to meet her here."

"And if she doesn't come?" Murphy asked.

"She'll come," Gabriel predicted. "Knowing Rebecca, she'll convince herself he wants to elope with her." Closing his eyes, Gabriel wondered how he'd ever thought he could live happily with the woman.

An hour passed, then two, then three. The afternoon was giving way to evening, and though Gabriel felt confident that his ruse would succeed in luring Rebecca to them, he was impatient to have this business finished so they could get on to the urgent matter of China's rescue.

"She ain't comin'," Murphy groused, shifting on the matted pile of straw. "We should've gone to the plantation and—"

"And ended up on the gallows with a noose about our necks?" Gabriel interrupted. "I've been there once already, Murphy. I'm not about to risk it again."

"Even so," the pirate went on. "If ye're askin' me—"

Gabriel silenced him with a wave of his hand. Hoofbeats pounding on the hard-packed ground were growing louder. He peered out between two broken slats and saw Rebecca approaching, riding sidesaddle on a roan mare.

"Is it . . . ?" Le Corbeau began.

"It is," Gabriel confirmed. He turned back to them. "I'll confront her, get her to admit it. And then, damn it, we'll go after China. Your word?"

"My word," Le Corbeau agreed.

"Aye, cap'n," Murphy promised.

Nodding, Gabriel looked out again. Rebecca had dismounted and tied the reins of her horse to a tree. Glancing around, she looked for Joshua Sayer.

"Joshua?" she called. "Come out." Frowning, she wandered closer to the storehouse. "Don't be a child! I'm here. Why are you hiding?"

Waiting until she was within reach, Gabriel threw open the door and stepped out. As Rebecca would have turned to run, he seized her arm and pulled her back. They were well within earshot of the men still in hiding.

"Gabriel!" Rebecca breathed. "What are you doing here? Did you send that man to Montcalm?"

"I did," he admitted. "I didn't think you'd come if I'd sent for you myself."

"You were right!" she snapped. "I wouldn't have come!"

"But your friend from Williamsburg might have."

"He broke his leg, you know, when his horse threw him."

Gabriel arched a brow. "I'm so sorry. It must have been painful—but not nearly as painful as when that pistol ball dug a path through my arm!"

"What do you want?" she snarled. "Why have you brought me here?"

"For the truth," he snarled. "Once and for all, I want to hear it from your own lips."

"What truth?" she challenged.

"That it was you who betrayed me to Spotwood's men. That you betrayed my crew; told them where to find them. That you pretended to be China and signed the deposition against me."

"I don't know what you're talking about," she declared.

Gabriel's eyes blazed. China's life—if, indeed, she still lived—depended on wringing the truth out of this vindictive little bitch.

"It's useless to deny it," he persisted. "I know it was you. You're the cause of all the pain and suffering and death that's gone on. Because of your jealousy and bitterness an innocent woman—"

"Innocent? China?" Rebecca screeched. "She took my fiancé from me! She ruined everything! She stole your love from me!"

"How could she?" Gabriel taunted. "When it was never yours to begin with."

"Damn you!" Rebecca flew at him, hands curved into talons, determined to claw that handsome face to ribbons. "I hate you! Hate you! I wish you had died on the gallows!"

Gabriel held her hands in his merciless grasp. He held her away from him so she could not kick him.

"Admit it!" he ordered, hoping her fury would drive her to recklessness. "You pretended to be China. You signed her name on the deposition!"

"Aye!" Rebecca screeched. "I did it! I admit it!"

She stared up at Gabriel, the fury draining out of her, being replaced by fear. "I did it," she repeated softly. "What will you do with me? Are you going to kill me?"

"No." Gabriel could not speak for the men in the storehouse, but for himself he had had enough of killing. "I'm not going to hurt you. I only want to hear the truth from you."

"Where is China?" Rebecca wanted to know. "Is she here with you?"

Gabriel shook his head, pained at the thought of China and what this delay might be costing her.

"I don't know where China is," he told her honestly. "I don't know if I'll ever see her again."

Rebecca stared at him, triumph glittering in her eyes. He had left her for China, but apparently China had left him. "Was there another man?" she purred sarcastically. "Poor Gabriel."

Gabriel resisted the temptation to throttle her and went on as if she'd not spoken. "Tell me why you did this, Rebecca. Jealousy is a petty emotion."

"It wasn't only jealousy," she told him. "Not after I heard you with China—not after I heard you tell her you never loved me, that you only thought of marrying me to get a mistress for your home, a mother for your children. It wasn't jealousy then, it was hatred. Cold, hard, bitter hatred. I decided that if I could not have you, neither could China. I knew you loved her—I had to destroy that love. I thought if you believed she had betrayed you, your love would wither and die. You would hate her as I hated you . . ."

Gabriel cringed, remembering the murderous fury he had felt when he'd thought China had set Spotswood's men on him and his crew.

"So you went to them; gave them the evidence they used at the trial?" he prompted.

"I did," she confirmed. "China was leaving for England. She would be gone before you came to trial. She couldn't come forward and deny she had been the one who gave the deposition."

Gabriel stared out over her head toward the ruins of the house. "I don't know," he said quietly, "how I ever believed you were the sort of woman I could marry. Thank God I didn't marry you. Thank God I found China before . . ."

"China!" Rebecca's blue eyes glittered with malice. "I didn't exist for you after you met China. I would have been a good wife to you. I loved you so much. But all you could see was China. I hate you now, Gabriel! I hate you and I hate China! I hope you both rot in hell!"

"Believe me," he replied, "I feel the same way about you."

They stood there staring at one another, torn between disgust and regret. At last Rebecca broke the silence to say:

"Is there anything else you wanted to

know? I told my mother I was going into Yorktown for a fitting. She'll worry if I'm not back before dark."

Gabriel had no doubts that Murphy and Le Corbeau, having heard everything, were fuming, dying to get their hands on the imperious girl standing before him, fists firmly planted on her hips. But he had their promise that there would be no more delays in sailing to wherever it was they had left China. If they wanted their revenge at some later time, there was nothing he could do to stop them.

"Well?" Rebecca prompted impatiently. She tilted her chin at him, haughty, cold, but inside she was terrified. She wanted nothing more than to be away from this lonely, deserted place and away from the tall, powerful man who stood before her, no doubt longing to wring her neck. "Can I go now?"

Nodding, Gabriel waved her away. "Go on," he told her. "And I pray our paths may never cross again."

"You can't possibly wish for that any more than I do," she told him.

With a swish of her blue velvet riding skirt, she returned to her horse, trying hard not to break and run. Standing on a stump, she swung herself up into the saddle. She glanced back at Gabriel, but he did not look up. With a slap of the reins, she set the horse into a gallop.

As she disappeared into the forest, Gabriel returned to the storehouse. Murphy and *Le Corbeau* were standing near the door.

"Did you hear it all?" Gabriel asked them.

Murphy nodded. "The scheming bitch! I'd have put a pistol ball between her bloody eyes, but the cap'n wouldn't let me."

Gabriel said nothing as they walked back to their horses and mounted. As they rode off, retracing their path toward the shore where their boat was waiting to take them back to the *Golden Fortune*, Le Corbeau spurred his horse forward till he was abreast of Gabriel.

"I stopped Murphy from killing the girl," he told Gabriel. "But you know, when the others find out about this, they will want to kill her."

Gabriel nodded. "I expect they will," he admitted. "And I can't say I'd blame them. God knows I wanted China dead when I thought she'd been the one who sent me to the gallows." He gazed off into the distance. "I will leave it to you, my friend, to decide Rebecca's fate. I know that if the men want her, you won't be able to stop them. The code of honor among pirates deals harshly with traitors."

"Blackbeard would have skewered her," Murphy chimed in.

"At the very least," Gabriel agreed. He shrugged and went on, "Once we've gone to wherever the hell you left China—regardless of what we find when we get there—I intend to return to Fox Meadow. I'm done with the sea, done with pirating. All I want now is to live out my life at Fox Meadow . . ." With China, he thought, but did not even dare to hope for that. "What you do about Rebecca is up to you," he finished.

As the anchor was pulled up and the *Golden Fortune* sailed out of Chesapeake Bay bound for the Bahamas, Gabriel stood on the fo'c'sle deck, the sea spray on his face, the wind in his hair, trying desperately to keep alive his dwindling hopes of reaching China in time.

On the barren dot of land where the pirates had left her, China lay wishing with all her heart to die. She was starving, dehydrated. The few brief storms that had poured down upon her seemed little more than cruel taunts, an evil joke played upon her by a merciless Nature.

She lay weak, sliding in and out of delirium, beneath the tattered canopy of silk that was all that remained of her gown. But though she could no longer stand, though her skin seemed like a sheet of harrowing pain, though she had discarded the last of her clothing, her ragged, dirty chemise, because she could not stand the touch of it against her inflamed, festering flesh, China could not bring herself to put an end to her own suffering.

In her more lucid moments, she stretched out a frail, trembling hand to touch the hilt of the weapon. She knew a single slash across one of her wrists would spell the end of her agony. But she could not do it. Sometimes she wept, soundlessly, without tears, and wished the morning sun would find her there, an empty shell, her spirit having fled. But she could not force herself to use the knife.

She did not know how long she had been there. She could not guess how many days had passed. One day melded into another, a symphony of pain. Only the nights brought any meager respite. Only the darkness, the comforting twinkle of the stars overhead, the silver-cool glow of the moon on the water, gave her any measure of relief.

She looked up now, awakening from an hour's blessed unconsciousness. The sun was lowering toward the horizon. Night was approaching, and China prayed yet again that it would be her last.

She gazed out over the endless ocean. It stretched away to the sky, empty, lonely, with nothing there to mar its blue perfection—

She frowned at the speck gliding into view. It was dark, long . . . The sails were pale mauve in the glow of the setting sun.

A ship . . . With a soft moan, China laid

her head down. It was another delusion, no more. She'd had many of them. Ships, Gabriel, Fox Meadow . . . mirages, hallucinations, nothing more. But the pain of realizing they were merely illusions hurt more than the pain of her burned skin, her parched throat, her empty stomach, all put together.

I won't look at it, she told herself. It will go away. I won't look, I won't—

Through his spyglass, Gabriel searched the speck of land Le Corbeau pointed out to him.

"There's nothing," he said, "I don't see—" In the gathering darkness, it was hard to pick out anything against the background of the island. But then he saw it, the rippling silk of China's ragged shelter. "Wait! There is something! Get me over there, Le Corbeau, get a boat lowered. I'm going ashore."

Without question, the swarthy pirate went to do Gabriel's bidding. He, too, had seen the makeshift tent on the island and the prone figure lying beneath it. He feared what Gabriel would find when he was rowed ashore. He could only hope the shock of it all would not be too much for Gabriel's taut nerves to handle.

On the island, China heard the snap of the wind in the sails, the splash of the tender boat being lowered into the sea, the shouting of orders as two crewmen joined Gabriel to row him ashore.

I won't look, she repeated, certain now

that Fate had decided to save the cruelest delusion of all for the last. Please, please, she said to herself, make it go away.

"Row!" Gabriel snarled, shading his eyes and gazing toward the island. "Put your backs into it, damn you!"

The bottom of the boat had not yet touched sand when Gabriel leaped out and splashed ashore. He carried with him a flask of water knowing it was likely futile but unable to abandon hope until he had no other choice.

He stopped as he came in sight of China's pitiful shelter. He saw the basin she'd made to try to save the rainwater that was her only sustenance. It was empty, dry. He saw the discarded rags that were all that remained of her clothing. He saw her lying there, her flesh blistered, raw, with angry festering patches. Her bones jutted against her skin, her hair lay spread on the sand limp, lifeless, dull.

Standing there, trembling, Gabriel did not want to go to her. He did not want to turn her over, see the ravages of her agony. She did not move; he could not see even the slightest sign that she was breathing.

Too late, he thought, something fragile dying inside him. He wanted to scream, to curse, to weep.

Moving slowly, reluctantly, he forced himself to go to her. He knelt beside her and reached out to turn her over.

The touch of his hand as he took her upper arm and pulled her over was excruciating. As he rolled her onto her back, a scream tore itself out of China's throat, her dry lips cracked as she railed against the pain of his touch.

Through slitted eyes, she saw him beside her. She would not have believed it was him and not a dream but for the pain that still wracked her, telling her she was alive.

"Gabriel," she murmured, the word slurred through swollen lips. Weakly she tried to raise a hand to touch him but it fell to her side.

Gabriel felt tears flooding into his eyes, blurring his vision. "I've come for you," he whispered. "I was afraid . . . so afraid . . . it would be too late. I'm going to take you home, China. You'll be well again. We'll—"

"No." China closed her eyes. "No more," she breathed. "I can't bear your mistrust, your doubts. I'd rather die." She reached a shaking hand toward Le Corbeau's knife. "You must end it for me, Gabriel. The pain . . ."

Snatching up the knife, Gabriel threw it out over the water. It disappeared beneath the waves with a soft splash.

"You're not going to die," he said fiercely. "Damn it, China, you're not!"

She gazed up at him while he uncapped

the flask of water and tenderly wet her lips. Gently, carefully, he helped her drink. He bathed her tormented flesh as best he could, hoping the water would soothe her.

"I have to pick you up," he told her apologetically, knowing what agony it was going to be for her. "I'm sorry, China." He swallowed hard, knowing he could never make amends to her for the pain his doubts had caused her. "I'm so sorry."

Shivering from the chill of the evening breeze on her dampened flesh, China raised a quaking hand to touch his arm.

"Gabriel," she whispered, touching him gently. She saw that he knew the truth. She suddenly realized that the old doubts, the old suspicions that had driven them apart and so nearly brought them to disaster and death no longer existed. They could begin again with nothing to come between them and mar the love they had felt for one another since the beginning. "Gabriel," she repeated, and her blue eyes met his agonized gaze. "Take me home."

Relieved, not quite daring to believe that she had been restored to him, that he had been given another chance at love, Gabriel lifted her as gently as he could and took her to the tender boat. The crewmen rowed them out toward the *Golden Fortune*. It would take them home to Fox Meadow where their future together awaited them.

Epilogue

Fox Meadow, Five years later

China St. Jon, Mistress of Fox Meadow, sat on the wide veranda surveying her home. The plantation was prosperous beyond the dreams of even Gabriel, whose grand ambitions had once seemed unattainable.

She smiled tenderly as she reached out and touched the petal-soft, downy cheek of her month-old daughter, Brianna. The child had Gabriel's sable hair and her mother's blue topaz eyes. She would, so her proud father asserted, grow to be as great a beauty as her mother. China sighed, tucking the blanket around her sleeping daughter. She had never imagined that life could be so blissful, that she could be so utterly, completely content.

There had been changes in the past five

years. Piracy, for one thing, had nearly disappeared. Governor Spotswood had sent ships against Blackbeard. The pirate who had made himself the scourge of the colonial coast had been defeated and gruesomely executed. His death had sounded the death knell for the great age of piracy off the American coast. Le Corbeau had retired to Martinique. He occasionally wrote to Gabriel, lazily amused that the two of them had ended as gentlemen-farmers steeped in respectability.

Thoughts of pirates and the past inevitably brought memories of Rebecca. She had married Joshua Sayer not long after Gabriel's rescue of China. And though Rebecca had lived in terror that she might be captured and killed for her betrayal of her one-time fiancé and his men, Spotswood's war on piracy had saved her from the hideous fate that had so nearly cost China her life.

A movement at the edge of the forest caught China's eye. She saw Gabriel astride his chestnut stallion riding toward her. Before him in the saddle he held their son, Rafe—short for Raphael—who would be four years old in the autumn.

The child, seeing his mother, laughed and waved, happily secure in his father's arms atop the huge animal. Gabriel, looking toward her, smiled, and China's heart melted. She loved him more with every passing year.

A groom came running up to take the horse's reins, and Gabriel, his son in his arms, strode toward the veranda where China sat.

China knew he was happy, knew he loved Fox Meadow and their life there. But for all that he was the respected master of a great plantation, received in the finest homes, for all that he was a loving husband, a doting father, she saw sometimes in the glint in those beloved green eyes, in the way he walked, in his very stance, that Gabriel Fortune, the reckless buccaneer who had won her with the turn of a card, who had followed her halfway around the world and back again, who had nearly met a pirate's death at the end of a hangman's rope, was alive and well in his heart.

She heard it in his voice, she saw it in his glance, she felt it when they touched and the passion, still wild and fierce, leapt through their veins like quicksilver.

THE END